The
WOLF
at the
DOOR

The
WOLF
at the
DOOR

A Novel
by Graham Shelby

Doubleday & Company, Inc.
Garden City, New York
1975

Library of Congress Cataloging in Publication Data
Shelby, Graham, 1939–
The wolf at the door.
1. John, King of England, 1167?–1216—Fiction.
I. Title.
PZ4.S5433Wo3 [PR6069.H42]   823'.9'14
ISBN 0-385-09437-X
LIBRARY OF CONGRESS CATALOG CARD NUMBER 73–10973

For Peter and Roslyn

Contents

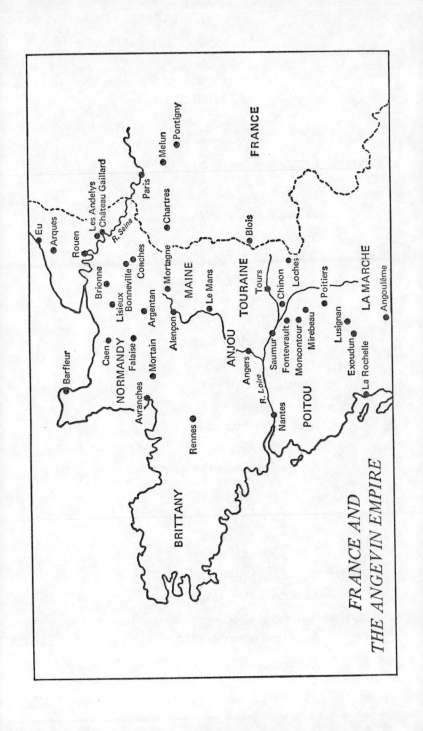

FRANCE AND
THE ANGEVIN EMPIRE

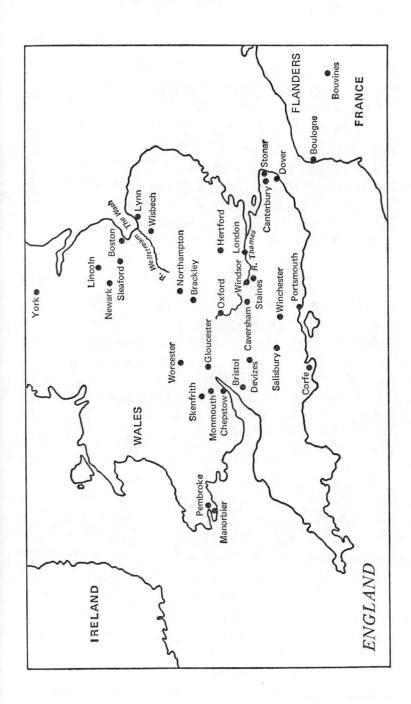

Principal Characters

JOHN   King of England
PHILIP AUGUSTUS   King of France
ELEANOR OF AQUITAINE   Dowager Queen
ISABELLE OF ANGOULÊME   Queen of England
WILLIAM MARSHAL   Earl of Pembroke
ISABEL DE CLARE   Wife of William Marshal
ARTHUR   Duke of Brittany

WILLIAM OF BRIOUZE   Knight Commander
MAUD DE ST. VALÈRIE   Wife of Briouze
HUBERT WALTER   Archbishop of Canterbury
STEPHEN LANGTON   Later Archbishop of Canterbury

HUGH LE BRUN   Lord of Lusignan
RALF OF EXOUDUN   Brother of Hugh le Brun
ROGER LACY   Castellan of Château Gaillard
SALDON   Constable of Corfe Castle
ROBERT FITZWALTER   Rebel Leader

The
WOLF
at the
DOOR

1

THEFT
June, July 1200

For the fourth time that morning the lookout unsheathed his knife and turned the blade until it caught the sun. The warning flash was acknowledged by the horsemen clustered below him on the plateau, and they urged their mounts into the forest.

The lookout remained for a while on the crest of the hill, peering in the direction of the approaching dust cloud. It was now less than a mile to the east, and it all but obscured the triple-towered castle of Moncontour. Nevertheless, the horses that stirred the dust had undoubtedly come from the vicinity of the castle—reason enough for the ambushers to take cover.

Satisfied that the riders would eventually descend to the plateau, the lookout scrambled down the western slope of the hill, reclaimed his horse and followed his companions among the trees.

The fifty or so ambushers all wore enclosed helmets, strange headgear for a hot June day. The heavy iron casques were pierced by ventilation holes and narrow eye-slits, and the men were dressed in rough, full-length surcoats, devoid of markings. Their leaf-shaped shields had been smeared with mud, obliterating all blazons, and plain swords had been substituted for any with an engraved inscription. There was no way of telling one man from the next, for anonymity was essential to the plan.

As on the three previous occasions someone asked, "Are you certain it's them?" And, as before, the lookout shrugged irritably. His voice dinned inside the protective mask as he retorted, "How many times must I tell you? If I wait to identify them, I'll be spotted. No, I am not certain. It could be them; it could be any-one. If your eyes are so damn sharp, you go up there!" he raised his arm in an angry gesture toward the hill, then guided his horse deeper into the forest. He had been chosen as lookout because he was the best man for the job, *which meant the man with the best eyesight.* But what did he get for his pains, crouched hour after hour in the sun? Stupid questions from those who had sat rolling dice in the shade. Well, the next time he was chosen he'd rub dirt in his eyes, and let someone else roast on the hill-side.

None of the ambushers accepted his challenge. Instead, they quietened their horses and sat silent, squinting through the trees.

Before long they saw the dust rise above the crest, and heard the drum of hooves, the chink of metal, the murmur of voices. Six voices at least and, the best indication of all, a sudden light laugh.

Thirty miles to the north, in the Long Hall at Chinon, the King of England fidgeted with impatience. Audemar was now an hour overdue, and his tardiness bordered on contempt. If he did not arrive soon he would find himself in serious trouble, regardless of his age or failing health. One more hour, the king decided, and then Audemar's name would be added to his list of enemies.

He nodded agreement with himself and gazed along the table at his commanders. They were there in their dozens, the warlords of England and her continental possessions. Men from Normandy and Anjou, Maine and Brittany, Aquitaine and Poitou, together with the local barons of Touraine. On the face of it, a rewarding show of strength for the new king, and an intimidating welcome for Audemar.

It was true that some of the barons had responded out of loyalty to the Crown, though most were simply curious to see how he would handle the first major crisis of his reign. However, few of them held out much hope of success, for the world already knew the king by his freshly coined nickname, John Softsword.

He leaned forward in his high-backed chair and said, "Pass that candle up to me. If Audemar is not here by the time it burns down to the next ring, he'll be found guilty *in absentia* and join the others on the list." Aware that the statement sounded peevish, he added, "He's an old man, that's why I'm allowing him the extra time. Old men move slowly."

The thick tallow shaft was pushed closer, and one of the barons cursed as hot fat splashed his hand. He was uncomfortable enough in his link-mail hauberk and embroidered surcoat, without having blistered fingers to suck. Smoke twisted up from the candle, mingling with that of pitch torches and unmarked tapers. No matter how trivial or serious the situation, the occupants of the Long Hall were perpetually under a cloud.

The laughter was still in the air as the riders reached the crest. They checked their advance, gazed down at the silent, tree-filled plateau, then descended the slope. They noticed the absence of birdsong, but blamed it on their own noisy approach. The horses moved faster on the incline, and the leading members of the escort were careful to let their palfreys run on, so the others would not be bunched as they reached the plateau. . . .

Hidden among the trees, the anonymous ambushers identified Hugh le Brun of Lusignan, Count of La Marche; his brother Ralf of Exoudun, Count of Eu, and between them, the prize they had come to collect, Isabelle of Angoulême, le Brun's bride-to-be. The girl was tall and slender and sat well in the saddle. It did not seem possible that she was only twelve years old.

The ambush had been rehearsed three times a day for a week. It was too much to expect that fifty horsemen would charge forward through bracken and between trees on a single word of command, so it was left to those at the edge of the forest to secure the victory. There would be a shout, and those who heard it would respond, and it was up to them to spur clear of the trees and destroy the escort.

And after that initial shout there was to be absolute silence, save from the one elected spokesman. The others were not to utter a word, on pain of death, and it was this prohibition, more than the charge itself, that had necessitated twenty rehearsals.

Like any trained chevaliers, the ambushers had been brought up to announce themselves on the field, for a man was nothing if he did not declare himself to the enemy. The war cries were simple—one's name, one's fief, one's liege lord—anything that would separate friend from foe. But today's work was to be done in silence, and it had taken a week to convince the ambushers that their closed helmets and muddied shields would be valueless if they emerged from the trees yelling their names.

But practice, and the shadow of the gibbet, had finally fastened their tongues.

The last of the approaching riders reached the plateau. As they joined the column and milled about, not yet in formation, they heard a single word roared from the forest.

"Avaunt!"

It was enough to alert them, but there was no time to close ranks. The ambushers streamed out, slashing at the escort, not caring if the men were killed or wounded or merely unhorsed. The prime objective was to isolate Isabelle and the Lusignan brothers, and it was done with murderous efficiency. The quiet June day was torn apart. Men and horses crashed to the ground, or staggered away from the contracting circle as more assailants plunged from the forest. It was a nightmare that had slept on fitfully until midday.

Hugh and Ralf could do no more than heft their swords and let their astonishment flare into anger, then burn away in frustration. They belonged to one of the greatest families in Christendom. They counted among their ancestors kings of Jerusalem and Cyprus, whilst they themselves were dominant figures in the West, and had survived countless ambuscades. But even the Lusignan brothers did not value themselves as high as fifteen to one.

Even so, Hugh swung at one of the attackers, and the man leaned away, as though despising a fight. Ralf also struck out blindly, but the ambushers circled wide, refusing to engage. While the brothers howled their chagrin, Isabelle hunched down in her saddle, sure that one or other of them would catch her with his free-swinging blade. God knew, most war wounds were inflicted by chance.

Hugh was the first to bring his fury under control, and he leaned across to steady his impetuous kinsman. "Leave it be, brother. They've insulted us enough." He transferred his attention to Isabelle, resting his hand on her arm as he glared at the ring of barrel helms and drab gray surcoats. His frustration had burned to ashes, and he was ready to accept the truth. For the first time in memory the warlords of Lusignan had been taken by surprise.

Count Audemar was carried into the Long Hall on a litter. It was a cleverly designed affair, with legs that swung down at one end, enabling the old man to lie with his head raised, as though on a cushioned couch. This and his appearance explained the delay; he was sixty years old, and his legs were now completely paralyzed.

The litter was borne by two sturdy young knights, and their constant attendance had given rise to various vile rumors. But they were not Audemar's lovers, nor his illegitimate offspring, nor were they unnaturally attracted to each other. It was mere coincidence that had brought them to his castle within the same week, two youths with the dark, curly hair of Aquitaine and the desire to earn themselves the eventual buffet of knighthood.

When they first arrived they were ignorant and uncouth, armed only with letters of recommendation. Audemar had been on his feet in those days, and had accepted them into his service with the salutary warning that they would be trained as rigorously as any Templar or Hospitaller. They would be expected to wait at table, study the songs and poetry of the region and master the brutal arts of warfare. They would not complain when his sergeants cuffed them silly in the yard, nor when his jongleurs made them pick at the strings of the citole until their fingers bled. They would clean dung from the stables, stand a full night's guard in any weather and remain at all times fully obedient to their seniors. In short, they would do as they were told, and learn whatever they were taught.

They would, for example, accord an unwashed cripple the same respect as a nobleman. They would show a peasant woman the courtesy due to a chatelaine. They would care for an urchin child as for any prince of the realm. And, if they were ever found guilty of cruelty, theft or disloyalty—all-embracing terms—they would be whipped raw in the presence of the entire garrison. Should there be any repetition of the crime, Audemar would personally brand them on the palms of their hands and evict them naked into the world. He was glad they did not smile at his promise, for they could surely believe he would keep it.

However, if the clumsy, slipshod youths survived their training with honor, they would find their blood purified, their minds sharpened and their hearts imbued with chivalry. No Christian house would be closed to them, and they would be valued for their rarity, as men of the world.

And, he told them with justifiable pride, they would receive the buffet—the stinging slap of a gauntlet—from Audemar Taillefer, the Iron-Cutter. It would be the last blow they need ever accept, a final test of humility, and a reminder of their fealty. The next man to strike them or their master had better beware, for by then they would be knights of the realm, the martial servants of God, and handy with any kind of blade.

Three years later, the young men had been dubbed by the warlord and given small fiefs on his domain. He promised that, in time, he would find wives for them and allow them to purchase more land. But for the present they would continue in his service and take the lowest seats at table. They did so without demur. They were his men, his gentlemen, but they acknowledged that they still had a lot to learn.

Known now by the names of the villages on their fiefs, Peter de Vars and Alan d'Anville set the tilted litter on the floor. King John had already half-risen from his chair, his impatient expression melting hurriedly into one of polite concern. He had not known that the old man's body was so far gone. Had Audemar been thrown from his horse, or poisoned by bad meat, or what? Someone should have informed him, not allowed him to make threats about guilt *in absentia* without first knowing the warlord's condition. He should have been told. God's eyes, it cost him enough to retain his legions of informers and spies. They should have found out. That's why they were paid.

He moved away from the chair, glanced at Audemar's darkhaired watchdogs, then at the rest of his entourage. Fifteen of the Angoumois nobility, a grim, big-bellied pack.

The visitors gazed, in reply, at the King of England. They knew a few things about him and had heard a thousand rumors, though they had discounted most of the tales as so much exaggeration. They had heard, for instance, that Softsword was a dwarf, and thin as a vine pole, and that his arms were made pendulous by the weight of rings on his fingers. But that was nonsense, of course, for King John was no midget monkey.

He was, however, less than five and a half feet in height. . . .

And the heels of his boots were cut from a dozen slices of colored leather, lifting him three inches from the ground. . . . And every finger was encircled, and there were bracelets on his wrists, and a pendant seal on a chain around his neck. . . . And his cloak, embroidered with scenes of court life, hung from his shoulders like a struck tent.

His brother had been Richard Coeur de Lion, the Lionheart, the Plantagenet giant who had led the Great Crusade against Sultan Saladin and the assembled might of Islam. Richard of England, who had wielded a double-headed ax with the ease that most men swung a sword. Richard, master of the crossbow and the springy, twelve-foot lance; a man of prodigious strength and magnetic personality, of extraordinary physical courage, and with an insatiable desire to be at the head of any cavalry charge or victory parade. He'd loved a parade, the Lionheart, and the cheers that fenced it in.

Understandably, his vices had been as vivid as his virtues. Overbearing pride, an obsessive greed for money, a well-mined vein of cruelty and an intimate predilection for men. The only woman who had pleased him had been his mother, the magnificent Eleanor of Aquitaine, but even she had failed to control his appetites. He had fathered no children, in or out of wedlock, and his death from arrow shot had left England without an heir.

Save for his diminutive, high-heeled brother, John Softsword.

Audemar's barons watched the king approach their master. John had worn the crown for little more than a year, but he had only recently come south to Chinon, and few of the visitors had ever seen him before. At first sight, they did not like what they saw.

He bowed curtly to Audemar. "I'm sorry to find you laid low, my lord. I trust it's a passing blight, and you will soon—"

"It isn't," Audemar said. "The legs have died ahead of the body, that's all." He brushed the subject aside and asked, "Why am I brought here, King John? Your emissary was as impolite as your summons. I thought I had made it clear that I was not yet ready to pledge allegiance to you. I owe nothing to the English cause, nor to the ambitions of your enemy, Philip of France. I hold myself aloof from your quarrels, as I did from those of Coeur de Lion. If you, or Philip Augustus, want me for an ally, you must buy me with reasons, not dictates. I am the master of my domains, and content with them. Why should I be dragged behind the walls of England or the palisades of France? Can you tell me that, lord king? Can you tell me why your war should become mine?"

John stared down at him, then looked away, frowning, as though he had misheard the words. His thin face reddened, and he rubbed his hands together, a closed fist against an open palm. Those who knew him knew the signs.

Like his father, the dead King Henry, and his brother, the dead King Richard, John Softsword suffered from what many termed the Angevin sickness—a mindless loss of temper. A dozen times in the past he had hurled himself to the ground, thrashing and kicking, or drawn his sword to slash indiscriminately at the furnishings. Afterward, he could not remember what he had done, though horrified witnesses told him that spittle had leaked from his mouth, and that a blood-chilling scream had found its way between clenched teeth. Once, years before, he had been involved in a chess game with a friend. His opponent had made some winning move, and John had promptly snatched one of the solid stone pieces and bludgeoned him senseless. Fortunately, an onlooker had wrested the chessman from his grasp before he could strike another blow, but John had then broken free, smashed the inlaid table and careered across the room with such force that he had dented an iron shield propped against the wall.

Next day, he had sent his friend an emerald ring, though he could not bring himself to voice an apology. And, needless to say, they had never again played chess.

Beyond a certain point, the king could no longer rein in his temper. But today he had good reason to try. He found it incredible that the bedridden cripple could lie there and announce that he owed nothing to England, and lecture him on the form and content of his summons, and demand reasons from a king. Well, the devil's dung on that! Audemar *would* pledge allegiance, and he *would* ally himself with England, even if he was hauled behind the walls by his legs! By Christ's wounds, he would. . . . Oh, yes. . . . Oh, yes. . . .

He waited, his head throbbing, his palm rubbed sore by the rings. Then, gradually, the blood drained from his face, and he trusted himself to address the warlord.

"Reasons, eh, Taillefer? Yes, why not, I'll give you reasons.

Your young porters can bring you up beside my chair, and we'll take some wine and talk. Your own entourage may be seated, by seniority, alongside mine, or, if you prefer, together at one side of the table. As you wish." Once more in control of himself, he told the assembly, "Lord Audemar may be assured, we will not chew a fingernail against his will." He nodded at Peter de Vars and Alan d'Anville, and waited for them to lift the litter. They did so when Audemar said, "Very well. We'll take one side of the table, without preference."

While John's commanders made room for the Angoumois, servants appeared with glass goblets—a present from Germany— and stone bottles brought up from the riverside cellars of Chinon. The king resumed his place at the head of the table. He indicated that Audemar was to be served first. Then, when his own glass had been filled, he raised it in salute to the Iron-Cutter, and sprang his trap.

On the tree-filled plateau near Moncontour the ambush had gone as planned. The Lusignans had been surrounded, their escort cut down or disarmed, the twelve-year-old Isabelle there for the taking.

From within one of the enclosed helmets a voice said, "Give her over, le Brun. You cannot defend her. Let her come forward."

Hugh glanced at the girl, then at his gray-garbed assailants. He could not be sure which man had spoken. Perhaps that one, or the one to his right or left. Satan scar them, they were too well disguised. The same surcoats, the same mud-smeared shields, the ring of anonymous barrel helms. And yet—there *were* differences, if one looked carefully enough, and he memorized them against the future. If he ever met a man with three shallow notches in the top of his shield, or with a mustache etched above the mouth-slit of his helmet, or with a flat-topped casque dented beside the left temple . . .

"Give her over, le Brun." There was finality in the tone, and the circle contracted.

Always the more impetuous of the two, Ralf of Exoudun cursed the ambushers as the issue of dripping demons and of rabbits swollen by disease. It was well known that devils could mate with animals, or, assuming the human forms of incubi and succubi,

pass as mortals. Their offspring were hideously deformed—men
with the body of a toad, women with bat's wings that had to be
bandaged down, lest they spread during the night. Everybody
had glimpsed them, skulking in the shadows, or moving about
the country under cover of mist and rain.

It was not an age in which such an insult could be ignored, and
the ambushers reached for their helmets. Their thrice-a-day rehearsals were forgotten and, if their spokesman had not snarled a
warning, they would have shed their masks and proved Ralf the
liar he was. No demon had sired them, and the damned Exoudun
would do well to acknowledge it!

As soon as he had managed to restrain his men, the spokesman
again demanded that Hugh surrender the heiress. "We will kill
you both, Lusignans, if we must. We've been given the license. Let
the Lady Isabelle come forward, or we'll dispatch you and take her
anyway. You have no choice, and we'd as willingly kill you as let
you go on tainting the air. Give her over, le Brun, or be finished
with."

Hugh and Ralf exchanged an agonized glance, then turned
away before Isabelle could catch their eyes. They had their enemies, of course, who did not, and they could name fifty without
drawing breath. But why would anyone wish to harm the heiress
of Angoulême? Who, on God's earth, had fifty masked enemies
at the age of twelve?

The brothers did not speak, though each privately decided that
the girl was being taken for ransom. The ambushers were merely
brigands, who had murdered unsuspecting knights and robbed
them of their armor. Or perhaps they were, themselves, dishonored
knights, who found ransom more attractive than reward. Either
way, Isabelle would be freed in a week or two, for a price.

The spokesman told them to discard their belts and *main-
gauche* daggers. "Now move apart." He nodded cumbersomely
to the men beside him. "Escort the lady. If the Lusignans resist,
cut them away."

The girl began to whimper. She crossed her arms in front of her
face, as though to repel the devil. Then she sat still, a faithful,
pathetic figure.

His eyes on the attackers, Hugh said, "Don't distress yourself,
lady. They dare not harm you. You've been taken for ransom,

that's all. You will be returned to me within—" He raised his voice to address the spokesman, whom he had identified by the nod. "What is your price, brigand? How long *do* you allow us to raise the money?" He glared at the narrow eye-slits and punctured face-plate. "Well, pig? State your terms."

The man did not reply, but waggled the point of his sword in ominous warning. Then, as the brothers surrendered their belts and daggers, he told his companions to collect all the sound horses. It was unfortunate for those members of Hugh's party who had been wounded. They would have to return on foot to Moncontour, or wait for a cart to be sent out from the castle.

The Lusignans dismounted, and Ralf launched into another flow of invective. But this time the ambushers did not rise to the bait. Exoudun could believe what he liked; *they* knew they had not not been spawned by devils. Nevertheless, they hoped that one day they could meet Ralf face to face, blade on blade, and prove it.

As Isabelle was led forward, rigid in the saddle, her arms still crossed, the uninjured horses were divided out, one to a rider, and the withdrawal began. Hugh and Ralf stood together, a natural rallying point for their escort. The grass at the foot of the hill was flecked with blood and littered with the bodies of the dead and wounded. At a glance, five of the escort had been slain in the initial attack, a further five or six cut from the saddle. Most of the injured palfreys would have to be destroyed, and it was with this in mind that Hugh roared, "For pity's sake! Leave one knife with us! Your killing may be over for the day, but ours is not."

The spokesman held his position, the last to withdraw. The heavy barrel helm turned and he gazed at le Brun. "Horses are valuable," he said. "It is a pity they had to suffer. I would much rather it was you." Then he drew his own commonplace dagger, and sent it wheeling toward the edge of the forest. He did not want his act of mercy rewarded with a knife in the back.

Members of the escort went off to search the undergrowth, while the brothers watched their assailants trot away among the trees. When they had gone, Ralf said, "Have you no idea who they—" then stopped, because there were too many suspects. If brigands, it could be anyone. If known enemies, well, as they had decided earlier, there were fifty to choose from without pausing for breath.

Once clear of the plateau, the ambushers picked up speed. The countryside was still thickly wooded, but there were paths and, for the last fifteen miles, a well-ridden track. Obedient to orders, the riders remained silent and anonymous, their leather gambesons slimy with the sweat that trickled from beneath their helmets. However, they were prepared to tolerate a few more hours' discomfort, for they had fulfilled their mission and looked forward to the promised recompense. Each uninjured man would receive three marks apiece and attend a celebration banquet, to which he could bring his wife, mistress, or a whore from the town. Those who had been wounded, and there were three or four who had sustained superficial cuts, would be given an extra coin and excused duty until their wounds had healed; generous compensation for such an everyday hazard.

The heiress had stopped crying and resigned herself to her fate. She did not not know who had abducted her, or why, only that the pleasant morning ride had ended in bloodshed, and that neither her future husband, nor his ill-tempered brother, had lifted a blade to save her. Perhaps, as le Brun had said, she was being taken for ransom, though she was no longer convinced that her abductors were mere brigands. Her greatest fear, at first, was that she would be raped and defiled, but that, too, seemed unlikely. The discipline of the riders was too strong. Brigands would never have kept silent after an ambush. And if they had intended to ravish her, they would have done so by now, their lust emboldened by the darkness and secrecy of the forest. Nor, she realized, would common felons be riding three by three, without jostling or falling back. These men, these murderous thieves, were soldiers of a sort, albeit rancid ones.

Audemar's late arrival at Chinon had upset John's calculations; that and the old man's arrogance. The king had originally intended to treat the warlord as a victim of circumstances, and appeal to him to reconsider his position. He would only exert pressure if the Iron-Cutter proved intransigent.

But Audemar had not appeared until midday, and had then

lain on his tilted bed like some Eastern potentate, critical of the summons and claiming to be aloof from the problems of England. Things had started badly and, as a result, John's courtesy stopped with the offer of wine.

The meeting was twice interrupted by an exchange of blows, the first as one of Audemar's barons struck out at some grunted insult from the other side of the table, the next because a courtier objected to the suggestion that King John would do better to give *his* allegiance to Taillefer. The scuffles had stopped short of swordplay, but the atmosphere remained tense.

From time to time John glanced at the main door, and the visitors prepared to jump back from the table, suspicious that he had reinforcements crouched outside. Audemar's two young watchdogs made ready to drag their master into a corner, where they could best protect him from attack. They had both refused the wine, for fear it was poisoned, and had remained silent and watchful at the head of the litter.

Broken only by the two outbursts of violence, the discussion continued throughout the afternoon. Those barons who were loyal to the king applauded his views, whilst the visitors shrugged aside his offers and ignored his threats. The mass of the assembly said little, for their curiosity would only be satisfied by results. If John could gain Audemar's allegiance, well and good. But so far the high-heeled king had made little impression on the warlord. He would have to do better than this if he was to earn the respect of Normandy and Anjou and the rest. A lot better, for at the moment all they could see was John Softsword, outwitted by a cripple on a couch.

The light in the narrow windows had weakened when the king left his chair and spoke with someone at the door. Audemar's men acknowledged that the caller was alone, though they did not share John's brief smile of satisfaction as he returned to his seat. "So," he told them, "we've been around and around and agreed on nothing. I have stated my position and made my offers, and they've been rejected. However, I will outline the situation one last time, and you'd do well to listen." His voice was firm, and it was clear that whatever he had heard at the door had imbued him with fresh confidence. The assembly waited in silence, while

Audemar beckoned to his watchdogs, who hauled him upright on the bed. Then the king said his piece.

"Some four months ago," he reiterated, "my mother, the dowager Queen Eleanor, was held against her will in the castle of Lusignan, in Poitou. She was restricted there by that self-seeking troublemaker, Hugh le Brun. And he, as ever, was abetted by the tragedy of Exoudun, his brother Ralf. Now, as I told you earlier —as you know without my telling you—my mother is not only Duchess of Aquitaine, but also Countess of La Marche. And, as again you're aware, La Marche shares a common border with Lusignan, and it has long been Hugh's desire to secure that fertile county for himself.

"Well, messires, four months ago he achieved his desire. My mother was on her way back from a visit to La Marche, and was, of necessity, passing through Lusignan. Hugh invited her to stay the night at his castle, and she accepted. It was naïve of her, perhaps, but let me remind you, my lords, Queen Eleanor is seventy-nine years old." He let his gaze slide from courtier to visitor, from the suzerains at the table to the guard sergeants who flanked the door. "I doubt if any of you know a woman who's so advanced in age. Within her eightieth year, and no longer keeping pace with deceit. She grows weary and welcomes a fire and a warm bed. She does not expect to find the door barred in the morning, nor her servants locked away in some other part of the castle. But that's how it was at Lusignan, thanks to le Brun."

The baron gazed at him, expressionless. Eleanor of Aquitaine was, indeed, the woman of her time. Once married to King Louis of France, she had divorced him, turned on her heel and married King Henry of England. She'd borne two children by King Louis, and then during her marriage to King Henry she had given birth to Richard, John and seven other offspring. She was everything Softsword claimed; still elegant and clear-eyed and armed with a coruscating wit. Yet the occupants of the Long Hall were surprised by this display of filial devotion, for the world knew that Eleanor despised him, regarding him as so much dust on Richard's grave.

The king leaned forward, not quite able to reach the table, then turned to Audemar and smiled an apology. "I'm carried away by personal— It's just that I see her there, trapped in that place, too frail to hammer on the door. She will be eighty years old in a few months and—"

"So you said," Audemar growled. "Almost eighty, and lagging behind deceit."

John nodded. "Yes, that's so." Then he said yes again, and his smile shriveled as he realized that the cripple did not think him sincere. *Ah, well, Audemar, I've not yet reached the best part of the tale, the part none of you know. . . .*

He sat back again, arranged his robes and decided how best to impart the news. "Yes," he repeated, "too frail to pound on the door, and held prisoner until she agreed to surrender La Marche. And now what, Taillefer? What to do now that my mother's property is in the hands of the Lusignans? What position should we take, eh, you and I?"

"I answered that question hours ago, and I've echoed it a dozen times since. I am not involved. Four simple words, my lord king. I am not involved. Neither in your quarrel with le Brun, nor in England's conflict with France."

"You puzzle me," John said. "You refuse to give me your allegiance, and expect me to overlook what is an act of defiance, a direct challenge to the Crown. Don't you think your refusal arouses our suspicions? If you will not swear fealty to England, it might well be because you have already done so to Philip Augustus."

"Though I have not."

"Ah, we have your word for it, and are supposed to be satisfied."

"I cannot say what will satisfy you, lord king—"

John nodded quickly and flapped a hand. "Very well, we'll leave that for the moment. Let's turn to your connection with Hugh le Brun. You are his neighbor—"

"If you mean my domain lies south of his, yes, that's true."

"I mean far more than that. I mean that you and— Well, I'll put it another way. Le Brun is my sworn enemy, the creature who held Queen Eleanor against her will until, under duress, she relinquished La Marche. I shall recapture that county in time, and return it to my mother. But first, it was necessary to balance the scales. To take pebble for pebble, so to speak."

Audemar realized what was coming. He heaved himself forward, threatening to topple from the bed. "What are you saying, Angevin? *What are you saying?*"

"That I have repaid le Brun in kind. The only difference is one of relationship and age. He seized my mother, and now I, in turn, have taken his betrothed. You say you are not involved—your simple words—but what choice have you, when the bride-to-be is your daughter, Isabelle of Angoulême?"

He allowed Audemar's knights to steady him on the litter, and listened to the stir of astonishment among the barons. How attentive they were now. How eager to share the victory. How well behaved.

He pointed down at his visitor. "We *know* you, Taillefer! We know you have wrapped yourself in alliance with Hugh of Lusignan, terrified lest he follow his seizure of La Marche with that of Angoulême. And worse, we know you gave le Brun your only daughter as surety for your protection, then let your pretty porters carry you here so that you could brazen it out. Christ's tears, Audemar, if you do not break with the Lusignans and side with me, I shall have your daughter walled up and turn Angoulême into a swamp!

"You may be called Iron-Cutter, but you'll be blunted if you go against me! I am young, and slight, and an easy target for nicknames, but that makes me all the more dangerous. Don't ever go for me, my Lord of Angoulême; I am a wolf in the forest, and I was raised among the shadows, how else would I have survived?

"Look at the table. It's ringed by influential men, intelligent men, yet not one of them anticipated my scheme. They see themselves as lions and bears and destriers, all fine, rampant beasts. But I have run around them, as I've run around you. Disavow your treaty with the Lusignans, and do it without delay. Otherwise, you never had a daughter, or a domain!"

Before he left Chinon, the old man swore fealty to the English Crown, thus breaking his alliance with Lusignan and La Marche.

Hugh and Ralf found the borders of Angoulême closed to them, and learned that Isabelle had been abducted on the orders of King John. They appealed to Audemar, who told them he was powerless to act. They appealed to John, who threw their letters on the fire and evicted their emissaries. Then, as a last resort, they rode north to Paris and appealed to the shrewd and chilly Philip Augustus, King of France.

Elsewhere, Queen Eleanor had heard of her son's vengeance, marveled at his devotion, then sent men to Chinon to learn the truth. Young Softsword might be anxious to drive a wedge between Audemar and the Lusignans, and he might possibly have sought to avenge his aged mother. But Eleanor told her scouts to look for another reason. With John there was always another reason.

"I do not think you'll need to squint and peer in order to find it. It will be as obvious as the castle itself. If it exists, you'll see it as soon as you get there. It'll stare you in the face."

She was right, understanding him better than anyone. When her scouts returned it was to tell her that Isabelle had been given the freedom of the district, yet showed no inclination to leave the castle. She was escorted everywhere, but not by men in mail. It was John who guided her arm, referring to her as the Sparrowhawk, his diminutive bird of prey. She wore two of his rings, trilled at his jokes and disported herself as though she was the chatelaine of Chinon.

"That," Eleanor remarked sourly, "or the next Queen of England."

2

THE ZEPHYR BLOWS CHILL
March, April 1201

The undergrowth had been cleared and boards tied to the surrounding trees, and there was now a level, fenced-off area deep in the forest. Its existence was known only to King John, a handful of his advisers and those workmen who had grubbed the bushes and constructed the fence. The workmen had been sworn to secrecy, on pain of having their tongues clipped, though they could think of no one who would be interested in such a trivial accomplishment.

". . . Listen. You know what lies in the forest south of Chinon? A fenced clearing! I swear it. A path of ground in the trees." No, they decided, the information had little market value.

Nevertheless, it was important to John that the whereabouts of the clearing be kept secret, and the path to it remain unmarked. Empty, it was just a shadowed enclosure, a pen in which to herd stray sheep and pigs. But it would not be empty for long, and men were already converging on it from every part of the country. They, too, had been sworn to secrecy, and told that on no account were they to show themselves at the castle. Instead, they were to make their way to a ruined monastery on the south bank of the Vienne, from whence they would be conducted to the clearing. Once there, they would make obeisance to the king and display their special skills.

Of the twenty or so that had been summoned, three would be chosen, and of these, two would eventually perform. The third would be retained in case either of his companions fell ill or deserted.

One other who was privy to the secret was Isabelle of Angoulême, or, more correctly, Queen Isabelle of England. In this, too, Eleanor had been right, for John had married the girl in August, two months after her abduction and, in October, she had been crowned in Westminster Abbey. The English barons found the child-queen uncomfortably strong-willed, but they prayed that she would curb John's vile temper and help allay his sense of persecution. If anyone could calm him, it would surely be his Sparrowhawk.

On the other side of the Channel the nobility were less optimistic, and queried the speed with which John had taken her as his wife and queen. Had she really been abducted—pebble for pebble—in response to the Lusignans' treatment of Eleanor, or had John previously taken a fancy to the girl and stolen her for himself? The situation was serious enough, for the theft had alienated not only Hugh and Ralf, but many of their supporters. The crippled Audemar had isolated himself in Angoulême, while, in Paris, Philip Augustus weighed the Lusignans' appeal. Serious enough, the barons agreed, but what if the king had stolen the girl merely to gratify his personal desires? He would then have hoodwinked his enemies *and* his friends, this wolf from the forest.

When the Sparrowhawk learned why the ground had been cleared, she insisted on attending the display. She told her husband, "I can be of value to you, when you make your selection."

"There'll be no pennants," John said. "It's not an entertainment."

"I know. We have our own yards for that."

"And there'll be blood. It's unavoidable."

With chilling accuracy, she said, "But that's the issue, isn't it?"

Unwilling to agree, he closed his hand over hers. "Very well, keep me company. But before the selection there's another problem to be dealt with. Amongst all my advisers, can you guess which one is most opposed to the scheme?"

She nodded immediately. "Yes, though the question that does defeat me is why you continue to listen to him. He's an old man, old and I'd have thought served out. Every day you speak ill of him, complain about him, step wide of him. It's become a ritual

with you, my lord"—she withdrew her hand and raised it to forestall his denial—"a ritual to curse him when we're alone." She
did not add that the ritual was most often enacted at night, to be
followed by a bout of ferocious lovemaking, as though by drawing
cries from his wife, John could somehow expunge his fears. "Why
not dispense with him. He brings you more distress than—"

"Sweet Christ!" John erupted. "You do no better than my
friends. If I were to list— If I described the ways and methods that
have suggested themselves to me. From banishment to sinecure;
sent off as emissary to the East, in the hopes that he would fall
prey to disease or some Saracen arrow. Yes, and a backstairs murder not least among them. Dispense with him? Oh, yes, Isabelle,
I'll dispense with him. When a ship can do without sails."

The outburst left him with his mouth twisted in irony and with
one hand pressed to his head, a mannerism he had long since
been unable to control. The gesture had begun as a way of dis-
playing his elegant, bejeweled fingers on a mat of reddish hair,
but time and tension had transformed it into an instinctive clamp
of despair.

Isabelle watched, appalled that even now, in the sanctuary of
their private chambers, the king could be so cowed. His air of
resignation made her careless, and she shouted back at him, "I *am*
better than your friends, for I know best of all what he does to
you. He countermands your authority and blocks your way. He
comes between you and half the things you would achieve. He
brings you awake at night, sweating out the problems that he has
set. He has you shivering, my lord, and clutching your skull. Yet
you allow all this, and still regard him as, what did you call it, the
sail for your ship?"

In a weak attempt at humor, John said, "I meant the wind. As
king, I can afford to buy the sails, but only he, it seems, has the
knack of raising the wind."

"Maybe so," she continued, "but I have never heard this special
wind that drives you all along. We trade ten words a day, he and I.
Cold courtesies, for that's all he'll afford me. Oh, I find no fault
with his greetings or farewells. He bows just deep enough, and
he'd catch me if I stumbled on the steps. But I know what he
thinks of his new queen, and I can tell you how I see *him*."

"Don't," John murmured. "You are angry on my behalf, and for yourself, but you do not know him, so—"

"A lean, dried-out scabbard, with its sword rusted away."

"You don't know him," John repeated. "I like him less than you do, and yes, he certainly blocks my path. But he is necessary to me, and—"

"Then let me learn."

"What?"

"If I don't know him, let me find out. You say there's a problem to be resolved. Well, let me be there when you resolve it. I'd like to see how he fills the sails."

The king started to shake his head, then turned the movement into a shrug. Why not? The experience might make Isabelle more tolerant of his nightmares. Yes, it was probably time she put to sea with William Marshal.

He had been up on the wall walk, and was still dressed in his link-mail hauberk and studded gauntlets. The latter were too new for comfort, the leather inflexible, the metal sharp from the anvil. It would need a few weeks of sweat and rain to mold the gloves to his hands, a dozen applications of oil before the scraped ox-hide became supple. Once they had taken shape, they would be welcome protection against the cold and the sudden wrench of a sword grip.

The previous pair had lasted more than a year, but they had eventually rotted to their fibers and were now in his weapons chest, with other discarded equipment. Early years of poverty had taught him to abandon nothing; a split belt was still good for its buckle, or as laces, while the arms of a leather gambeson could be unstitched, then attached to a sleeveless tunic. He was no longer poor, far from it, but the habit had never left him, witness the pile of mildewed clothes.

He shut the chamber door, hung his helmet from a hook above the chest, then tugged wearily at his gauntlets. He had walked the entire length of the ramparts, climbed the narrow stairways of every tower, and exchanged a nod or a comment with each of the sixty lookouts. He was neither the constable of Chinon, nor sergeant of the guard, and was under no obligation to patrol the mile-long wall. Yet he did so at every change of the watch, albeit pausing longer and more often to catch his breath. If the guards noticed the lengthening interruptions, they welcomed them as the chance to spend more time in the company of their hero, William Marshal. These days, there were few malingerers among the wall guards of Chinon.

He had freed one hand from his glove when he heard a heel tap on the flagstones, and he swung around to see King John emerge from the deep recess beside the fire. As in most rooms in the castle, logs smoldered day and night, summer and winter, in an attempt to combat the dampness drawn up from the Vienne. But during Marshal's tour of the defenses the fire had gone unattended, and the flames had died down, no longer illuminating the stone benches that lined the recess.

From the other side of the alcove came Queen Isabelle, her eyes reddened by smoke, her expression a mixture of discomfort and triumph. It was obvious that Marshal had been caught unawares, the way the king's footsteps had startled him. The mighty Earl of Pembroke, to whom Christendom supposedly clung for color, and here he was, surprised at his own fireside.

It's his age, Isabelle thought. It must have smothered his senses, to leave him so vulnerable. What if we had been assassins? He'd be dead by now, with one gauntlet still hanging from his hand. A ludicrous sight, not at all what the devoted garrison would expect from their exemplar.

John acknowledged an unsmiling welcome and said, "We sent word we were coming, Earl Marshal. The messengers are probably still tramping the length of Chinon. You were in one of the turrets, I daresay."

"I was in all of them," Marshal told him, "and I am still waiting to see evidence of the repairwork I suggested. The list grows, King, and the weak spots become more apparent. Your father called this place 'a stone crown on a stone head,' and did more than anyone to improve its defenses—"

"I told you before, my architects are examining your reports. These things take time."

"And effort," Marshal emphasized. "But so long as none of the architects turn traitor and tell the enemy where best to place their ladders . . . A stone crown was King Henry's description, not a patchwork cap." He dragged off the second glove and tossed the pair into the open chest. He was impatient to shed his heavy mail tunic, but he resigned himself to another hour of clinking irritation. Perhaps less than an hour; perhaps the rest of the day. It depended on his visitors.

"You're right to hound me," John placated. "Chinon must remain impregnable, as must Château Gaillard and Loches and our other frontier fortresses. If we lost Chinon"—a sudden grin, boyish and charming, a valuable weapon in his armory—"well, you'd be deprived of your promenades, eh, Marshal? There are no other walls in the region as extensive as—" But his humor evaporated beneath the warlord's gaze, and he turned away to motion Isabelle into a chair. "No more pleasantries," he told her. "We'll say our piece and go. The Earl of Pembroke was never one for uninvited guests."

The chair was too large for the young queen, as it would have been for John, and she was forced to sit well forward, as though eager to hear what was being said. She hoped John would notice her plight and forage for some cushions, but he stayed where he was, his eyes on Marshal.

"It's been a disturbed year, so far," the king said. "The Lusignans ran squealing to King Philip and, when he rejected their complaints, they took the law into their own hands."

"He did not reject them," Marshal countered. "He set them aside in favor of more pressing business. If you're here to discuss recent events, lord king, you must be more precise. Philip Augustus rejects no one. The word does not apply."

"Very well. The brothers were set aside. They were put off. Their complaints were held in abeyance. However you care to phrase it. But you would agree that since then they've fomented trouble in Poitou and Normandy. You *would* accept that they've made the law their own?"

"Yes, I would. In return for which you have installed your own commanders in La Marche and all but driven Ralf from his holdings in Normandy."

"God's sight!" John snapped. "You say that with disapproval. Of course I invaded their lands! They are traitors to the Crown, they and all who support them. They refused to pledge allegiance to England, maltreated my mother in order to secure La Marche and now they're in open revolt against me. Of course I attack them! Or does that word not apply!" He had begun to slap the flat of his hand against the chair arm, a rhythmical overture to fury, symptoms of the Angevin sickness.

Isabelle murmured, "Don't let him blow you about, my lord." Then, in her first informal address to Marshal, "Do you know, Pembroke, there's a smell that pervades this chamber? It's you, I think, reeking of reason. How you love to sit in judgment on the king's actions, only stirring yourself to prowl the walls. Yet I did not see *you* lead the invasion into La Marche—" She felt John's hand on her shoulder and glanced up as he mouthed, "Leave it be. You do not know him. Now leave it be."

But she would not be dissuaded. True, she was sublimely ignorant of Marshal's achievements, but she would not let him stand there—a picture of hawk-nosed severity—and imply that the king himself held the law on a loose rein. If William Marshal had the power to raise the wind, she had yet to see him do it.

"Nor did you accompany King John on his recent visit to Philip Augustus. Indeed, I have not been witness to anything you've done, unless it's to cast yourself as the Zephyr. Is that the part you take, Pembroke, the god of the west wind, blowing us about?" It only required her to stamp her foot, and it would have been perfect. But she lacked her husband's high heels, and could not quite reach the floor.

John interceded. "There's no value in this. Queen Isabelle has mentioned the meeting with Philip, at which I agreed to grant the Lusignans a fair hearing. We merely want your opinion, Marshal, on how best to summon them."

He tried another disarming grin, but again it failed, and he let his gaze edge down to Isabelle. Too late now, the list of Marshal's accomplishments unrolled in his mind, and he blamed himself for having kept the Sparrowhawk in ignorance. He had meant to apprise her, but, each time the opportunity had arisen, he'd found himself unable to speak well of the man who made him sweat in his sleep.

Nevertheless, to hear his wife suggest that William Marshal only walked the walls, that he cast himself as a god, but had otherwise not done much . . .

He had spent his youth on horseback, traveling the length and breadth of Europe, the undefeated champion of a hundred brutal tourneys. . . . If nothing else, he had visited as many countries as a messenger, or a pilgrim. . . . If nothing else, his success in the lists and against the quintain remained unsurpassed. . . . If nothing else, his name was known throughout the West by the time he was twenty. . . .

But he had then gone on to serve the volatile King Henry, choosing to remain landless whilst his companions scrambled in search of manors or fiefs. . . . They had grown rich around him and, growing rich, had grown fat.

At forty-three he was still single, and had then married a woman of nineteen, the enchanting Isabel de Clare, heiress of Pembroke and Striguil. . . . With the peal of the wedding bells the impoverished knight had become one of the most powerful noblemen in England, and would never again need to patch thread-bare tunics.

The companions of his early life were fattened for the grave, but another ten years had passed, during which he had sired five sons and guided the tempestuous Richard Lionheart, daring to contradict him when others acquiesced.

And now, as Henry had bequeathed him to Richard, so Richard had charged him to guide the fortunes of brother John. . . . But it remained to be seen if the heroic William Marshal, the arid, dried-out scabbard, was still firm enough to hold Softsword. . . . Henry and Richard had been problematic enough, but they were lions, and here was a wolf.

Isabelle's accusations had earned her one of Marshal's rare, dry smiles, and he made no attempt to defend himself. Instead, he nodded at John's hurried explanation and said, "How best to summon the Lusignans? At swordpoint, I should think. They'll never come otherwise."

"And why not? They are being offered the justice of the court."

Marshal shifted in his heavy mail coat. "Is that why the ground has been cleared in the forest? An open-air hearing? The scent of spring?"

"You know what it's for, so don't play the innocent."

"Yes, King, I do, and so will they within the week. And then how will they react to your talk of a fair hearing? Why not ask it of yourself? Ask how you would react if you learned that

Philip Augustus had fenced off a Paris square with you in mind. Would *you* take the risk? No, my lord, you'd do better to have the boards dismantled, and think again. If not, you will drive the Lusignans even deeper into rebellion and closer to France."

John stared at the lean, dark-skinned commander. Marshal's adzed features and bird's beak nose reminded men of the Bedouin, the Saracens, the ferocious disciples of Mohammed. For the thousandth time the king wished it had been so; that Marshal *had* been an Arab, and slain by a crusader.

Turning slightly to gain his wife's tacit support, he said, "I cannot accept your reasoning. If the Lusignans reject the summons—and only you say they will—they'll be branded as cowards throughout the West."

"On the contrary," Marshal told him, "they'll be praised for their damn good sense."

"Oh, not by Philip, they won't. His own words to me in Paris: 'I have no wish to intervene in your dispute, so long as there is the chance of your being reconciled with Hugh le Brun.' Philip has encouraged this hearing from the outset—"

"As part of his strategy."

"—and, if the Lusignans stay away, he'll disavow them, nobles who are afraid to face justice."

"That's another word out of keeping," Marshal sighed. "The King of France would not disavow Satan himself, if there was a profit to be made from the alliance. He has not intervened yet, because he's waiting to see the nature of your summons. You promised him a fair hearing for the Lusignans, but I doubt if you mentioned the diversion you have planned for them in the forest."

"So you think I've been led along, do you? You see them hand in hand, Philip and the Lusignans?"

"They've been hand in hand all year. But I'm more worried that, unless you abandon your scheme, we shall see them horse by horse on English soil."

Isabelle came forward abruptly from her chair. "Now the Zephyr blows chill. Listen to him long enough, and he'll have Philip knocking on the gate. God knows it, the French have no need to raise an army. Marshal will do their work for them, with his forecasts of doom. I say we should issue the summons. Neither

Hugh nor Ralf are as fainthearted as Pembroke believes. They'll come." She glared up at Marshal and with sudden spite told him to walk the walls again. "You might see the enemy fording the Vienne."

John escorted her from the chamber. In the doorway he glanced back, but it was impossible to gauge his expression, for he had one hand raised, his fingers splayed across his head.

So the selection took place. It continued for three days, though Queen Isabelle could stomach no more than the first bloody morning. Whatever stirrings of excitement she may have felt were quickly curdled by the horrors of the scene, and she was led from the clearing with vomit on her gown. John had warned her not to expect an entertainment, but not even he had imagined the carnage that would ensue.

The Sparrowhawk's sudden departure had brought the contest to a standstill. From the start, her presence at the board fence had embarrassed the participants. It was no place for a lady, and King John should have realized it. However, it seemed unlikely she'd return, so perhaps they could get on with the job they'd been brought here to do. They waited for the sergeant to rap the shield.

He did so as John nodded assent, and two fully accoutered knights lumbered forward from opposite corners of the clearing. Their dress was as anonymous as that worn by the ambushers near Moncontour—enclosed helmets, plain tunics, commonplace swords and bucklers. The arms and armor had been supplied by the king. The contestants had merely been required to find their way to the ruined monastery, from whence they had been taken to different parts of the forest. There, attended by one of John's barons, each of the arrivals had been installed in a crude shelter and told to await his summons. The men were not the type to complain about their lodgings; they had food and wine and the promise of reward, and all they had to do for it was fight.

Isabelle's departure had delayed the start of the fourth individual bout, so it was clear that her revulsion had arisen from one of the previous contests. Perhaps the first, when a man had leaned down and, with his left hand, scooped up the sliced-off fingers of his right. Or the last, in which one of the unidentified warriors had had his head wrenched back, leaving space for his opponent's blade to go in between helmet rim and circlet. The onlookers agreed that the winner had made a messy job of it, for his victim had flailed about with half a sword's length in his windpipe. By the time the man had accepted his death, the queen had vomited and fled.

The fourth duel was a give-and-take affair. The contestants were too well matched, too stubborn to surrender, too greedy for reward. They swung at each other in a dull carillon, trading blows in rhythm. Blood seeped through their armor and ran from beneath their helmets, and their clumsy movements showed that bones had been shattered. The onlookers had witnessed grislier sights than this, though it was obvious that neither man would be chosen, and they shouted at the sergeant to stop the fight. Then, before he could do so, one of the combatants tore his helmet from his head and croaked surrender. His face was so badly battered that even now he was unrecognizable.

Physicians climbed through the fence to tend the disfigured warriors, while the barons turned their gaze to the king. The bloody spectacle had been his idea. Bejeweled and embroidered, he was the one who'd dreamed up the plan. It was Softsword who had decided to summon the Lusignans to a fair hearing, then challenge them to a trial by combat, and it was he who had secretly invited the twenty mercenaries and brigands to prove themselves in the arena. The best of these would be his champions, meting out his special version of justice. The truth unearthed with the edge of a pitted sword.

Emboldened by wine, the king forced himself to attend the subsequent bouts. He asked Marshal to keep him company, but the earl refused and his absence acted as a magnet on the spectators. By the time the last blow had been struck, two days later, there were more physicians than barons at the fence. The king chose his champions, paid off the others and returned, sickened, to the castle. The boards were left to rot.

In the third week of March, Hugh of Lusignan and Ralf of Exoudun received their summons. No mention was made of a trial by combat, but they had already learned what lay in store for them and immediately took their complaints to King Philip.

He registered astonishment at John's deceit and sympathized with the indignant brothers.

"The Plantagenets were always unpredictable," he told them. "My father would not trust King Henry out of his sight, and for my part I doubted Coeur de Lion, even in the clarity of noon. He was known as Yea-and-Nay when he was younger, and I always thought it a more suitable name than Lionheart."

Escorting the Lusignans on a tour of the Louvre palace, he continued, "Of them all, John is the worst, for he's more cunning than Henry or Richard ever were. And something else to bear in mind in one's dealings with Softsword—he has never been restricted by pride. The feeling's unknown to him." He took Hugh and Ralf by the arm, flattered them with his touch, then guided them through the newly built cloisters that abutted the palace. The three men stepped carefully, for the flagstones had not yet had time to settle. In a week or so the masons would go around with mallets, tapping the flags into the beds of sand. Gardeners, too, would periodically check the open, central area to make sure the transplanted bushes had taken root. A year from now, and the cloisters would make a welcome retreat for monarch and monks.

"This trap of his," Philip said, "it runs counter to everything the world demands of a king, yet it fits his character like a key in a lock. If the information is correct, and, as I say, it has the click of truth, then it's intolerable that you should be lured to Chinon to face paid felons. I know you are anxious to defend your honor, but I cannot allow you to submit yourselves to his terms." He glanced at them, aware that they were both greedy for praise, yet touchy on the subject of courage. They must not think they were being protected, least of all from Softsword and his mercenaries. It would never do if the lords of Lusignan and Exoudun believed they were being denied a fight.

"There is not the slightest doubt," Philip larded, "that you'd each win your contests, no matter who Softsword sent against you. But if we descend to his level—if we accept that trial by combat is proof of guilt or innocence—then we give power to monsters. Speaking for myself, I would not last a moment in the arena, and I have no intention of proving my worth against baseborn soldiers." He paused, seeking the word, then said, "For men such as you, men of nobility, it would be unfitting. You will stay with me, messires, whilst we plan a proper response."

At thirty-five, the Capetian King of France was two years older than John. He was taller, even without the benefit of high heels, and almost totally bald. He was also blind in one eye, a disability that had left him with an expression of amused skepticism.

King Richard had spoken of him as a cold fish, his good eye as bleak as his bad. But the Lionheart's opinion had been distorted by his own uncontrollable desires, and his advances toward Philip had been rebuffed. After that, he would hear nothing good of the Frenchman. The fish was a bloodless schemer, whose only ambition was to enlarge the pond of his kingdom. Oh, *he* knew what Philip was about, let no one doubt it. Encircled by Flanders, the German states and the Angevin empire, France was anxious to spill over its banks and wash its neighbors into the nearest sea. And how the French fish would love it, if he could then turn his single eye on England.

With the bitterness of the spurned lover, Coeur de Lion had denied Philip's patience and tenacity, his unrivaled skill as a diplomat, his ability to make the most outlandish demands sound reasonable. But worse, he had instilled his prejudices in brother John, ensuring that the historic enmity between France and England continued unabated.

Philip Augustus was now in the twenty-second year of his reign. King Henry had managed to hold him at bay, but Richard had found himself outmaneuvered time and again. With the accession of John, the Plantagenet chain had reached its weakest link, and Philip prepared to snap it. Or, in terms that Softsword would more readily understand, the fish was about to make a splash.

3

MIREBEAU
April 1201–August 1202

John seemed genuinely surprised when the brothers rejected his summons. Their emissary informed him that the lords of Lusignan and Exoudun had learned of his duplicity and would on no account present themselves at Chinon. Unless, of course, the king chose to don armor and personally engage Hugh le Brun in single combat—

"That day may come," John snarled. "Once he's been tracked to his midden heap."

—whereupon the said Hugh le Brun would respond with alacrity—

"Yes, and ten thousand traitors."

—at a place to be mutually agreed. The King of England's attempt to lure Lord Hugh and Lord Ralf into his trap followed too closely upon that same king's unwarranted invasion of La Marche and his clandestine abduction of the Lady Isabelle of Angoulême. The world viewed with disfavor the secret and deceitful manner in which John of England—

"*And* of Lusignan! *And* of Exoudun!" He gestured irritably at his guards. "Take that man out of here. I go to priests if I'm in need of admonition; I do not accept it from the messengers of traitors."

As the emissary was being herded toward the door, John shouted after him, "Tell your masters our patience is off the leash! It is we who will respond with alacrity. And then let's see who's out of favor!"

He was heartened by the murmur of approval from his barons. They had doubted the wisdom of the ambush and, still more, the ill-conceived business in the clearing. But now, at last, the king had issued an open challenge to the troublemakers. If a punitive expedition could be mounted—yes, with alacrity—and the Lusignans tried and hanged, it would deter other would-be rebels and give the French fish pause for thought.

However, there were a few, among them a tight-lipped William Marshal, who heard another, more ominous sound—the satisfied chuckle of Philip Augustus.

During the past few months English spies had reported a growing state of preparedness within the French army. Mercenaries had been recruited from as far afield as Spain, Sweden and the distant principalities of Poland and Galicia, and Philip was not the type to squander money on idle soldiers. They had been hired for a purpose and, if the latest reports were to be believed, still more were being hired.

But for what purpose? Neither Flanders nor Germany posed any immediate threat to France, so Philip must be anticipating trouble from the west. Was he then expecting an Angevin invasion and merely strengthening his defenses, or was he himself about to launch an attack?

Marshal listened as the murmurs swelled to cheers. He could remember only one other occasion on which John had been so noisily acclaimed; his coronation, when his stewards had thrown money to the poor.

The earl pushed his way through the Long Hall, not caring who he bruised with his elbows. Of the seventy assembled barons, he counted ten as personal friends and knew that another twenty or so would give him support. But the word would soon be out; exaggerated as always. "King John rides in pursuit of the traitors! The Lusignans are at bay!" And then further contingents would rally to the royal standard, and even the moderate barons would be swayed, and Philip would have the pretext he needed.

As Marshal saw it, events had now gained the momentum of an avalanche. No one could say exactly when the slide had started; perhaps when the Lusignans had detained Queen Eleanor and forced her to surrender La Marche. John had immediately demanded restitution and their vow of allegiance, and then, failing in both, had abducted the child Isabelle.

A dangerous sequence, though not yet disastrous. Pebble for pebble, until the king had turned his captive into his queen.

And then the brothers had risen in open rebellion, and John had invaded their territories, and both sides had appealed to France. The pebbles had dislodged stones, disturbing rocks, which had in turn loosened the slabs. The landslide had gathered weight and force and speed, and the spectacle had begun to draw the crowds. Armed crowds that sailed from England, or marched from Cilicia.

And what next, now that Softsword's patience was off the leash? The Lusignans would once again appeal to Philip, demanding that he help them regain their honor and their lands. And from Hugh le Brun a special plea; the rescue and return of Isabelle.

At Chinon the militant barons would insist that John keep his word and track the brothers to their lair, be it a midden heap or the Palais du Louvre. To the devil with Philip's warnings that any incursion would be taken as an attack on France. If he chose to give sanctuary to traitors—well, he must expect the consequences.

What concerned Marshal was his growing conviction that the farsighted, half-blind Frenchman *did* expect the consequences, and was inviting them. It made the earl strike out harder as he elbowed a path to the door.

The following months were given over to vicious border skirmishes and the constant exchange of threats. John wisely stopped short of invasion, but continued to demand the surrender of Hugh and Ralf. Marshal urged his fellow barons to contain their impatience, though by doing so he left himself open to charges of timidity and failing powers. The once-great William Marshal would never have been seen at Chinon, counseling caution. He'd have been in Paris by now, his sword arm aching. Age had dampened his fires, that was the trouble, and only his contemporaries could remember how brightly he had blazed. As more barons rallied to the cause, more of them asked why the court paid so much heed to the Arab. God's eyes, he didn't even look like a Christian.

The winter saw more emissaries on the road, riding east and west with letters of complaint, appeals for reason, counterclaims and denials and fresh accusations. English soldiers had raped ten women at Blois, tying them down in the main square, their wrists and ankles pinioned to market weights. French mercenaries had struck deep into Touraine, disemboweling innocent peasants and throwing firebrands into every house en route. The English swine, the French carrion; the French, the English, carrion and swine.

It was Philip who added fresh ingredients to the pot.

The border conflict was costly, and so far neither side had made any significant gains. The moderates were frustrated in their attempts to bring the adversaries to the table, whilst the militants grew increasingly restive. If the situation was not resolved, one way or the other, swords would soon turn inward. It was time to thicken the stew, or let it cool.

He reminded his courtiers of the year-old dispute between the Lusignans and King John, then summoned John to Paris to defend himself against charges of abduction, the illegal seizure of La Marche, and of insulting the distinguished lords of Lusignan and Exoudun. The accusations had already gathered dust, but they provided the platform from which to issue his real challenge.

The underhanded ambush at Moncontour, the undeclared invasion of La Marche, the unsprung trap in the clearing near Chinon—these were all indications that John could not be trusted. Therefore his presence at the French court would no longer be enough. He would have to offer a more tangible token of good faith; say the massive fortresses of Falaise and Château Gaillard.

It was a brilliant and wholly unacceptable demand. Château Gaillard was a border stronghold and the very gateway to Normandy. It had been the brainchild of Richard Lionheart—his Insolent Castle—and the barons would no more have parted with it than with the crown of England.

Philip knew this, which is why he made the demand.

Falaise was much older—the handiwork of William the Conqueror—but for many years it had been deep within Angevin territory. Again, there was no thought of surrendering it to the French. If they hung their banners from the walls of Falaise, why not from Dover? Why not the Tower of London?

Philip knew this too, and awaited John's reply.

When it came—an angry rejection of the summons—it confirmed all French suspicions. Softsword had no intention of seeking peace. The very thing he claimed of the Lusignans was true of him; he dared not face justice. Give him his secret clearings and he would prowl about, like the wolf he was. Let him send his pack to lurk in ambush and delight would drip from his fangs. But call him into the open, and he was nowhere to be seen.

With a well-staged show of piety, Philip Augustus presided over a council of war. John was held in contempt, and the historic links between France and England were severed. Action would be taken to reclaim La Marche and secure its borders, along with those of Lusignan and Exoudun. No unnecessary incursions would be made into Angevin territory, though, naturally, force would be met with force. It was devoutly hoped that King John saw the error of his ways and sued for peace, else who could say where it would end?

For the past hour rain had softened the thin layer of topsoil, and the horses wallowed as their hooves sank through to the chalk. The twenty riders hunched in their saddles, the hoods of their traveling cloaks pulled forward, mud on the hems. Progress had slowed to a walk, and the escort commander suggested breaking the journey at the next village. Suggested, because one did not give orders to the dowager Queen Eleanor.

Her reply was curt and in character. "The next time I dismount will be in Poitiers, within arm's length of a fire. My bones are too brittle for these long excursions—"

"Then let's wait out the storm—"

"—but now I'm in the saddle I intend to stay here. Don't tempt me, messire. Once I dismount it'll be for a week."

"It's another fifteen miles, maybe more."

"Then speed us along," Eleanor told him, "speed us along. At our present rate it will be age that kills me, not the weather." She glimpsed his shrug of resignation and drew back the edge of her hood. Blinking against the rain, she said, "I can hear your thoughts, messire. 'She is a truculent old woman who spurns advice. The journey *will* kill her, but *I'll* be the one who's blamed.' Isn't that it?"

"I assure you, my lady—"

"But I agree. If the first occurs, the second will undoubtedly follow. So you'd better get me to Poitiers before I expire; it's your only salvation." Her voice carried the full weight of her years, yet the words were framed by the faintest smile, and the commander acknowledged that he would, somehow, deliver her safe to Poitiers. If the eighty-year-old Eleanor could preserve such a smile, then she, herself, must be preserved.

The column continued south and was still riding head on into the rain when it met the Lusignan patrol. There was comedy in the collision, for both parties assumed the other was friendly and disentangled with apologies. It was only when they had re-formed and passed on opposite sides of the track that a member of the patrol twisted in his saddle, growled to himself, "*Aliénor?*" then yelled at his companions, "*C'est elle! J'en suis sûr! C'est Aliénor!*"

The hiss of rain added to the confusion, for some of the patrol thought he had shouted "*C'est une alliance!*" So why the fuss? What was so unusual about friendly patrols passing on the road? Why scream and jabber when— What? *Aliénor d' Aquitaine?* Sweet Christ, how the brothers would love to seize her again! And how they'd reward those who brought her in!

The men of Lusignan wrenched at the reins, struggling to turn on the narrow path, then spurred back in pursuit.

But by now the patrol had also been identified. Eleanor's party wheeled aside and plunged down a steep, bracken-covered slope, riding without direction. Two knights flanked the dowager queen, bruising her with their legs, gripping her shoulders with metal gloves. The rain curtained their flight, but the horses had tracked mud down the slope and it would not take their pursuers long to find the trail. Poitiers was still twelve miles to the south and, even if they eluded this patrol, how many others churned the roads between here and the city?

They must find a more immediate sanctuary. The choice was obvious and limited. They would head for the nearby castle of Mirebeau and pray God they did not lose their way. . . .

There were three local men in the party, and the escort commander roared at them to take the lead. So long as the flight lasted, these three mounted archers would decide the route and issue whatever orders they chose. They were too hard pressed to think about it now, but if they survived to reach Mirebeau, they could tell their friends they'd saved and commanded Queen Eleanor and her knights.

Following the guides, the column plowed through the valley, swerved west along the edge of a dark, rain-pocked lake, then sent their palfreys racing across a series of natural causeways. Riders twice misjudged the direction of the high earth banks and ran their mounts into the water. Nothing could be done for the men and they drowned quickly, weighed down by their armor. The horses thrashed against the bank, or swam out into the lake.

The nightmare ride continued. The causeways widened, and then the fugitives were among the trees again and at the mercy of thorns and branches. A horseman was clubbed senseless, but he was well enough jammed in his saddle to be carried onward in the rush. The rain and slap of the leaves cloaked any sounds of pursuit, but there was no reason to think they'd outdistanced the patrol. After all, their pursuers might also be guided by men who knew the country.

The trees thinned and the riders reined in for a moment, their faces scratched and swollen. As the escort commander approached Eleanor he was horrified to see that she, too, bore the marks of passage. They both knew that his concern would achieve nothing, and she waved him away with a curt, "Take us on, messire. I don't welcome an arrow in the back."

He nodded, wiped at his own watered cuts and the column moved forward again, ascending the first of a dozen humpbacked hills. The guides faltered once and the party was forced to re-trace its steps. Then the horses were laboring up another incline and over another bald ridge. Eleanor swayed in the saddle and was immediately supported by the attendant knights. Rain drifted across the hills. The journey seemed endless, aimless, an enacted dream in which the party must be subjected to every natural hazard. Soon they would enter a land of fire and molten rock, or feel the piercing shards of ice carried on the wind. They were already numbed by the rain, battered by the lurch of their horses and the whip of branches, goaded on by the fear of death or capture. They had almost forgotten their destination. It might be a mile away or less, the small, insecure castle of Mirebeau. But however eagerly it beckoned, they could neither see nor imagine it. Before they reached Mirebeau, they must first sample the torments of the world.

The man who saw them emerge from the gloom fitted an arrow in his bow and shouted the alarm. The shout was relayed to others on the wall and more shafts were leveled at the riders. The gate guards slipped an arm through the leather brace of their shields, hefted their spears and ran forward to bar the way. A bell tolled, alerting the constable and his knights, and they strode from the isolated keep, incensed that anyone should choose to threaten the castle in weather like this.

The column slowed and halted. The three guides nodded wearily to each other, then, with some slight reluctance, waited for the escort commander to come forward and reclaim command. The guides had never spoken directly to Queen Eleanor, but they knew her well enough to accept that she would reward them for their achievement. Not today, perhaps, for they were all too tired. But as soon as she was strong enough she'd send them a few coins and a word of thanks. Worldly men that they were, they also knew they'd set aside one of the coins as a keepsake, then spend it when they needed money for a drink.

The escort commander went on alone to meet the constable of Mirebeau. Their exchange was short and to the point, for neither was anxious to leave Queen Eleanor out in the rain. The flurry of movement that had followed the first shouted alarm was repeated, but this time the gate guards formed a protective ring around the visitors, whilst the garrison archers directed their sights at the drifting rain clouds. God grant mercy to any innocent traveler who chose this time to reach Mirebeau, for he'd find himself with a chestful of arrows.

Eleanor entered the castle. Held in the saddle by her knights, she was escorted as far as the keep, then helped to the ground and all but carried indoors. The atmosphere at Mirebeau was compounded of sorrow, fury and embarrassment; sorrow for the old woman, her face torn and disfigured by the whip of the branches; fury with those devils who had hounded her, and embarrassment that the castle was unprepared for the arrival of the great dowager queen. There would be some hasty banking of fires and airing of beds, and the wine merchants in the nearby town had better produce their finest vintage, and by the barrel load. As for the garrison, as ever understrength, they could look forward to a wet and dismal night, on guard against the demons of Lusignan. If Queen Eleanor sickened and died . . . If the castle was attacked and overrun, and she was taken prisoner . . . Well, it had better not happen, that's all.

But prayers and determination were insufficient. There were too many loose stones in the outer walls, too few men to patrol the towers and ramparts. Estimates varied, but not by much; the garrison could hold out for a day, two days, maybe three. Of all the places in which Queen Eleanor might have sought refuge, Mirebeau was the least secure.

Whilst the queen's injuries were being dressed, the constable and escort commander retired to a private chamber to discuss the situation. An ugly and reliable bantam of a man, the constable suggested sending to Chinon or Saumur for help. "They're less than thirty miles from here. If a messenger rode nonstop, he'd reach them within— Why shake your head? There's a massive garrison at Chinon. The king himself—"

"The king went north weeks ago, lord constable. He made no noise about it, lest Philip or the Lusignans learn the true state of the defenses. You probably don't hear such things this far south, but the French are pressing us in Normandy, and King John has gone to Le Mans to rally the army. And," he added, "he's taken with him the garrisons of Chinon and Saumur. There's no point in sending a messenger to those castles; they're as undermanned as Mirebeau."

"Do I understand this?" the constable snapped. "King John has emptied his most powerful strongholds and marched the occupants all the way up to Le Mans? And, by doing so, he has left us to our own devices? Are you saying, messire, that we've been abandoned?"

"For the while, yes, we have. Any help must now come from Le Mans."

"But that's eighty or ninety miles away."

"So it is."

The bantam moved to the window, tightened the laces of the leather curtains, then for want of a proper enemy slapped at the stiff, boiled skins. Turning to his visitor, he asked, "And the Lusignans? Where do you place them?"

"I've no idea, though patrols do not generally roam far from home. At a guess, Hugh and Ralf—if they're working together—are within twenty miles of us."

"A day's fast ride.

The escort commander dabbed the seeping cuts on his face. "Yes," he said. "A day's ride, once they know where we are."

"So you think that this patrol you ran into, you think they tracked you here?"

"I'm sure of it. But, even if they did not see us ride through the gates, they'll guess our destination. With due respect, lord constable, Mirebeau is not the most formidable of castles, but it is the only one in the district. The patrol will assume we came here, and the brothers will know of it soon enough."

"Then we can expect an attack any time after dawn."

The escort commander gave an affirmative grunt, not needing to waste the words.

Nevertheless, the defenders took what precautions they could. More to inform King John that his mother had been captured than in any hope of rescue, they sent a messenger north to Le Mans. The man would ride all night and the following day and, even if the king assembled a relief column and dispatched it without delay, it would be a further three days on the road. However hard one prayed, Mirebeau would remain unaided for five or six days—double the most optimistic estimate.

Members of the garrison spent that first night commandeering food and weapons from the town. By dawn they were back within the walls, and trying hard to forget the time when an excited hound had run across the yard and cleared the outer defenses without touching the ramparts.

The messenger rode north through the forests of Poitou, crossed one of the shaky bridges that spanned the Loire, then spurred on into the duchy of Anjou. His thighs were rubbed raw from the exertion and he fell asleep in a village stable whilst a sour-tempered ostler saddled a fresh horse. When the man shook him awake, the messenger discovered that he had been bitten by red ants. Scratching and yawning, he rode on, aware that the sky had grown light in the east.

The Lusignans had reacted predictably to the news. It had been brought to Hugh le Brun as the senior overlord, and he had listened in silence to the patrol leader's account. The story had wandered some way from the truth, for the man had been unwilling to admit that his riders had passed within a sword's length of Queen Eleanor. As the leader told it, the groups had come upon each other unexpectedly, but had been separated by a deep, rain-filled ditch. It was this that had hindered the pursuit. Had it not been for the ditch, the patrol would certainly have captured the old woman and her escort. As it was, they'd chased the fugitives through forests and around lakes and over hills, and were almost within arrow range when the queen's party entered the castle of Mirebeau. That's where they'd taken refuge, Mirebeau. Less than fifteen miles away if one rode directly northwest. Mirebeau, which everyone knew was a child's castle, ill-knit and weak-walled, and famous for the dog that had vaulted it, clearing battlements and yard and keep. It must have been an exceptional hound to leap three hundred feet, but he'd done it and not once grazed his skin. Anyway, believe it or not, the Lord of Lusignan would have no trouble scaling the nursery blocks of Mirebeau.

Hugh had thanked him for his report, dismissed him and conferred with brother Ralf. They had sheltered in Hugh's damp pavilion, where they assessed their chances of taking the castle, and with it Queen Eleanor. In less than an hour they had reached a decision; they would postpone all attempts at general insurrection and concentrate upon the hurdle walls of Mirebeau. If Queen Eleanor was still there and they could capture her, she would be worth a score of minor castles, a duchy perhaps, why not a principality? Philip of France would bid for her, in the hopes of using her against King John, while Softsword himself would give anything to reclaim his mother. He'd offer lands and titles and wealth, but he might also relinquish his hold on Isabelle, for it was common knowledge that the Angevins loved their mothers more than their wives. If the Lusignans held the aged Eleanor, then they held power and could play her off against the two greatest monarchs in the West.

Sometime before midnight flames blossomed on a plateau in the disputed county of La Marche, and the brothers led their troops on a forced march, moving directly northwest. As they neared the end of their journey they saw the sky lighten around them.

Bloody and bitten, the messenger continued northward through Anjou and thence into Maine. He had stopped twice to change horses, but had otherwise been in the saddle for almost sixteen hours. He could not say how far he had come, nor even if he was on the most direct path to Le Mans, though he supposed he was, for whenever he croaked the question at farmers or passing travelers they nodded and pointed to the north, albeit with a nervous glance at the rider and his foam-flecked mount.

Sweat and the rub of his tunic had infected the ant bites, and at his last halt he had bought two flasks of rough local wine. He had already finished one, deadening his senses, and he trotted on, reciting ribald poetry and relieving himself in the saddle. He had long since ridden clear of the rain, and now the midsummer sun drew steam from his clothes and tightened its grip on his head and neck. From time to time he patted the leather wallet on his belt. If he did not drink himself insensible and fall from his horse, or succumb to blood poisoning or sunstroke or the knife wounds of a waiting brigand, then he would deliver the letter from the constable of Mirebeau to King John of England at Le Mans.

The town had provided everything for their needs. Ladders had been taken from a thatcher's yard, then tied two by two, extending them to the height of the outer wall. Crude grappling hooks had been forged in the smithy, plunged into the cooling trough, then attached to ropes. A loaded hay cart was found and small barrels of pitch brought up from the cooper's cellar. The barrels were lifted onto the cart and split open, so that the pitch oozed down among the hay. Doors were torn from their hinges and carried in the direction of the castle. Sheds had been wrecked to provide beams and stakes. The cart was dragged along the street that led to the barbican gate.

Three hours after dawn, when he was satisfied with the preparations, Hugh le Brun gave the signal to attack.

The castle of Mirebeau had once stood in isolation, but, as the town had grown, so the houses had crept closer to the walls. Now less than twenty yards separated the barbican gate from the youngest buildings, and several of Hugh's bowmen had already clambered onto the roofs and porches. At his signal they loosed a hail of arrows at the gate guards, whilst other bowmen ran from cover with the doors and shed beams. Propped up by the beams, the weathered doors served as shields behind which the archers could crouch to fit their arrows or mend snapped bowstrings. As each man was ready he leaned clear of the shield and let fly at the defenders.

The knights went in next, lumbering toward the gate, their own leaf-shaped shields held high, their swords not yet unsheathed. Instead, they carried stakes and mallets, or dragged two lengths of rope in their wake. Whilst the archers forced the gate guards to huddle below the battlements, the knights hammered the stakes deep into the ground on either side of the gateway, then hauled the ropes around the anchor posts. Above them a number of the defenders braved the hail of arrows to hurl down sharp-edged flints, and three of the knights collapsed beneath the avalanche. Their companions dragged them away, leaving the open ground littered with rocks and splintered shields. As they retreated, the knights continued to pay out the ropes, taking care to keep them taut around the posts.

Hugh and Ralf were waiting in the street. One end of the ropes had been fastened to the hay cart and, as the knights staggered to safety, more men ran forward to catch the rope tails. Hugh yelled, "Now! Fire it!" and flaming torches were thrust into the pitch-soaked hay. The contents of the cart were instantly ablaze, and the brothers led their teams along the street, hauling away from the castle.

Below the barbican the ropes quivered and slid around the posts. The cart rolled forward beneath a cloud of bituminous smoke, whilst the Lusignans roared encouragement at their men. The smoke billowed between the houses, then spread as the cart rumbled across the twenty yards of open ground. The gate guards stared in horror, or leaned out in an attempt to drop rocks directly on the anchor posts. Thus exposed, they were an easy target for Hugh's bowmen.

The cart was traveling fast when it hit the gate. Its weight alone was enough to splinter the studded planks, but that damage was concealed by the explosion of burning hay, pitch and barrel staves. The gate was immediately set alight and the smoke rolled upward, blinding the defenders. They had no choice but to abandon the barbican towers and make their stand on the lower walls. But by then the first grappling hooks had caught the inner edge of the battlements, and the first ladders were in place.

The imaginative use of the tow ropes had achieved a twofold purpose. The fire cart had been guided accurately against the gate and, protected by the houses, the hauliers had remained unscathed.

From then on the attack was more costly. In the next hour, twenty-three knights fell dead or wounded from the scaling ladders, and another dozen were cut down on the walls or inside the bailey. Ralf of Exoudun was hit by a ricocheting slingshot, but the stone had lost its impetus and he merely suffered the indignity of a bruised buttock. Hugh sported a shield in which were embedded three arrows, their shafts snapped short.

A number of Lusignan bowmen were also killed during the assault, along with innocent townsfolk who fell victim to stray arrows or far-flung stones. In all, the attackers lost thirty or forty men, but it was a low enough price for victory. By midday, the outer defenses of Mirebeau had been overrun and all but ten of the wall guards slain. There remained only the moatless, insubstantial keep.

The brothers interrogated their ten captives and learned that Queen Eleanor *was* still present and that her nearest savior was eighty miles away, holding court at Le Mans. Under torture the guards admitted that a messenger had left Mirebeau the previous evening, en route for the court of King John. But yes, they winced agreement, the messenger would not yet have reached the court, and yes, when he did get there King Softsword would scream and rage and totter about on his high heels. And yes, it was true that he would not dare start south without his army, and yes, the cumbersome force would be at least three days on the road. Yes,

yes, the king was too far away, and the journey would take too long, and he would arrive too late. Yes, they would admit it, there was no hope for Mirebeau.

Hugh and Ralf stood together beneath the fire-scarred arch of the barbican gate. They drank wine and studied the single shaft that comprised the keep. Ralf massaged his buttock and grinned at Hugh. "We'd best not stand here, brother."

"We're well beyond arrow shot."

"So we are, but we don't want the gateway falling on us. Look at it. A good fart and it'd crumble to powder." He moved away, laughing at his joke. Hugh watched him for a moment, then shook his head indulgently and followed him into the yard. Young Ralf's mind was a cesspit of vulgarity, but the soldiers worshiped him, and there was time enough in which to teach him good manners. As with the capture of Mirebeau—time enough and to spare.

They gave the constable until nightfall to surrender the keep and deliver up the dowager queen. He replied that he would give over neither his house nor its occupants to a pair of Poitevin brigands. "The countryside crawls with them. You two may bear the brands of nobility, but you move with the slyness of felons. Worse than that, you're simply wild dogs masquerading as hounds. The kennels are near the gate, and you'll find your way to them by the smell."

At dusk the brothers hanged five of their captives. Then they gave the constable until dawn, at which time the remaining five guards would be hanged, and with them five of the townsfolk.

Hugh decided that by now the messenger must have reached Le Mans and delivered his plea for help. Softsword would be grinding his teeth and stumbling about the court, or shrieking at his warlords to assemble their contingents, harness the siege machines, organize the stocks of food and weapons and wine. He would never go without his wine, nor his windbreaks or pavilions or brightly garbed troubadours. And even if he did, he would not dare set foot outside Le Mans without a ring of armored knights, ten deep and a half-mile long. Oh, he would come, determined to save his mother, but he would not set out to rescue the Virgin Mary herself unless he was first protected by iron.

At dawn the doors of the keep stayed shut, so five of the towns-folk were dragged from their beds and hanged, along with the wall guards.

Hugh and Ralf again conferred near the gate, and it was Ralf who suggested firing the keep. "Why spend time on the place? Stack a bundle of twigs against the door and they'll be out like rats from a barn. Do you think the constable will allow Eleanor to burn? You watch. The first sniff of smoke and that feeble tower will be empty. Leave it to me, brother. I'll have the old woman lifting the hem of her gown."

"No doubt," Hugh nodded, "but we'll warn them first. Eleanor is only of value to us while she lives, remember that." He studied Ralf's hard, greedy expression—*how he'd love to set Mirebeau alight*—then said, "I've seen siege fires before, and I've seen them run out of control. That keep is nothing more than a chimney; it's old, and the beams and flooring will be as dry as chaff. Make one mistake and your fire will engulf it, and we'll be left trading Eleanor's bones. She's an exceptional woman, Ralf, but she's not yet a saint. It's better we keep her alive and sell her off to John or Philip."

"You want to warn them first? Very well. And when we've warned them, we'll *warm* them, eh, brother?"

"That's right," Hugh encouraged. "We'll turn them out, or burn them out."

Ralf loved that. He sent forward a spokesman, protected by a white sheet tied to a pole, and the occupants of the keep were informed that they had until dusk to surrender. If they did so they would be treated honorably and their lives spared. Even the constable, who had been so generous with his insults. But the brigands would not slit his throat, nor would the wild dogs emerge from their kennels to savage him. Instead, his tongue and hands would be removed, as a lesson in manners.

However, if the defenders did not emerge, then sunlight would give way to flames. They had been warned.

A subversive riddle posed the question: "Which creature mounts an ox in the morning, and nests at night, yet is never seen in the field or orchard?"

It was a labored joke, but it brought a sly grin from those who knew the answer. King John was the one who mounted oxhide heels and made his nest with the Sparrowhawk, and it was he who had yet to take the field of battle and snatch the fruits of victory.

The riddle had gained wide, if whispered circulation, and there seemed no reason why it should not continue to spread. The king lacked both the stature and magnetism of Richard Lionheart. John was a thief, who had stolen another man's betrothed. He was a coward, absent from the ambush and the battlefield. And finally he was a monarch with neither scope nor purpose.

So the Lusignans were understandably surprised when a force of Angevin knights swept into Mirebeau two days early and with the King of England first through the gate arch.

The brothers were not together when it happened. Ralf of Exoudun was over by the east wall, supervising the men-at-arms who ran forward to stack bundles of kindling against the door of the keep. An occasional arrow flew from one of the cruciform slits, but it was loosed more as an act of defiance than in the hopes of deterring the attackers. Ralf's archers did not bother to reply; the rats would be smoked out soon enough.

A long trestle table had been set up near the barbican gate, and Hugh le Brun was still there, discussing with his commanders where best to hide Queen Eleanor. It pleased Ralf to lay his fire, but Hugh was convinced that at any moment the door of the keep would be pulled open and the defenders emerge to sue for peace. And then what to do with Softsword's mother?

The consensus of opinion was against holding her in a castle, for both Philip and John could bring their siege machines to bear on even the strongest walls. No, the answer lay in secrecy rather than strength. Install her somewhere out of the way; a small manor house, a mill in some distant corner of Poitou, a cave in the hills if need be. Somewhere that would not have to be defended, for it would never be discovered.

Hugh accepted the advice, rested his feet on the table and listened to the sound of thunder rolling across the dull gray sky. He had posted a number of guards on the walls, and they gazed down at the firewood detail. It would be dark soon, and then the Lord of Exoudun would remind le Brun that it was time to light the fire. A few of the guards glanced scowling in the direction of the thunder roll, anxious that the approaching storm should not drench the blaze.

They might have wondered that the sky was cloudless above Mirebeau and that no lightning stalked the horizon. They might have wondered that the thunder did not swell and break, but merely grew closer, as though exploring the terrain.

On the long table a pewter jug chinked against a dish. A shield that had been propped carelessly against the gatehouse fell to the ground. Hugh peered at the sky, then swung his feet from the table and placed his hands palm down on the boards. The wood trembled to the touch and he said, "It doesn't drum like that. It isn't thunder." He pushed himself erect, while his companions frowned at him or copied his movements. Then they realized the truth. As Hugh roared the alarm, the diners broke away from the table and went for their swords. Ralf saw them, heard his brother's warning cry and started running across the yard. The men-at-arms hesitated, then streamed after him, while the wall guards turned and yelled at what they saw.

Hugh le Brun had reached the fire-scarred gate arch when the first horse pounded through. A collision was unavoidable and, in the instant before the palfrey's broad chest sent him flailing backward, Hugh recognized the rider. It was John of England, the man who should have been at least two days distant, the man who had never yet led a charge. Pluck any name from the air—any name but John's—for it went against reason to put Softsword first in the battle line. Yet it *was* John, and, as though on cue, he had been met at the door by his avowed enemy, the master of Lusignan.

It was too great a coincidence, too extraordinary a compression of time and distance. It denied the world's knowledge of the indoor Angevin, for he should have been the last to enter Mirebeau, or, more likely, never have left Le Mans. How had he managed to cover more than eighty miles in a night and a day, unless by magic? And what spells had been cast that could transform the wolf into a lion? Surely there were none powerful enough to instill courage in a creature such as John, not even if they were conjured by the devil?

The thunder of hooves filled the yard. Three hundred horsemen followed their king through the gateway, then spread out to

trample the besiegers. No quarter was given to the common soldiery, and with the dying of the day went half the Lusignan force.
John dismounted and moved about, slashing indiscriminately at
the dead and wounded. By doing so he may have killed some of
his own battalion, though no one seemed prepared to stop him.
All the while he mouthed things about Eleanor, what he would do
if she had been harmed, what more if she was dead. His own life
was in danger, for the yard was committed to chaos and a number of Lusignan archers were still at large. Arrows flew in the
darkness, and men who had feigned dead sprang up in a desperate bid for freedom. Some who had already been seized produced hidden daggers and struck out at their captors, while one
fanatical group retreated to the steps of the keep, intent on firing
the wood. They were cut down by a dozen Angevin knights and
the kindling dragged from the doorway.

Ralf of Exoudun was cornered, though not immediately disarmed. He stood with his back to the wall, sword drawn, in-
ventively cursing the half-ring of knights. The edge of his left
hand had been cut, and he raised it to his mouth, licking the
wound. When he had finished he resembled some grotesque car-
nivore, his lips and chin shiny with blood. "Come on, filth, share
the profit. Six of you? Aren't you strong enough yet? Or dare you
not move for fear your bowels will empty? Come on, come ahead,
at least half of you will survive the encounter and— Ah, God, I
think someone's voided already."

His insults were almost too much for them, but they had strict
orders to take the Lusignans alive and were awaiting one of the
senior overlords. However, if he did not appear soon he'd have a
wasted journey. . . .

The rescuers had driven the enemy from the ramparts and the
lower end of the bailey, and several torches now burned in the wall
brackets and in tripods around the yard. Hugh le Brun had seen
nothing of the battle, for the collision with John's horse had flung
him against the gatehouse wall, and the second impact had
knocked him senseless. Fortunately, the king had not thought to
go back and finish him, so the Lord of Lusignan had suffered
nothing more than a battered chest and a thick ear. He still lay on
the ground, but robbed of his sword, belt and boots, and watched
over by three conscientious knights. He made one attempt to

move, then fell back, his arm numbed by the flat of a blade. The man who had struck him said, "No account has been taken of your wounds, my lord. We'll make the list as long as you like. You're to be kept alive, that's all. That's our only restraint."

Thirty yards away, brother Ralf complained about the stench, then stopped in mid-sentence. William Marshal shouldered his way into the semicircle and the two men looked at each other. Ralf's expression settling into a bloody smirk, Marshal betraying no emotion.

"It's over now, Exoudun. Reverse your sword."

"Who's that?" Ralf squinted. "Ah, yes, the Arab. It's difficult to see you in the dark, you're so akin to an Islamic pig. Well, Earl Arab, you weren't expected here so quick. How did you cover the miles?" He asked another question and lunged as he did so, his sword leveled at Marshal's chest. His tone of voice had not altered, but his expression had stiffened, and the Earl of Pembroke was already moving back. He retreated far enough to draw his enemy off-balance, then brought up his own sword, both hands around the grip and banged Ralf's blade aside. That done, he checked and went forward, his sword pommel serving as a ram. The pommel was in the shape of a simple iron mushroom and Marshal used it to break Ralf's nose. The Lord of Exoudun grunted with pain and, unable to stem the sudden rush of tears, lurched back against the wall. He felt his arms pinioned, his sword wrested from him, and then he heard Marshal's voice, low and pitiless. "Now you must believe it, Exoudun. You are at an end. And in all the years you live, all in a dungeon, you'll remember how it ended for you. Taken by surprise, then disarmed by—a pig?"

He turned away, sheathed his sword and went off to find the king. The knights who now held their prisoner thanked God they'd done nothing to upset Earl Marshal. He might be old—*was* old in years—and to those who had not seen him in action he might appear thin and dried out. In which case more fool they. Witness Exoudun, with his broken bridge.

The siege and relief of Mirebeau were over. The prisoners were rounded up and divided into two groups, the archers and common soldiery herded into the center of the bailey, the knights and nobility assembled near the barbican gate. The latter group was the larger, for no more than a handful of the infantry had been spared. They were, after all, worthless in terms of ransom, and no one would trouble to extract a promise of fealty from them. A place might be found for the sergeants, but the remainder would be hanged in the morning, or mutilated and set free. And from John's point of view, either fate was better than they deserved, for they had not merely risen against the Crown, but against his beloved mother. All Christendom knew how close they were, the king and dowager queen, even though appearances occasionally deceived. . . .

Lapped by the tide of cheers, mother and son embraced on the steps of the keep.

There had been an hour's delay, for the bantam-like constable had refused to let Eleanor leave until he'd been assured that every guardroom and outhouse in the bailey had been searched. "I know this place," he said. "I know where a man can hide. Drop a torch down the latrine shafts. Fork the hay in the stables. Check that your own men have not been infiltrated, and then I'll send her out. But I will not put her at the mercy of some wild assassin."

"And how many do you think we'll find disguised as hay sacks or Angevins?"

"Is the number significant, my lord king, so long as it exceeds none?"

In the event, they discovered three Lusignan archers, two of whom were still armed.

John's astonishment gave way to shuddering relief and, within a month, the constable of Mirebeau had been awarded fiefs in Touraine, Anjou and the English county of Kent. Nothing was too good for such a man, the king decided, not when his kind were so scarce upon the ground.

One public embrace would have satisfied Eleanor, but John clung to her, needing to believe that the rescue had been inspired by love. He had closed his mind to reason, aware that reason would say different. The dowager queen belonged less to her son than to the nobility of England. It was *they* who adored her, and *they* who would never have forgiven him had he left her to the mercy of the Lusignans. It was not filial devotion that had brought him down from Le Mans or sent him first through the gate arch to

Mirebeau; it was the knowledge that Queen Eleanor was too popular to lose and that, if he did lose her, he would soon afterward lose his throne.

Nevertheless, when the facts emerged they would reveal King John in a new and flattering light, for he had been the prime architect of the rescue and had led it from the start. For a while at least there would be no more talk of Softsword, or Couteau du Beurre.

He released Eleanor from his embrace and moved back, incensed by her appearance. Her face was still swollen by the whip of the branches, her eyes sunk deep with fatigue. What breed of animal would drive an eighty-year-old woman through the forest, hound her into a keep, then lay a fire at her door. What monsters would do this and dare call themselves Christians?

"Now, now," she said, "don't look so distressed. I'm no longer in any real pain, and my complexion deserted me years ago. But not, I warn you, my curiosity. I want to know how you accomplished this extraordinary mission. Were you really in Le Mans?"

He raised a hand as though to touch the scars on her face, then said, "Yes, we were. It's been the rallying point for the army. As you know, the French have invaded Normandy, and are now threatening our castles at Arques and Driencourt."

"Let's discuss that later," Eleanor deflected. "First tell me about the rescue. For instance, how you traveled so fast in full armor. You've only struck a night and a day from the calendar, the same time it took the messenger. How could your troops possibly have matched the speed of a single rider?"

John opened his mouth, then closed it without speaking. He had neither imagined nor experienced such success as today and he was determined not to squander his tale. Reason was reasserting itself again, and he was sure that if he told her how it had been, she would lean against the doorway, summon a smile and disbelieve him. *John could not have planned this, it isn't the way his mind turns. He would not be so inventive, unless he's lying. No, this is not my son's brew. It does not taste like him. There's too much flavor in it.*

She would have believed Richard, of course; she had always believed dear Richard. Everyone had accepted the word of Coeur de

Lion, for a creature as heroic as that was surely incapable of lying. But not so the Lionheart's brother, not so the wolf. If *he* was to be believed, he must first find someone to vouch for his story, a man of unblemished reputation and one for whom Eleanor had high regard.

There was an obvious candidate.

"Well?" she prompted. "Will you tell me how it was done?"

"Yes," he nodded, "but in the presence of a witness, I've recounted several things in the past that were not entirely true, but this time I must be sure you're convinced. It's too good a tale to waste." Then, as though changing the subject, he said, "Would you like to meet an old friend of yours, Lady Eleanor? I'll call him up here and—"

"Call who?"

"—we'll let him bear witness to the truth."

"Call who, John?"

"Earl Marshal, of course. We know he adores you, and there was ever a section of your heart railed off for him, wasn't there, my lady?" His triumphant expression was less smile than smirk. He had regained the initiative. His mother would believe him now.

She made an effort to shield her emotions, but it failed. William Marshal, whom she had championed for so many years, the spindly young knight who had once saved her life, then later delivered her from sixteen years of imprisonment—a gift from her husband King Henry. Oh, yes, she would like to see Marshal again. What did they call him—the Arab? Yes, she would love it if Marshal the Arab bore witness to John's victorious tale.

"By all means," she said, "summon him here." And then her voice trembled and she pleaded, "God in heaven, John! Bring him to the steps!"

While the rescuers were scouring the castle in search of leftover assassins, the Earl of Pembroke was compiling a list of the senior prisoners. One at a time they were led before the long trestle table, now cleared of its flasks and dishes, and interrogated as to their rank, titles and holdings. In this way the victors could assess each man's value in terms of ransom. It would take several months to verify the information, but when that had been done the prisoners would be offered the chance to purchase their freedom. Many of them would be left destitute, with no choice but to serve some minor baron, or join a crusade in the hopes of finding fortune in the East. But it was better to be poor and at liberty, than to go slowly blind in a dungeon.

Needless to say, the offer would not be extended to the lords of Lusignan or Exoudun. . . .

When the prisoners had supplied the initial information, they were granted a further period in which to recollect the extent of their holdings and those controlled by their wives and families. And the contents of their coffers. And the names of such friends as might be persuaded to contribute to the ransom. They had until morning to rack their brains, though Marshal reminded them of the dangers of deceit.

"It'd be foolish and perhaps fatal to undervalue yourselves. Don't imagine that King John will see your omissions as a mere oversight; he'll assume you tried to cheat him, and act accordingly. So if you have any salable horses, list them. Likewise the rents from your farms, the bracelets that decorate your ladies, the tapestries on your walls. Everything will be checked, then checked again, and it'll go hard with anyone whose poverty is disproved."

He gazed at the dull, scarred faces, then went on, "Most of you held your titles during the reign of Richard Lionheart, and those of you who knew him will remember his obsession with money. So you can believe me when I tell you—it's a family trait."

On that ominous note he left them to dredge their memories and decide whether or not they'd cheat King John. On balance they thought not.

Marshal had already informed the king that the Lusignan brothers were in custody and unharmed. He had made no mention of Hugh's stone-struck ear or Ralf's broken nose, for the traitors were unharmed in the sense that they would still beg for mercy, and that was all John cared to know. The warlord had then devoted himself to the list, stopping once as Queen Eleanor emerged from the torch-lit shaft. No clerks had accompanied the riders from Le Mans, so Marshal himself had inscribed the names and properties, drying the ink with sand. When he had finished—and delivered his warning to the grim-faced prisoners—he started in the direction of the keep. He was within earshot when Eleanor said, "God in heaven, John! Bring him to the steps!"

The king turned to dispatch one of his bodyguards, saw Marshal approach and said, "No wonder you love him; he's on us before the echoes fade." Then he moved aside and watched with amusement as the old friends met.

"What's this?" Eleanor queried. "Are you a clerk now, William Marshal?"

He bowed to her, straightened again and said, "It seems I am, my lady. Where I once rode in the lists, I now write them."

The queen smiled and nodded, then extended her hands, one laid over the other. Marshal raised them to his lips, holding them longer than mere courtesy dictated. He affected not to notice her injuries, though any faint trace of pity he had felt for the prisoners was immediately expunged. They could expect little mercy from King John, but neither could they count on it from the moderate William Marshal, not for a long while yet.

John had now squeezed all the amusement he could from the meeting. He moved up the steps until he had once more gained ascendancy over the warlord, then said, "Lady Eleanor has asked for an account of the rescue. You know how it went, Marshal, so you can bear me out."

"If you wish."

The king could not bring himself to invite Marshal alongside, so he continued to speak down and across, half the time to the Arab, half to his mother. "The messenger reached us last evening, sometime around dusk."

There was a short silence, until Marshal realized he was expected to signify accord.

"He did, King, an hour before dark."

"And brought with him a letter from the constable, explaining that Queen Eleanor had taken refuge here, and that an attack was imminent." He waited for his witness to agree, but Marshal said, "It'd be simpler if you told the story straight out. After all, it was your achievement."

John glanced at his mother to assure himself she'd heard. *My achievement, lady, from the lips of your oldest friend. Mine, so says the Arab.*

"Very well," he nodded. "By the time the messenger reached us, Mirebeau had already come under attack. We did not know where the enemy were quartered, but it was obviously close by. As the constable said in his letter, patrols do not usually venture far from home. Speed, then, was essential. The army grows daily stronger at Le Mans, but if Mirebeau was to be saved, and you, my lady, it would not be by a ponderous column of foot soldiers and mangonels. Nor even by a detachment of armored knights." He saw Eleanor frown and said, "Oh, yes, they were armored knights that followed me into the yard, though we looked rather different riding out from Le Mans." He treated them both to a triumphant grin. "I set as my target the time it had taken the messenger to reach us; some twenty-five hours. But, if we were to match his speed, we'd have to sit as lightly in the saddle. In other words, we'd have to undress for the part."

"Are you saying you set out without armor?"

"Less than that, my lady. Almost without clothes. In boots and shifts, that's all, and each of us with an extra horse in tow. Can you picture it? Three hundred riders, the flower of our chivalry, charging half-naked through the night?" He turned to Marshal and exclaimed, "I had not thought of it before, but now I thank God *we* didn't meet an enemy patrol!"

"And the armor?" Eleanor persisted. "Where was that obtained?"

"At Chinon," John told her. "Again my idea. The garrison there is depleted—well, the troops are all at Le Mans—but the armory is one of the largest around. We stopped once to change horses, and then again at Chinon. Look more closely, my lady, and you'll see that nothing quite fits us. Look at Marshal. Do you think he'd own a sword like that, with its swollen pommel and frayed grip? His is a masterpiece, perfectly balanced, yet he was content to leave it behind." With a characteristic touch of vanity, the king scratched at his link-mail tunic and said, "I assure you, my hauberks are better measured than this metal pavilion."

The dowager queen exchanged a glance with Marshal, then reached out to take John's hand. "I understand now why you thought it was necessary to summon a witness. It is an extraordinary achievement—"

"And more so because it came from me? Yes, of course. If it had been Marshal's doing, his or a hundred others, you'd have accepted it word for word, isn't that so? But for Lackland-cum-Softsword to have made his knights divest themselves of their armor, to have led them at a breakneck pace and then trampled le Brun in the gate? No, that would have imposed too high a tax on your beliefs." He seemed on the verge of withdrawing his hand, but his bitterness suddenly evaporated and he said, "The truth is, Lady Eleanor, that neither Marshal nor the others think as I do. Oh, they'd probably have rescued you, but not so quickly, for they'd never have asked their compeers to undress. Or would you, eh, Pembroke?"

The warlord could not explain to himself why it hurt so much to say no, he would not.

He presented the list of prisoners. "There are more details to be added in the morning, but there's one name that might be of special interest to you. Among the general group of knights and nobles, and we've taken almost two hundred, we found a boy of fourteen or so. I'd have dismissed him as a common squire, except that he was wearing a hauberk of pure silver. It was necessary to twist him a little before he'd tell us who he was, and I'm not yet convinced as to his identity. But if it's true, your achievement is really crowned. He says he's Arthur of Brittany, and would that not make him your nephew, and the claimant to your throne?"

4

THE ANGEVIN SICKNESS
August 1202–April 1203

The field hands stood silent, or sank to their knees amid the stubble. They knew better than to approach the wagon train, and were content to watch it pass and pray they'd be ignored. There was enough misery in evidence on the road, without tempting it across the verge.

This was not the only such train on the move today; a second had already turned off toward Angers, while a third was bound for the Norman county of Mortain. Each comprised five or six oxcarts, escorted by a hundred Angevin knights. There was no misery in that, but in the wake of the carts came the Lusignan prisoners, the knights and nobility, stumbling along head down, their necks encircled by heavy iron collars, their wrists shackled, each bracelet chained to the next. The captives had been stripped of their armor, and this, together with a pair of armed guards, formed the ballast of the carts.

Progress was slow, though it was still inadvisable to miss one's footing, for the chains were not long enough to let a man lie full-length on the ground. Those who had fallen—and so far there were three in this train—had been dragged along, arms in the air, their wrists broken.

The Angevin escort made no comment. They understood how King John had felt when he had seen his mother's branch-whipped face, and they acknowledged his desire for vengeance. They had willingly mutilated the enemy archers and men-at-arms, blinding the bowmen and releasing the infantry, minus their hands, and

they were only surprised that the king had not hanged Hugh and
Ralf from the gate arch at Mirebeau. But these others, dragged
like felons behind the carts, did they really merit such humiliation?
They were the enemy, yes, but they were still men of rank, and
each could find his equal among the escort. Victor or vanquished,
they were compeers, and the riders were perturbed by John's pitiless display.

His victory had been so complete. . . . The brilliance of his
strategy . . . The incredible speed of the rescue . . . The timely
collision with le Brun . . . The unexpected, yet heaven-sent dis-
covery of Duke Arthur . . . All this, raising King John on a level
with the legendary Lionheart. . . . All this, now sadly diminished
by his treatment of the captured chevaliers. It was unworthy, but
most disturbing of all it set a dangerous precedent, for how
would English knights fare when they next fell victim to Philip of
France?

Nevertheless, the riders kept their thoughts to themselves, and
the carts rumbled on, liming the prisoners with dust.

It would take the wagon train two weeks to reach its destination, the massive Norman fortress of Falaise. It seemed appro-
priate that Arthur and the Lusignans should be incarcerated there,
for Falaise was one of the castles that, six months ago, Philip had
demanded as a token of John's good faith. The news of it would
make the French fish wriggle.

John had divided the mass of prisoners with a purpose. Philip
Augustus would be distraught when he learned of the reversal at
Mirebeau, but, even with the loss of Hugh and Ralf and Arthur,
the French army was still rich in commanders. It also outnum-
bered anything the English could put in the field, and if the prisoners were known to be under one roof, an attempt might be
made to rescue them. But not so if they were scattered, some at
Angers, some at Mortain, a few at Falaise, a dozen in this place, a
dozen in that, and a further twenty-five transported to England.
Not even the cunning Augustus could raise a crop of armies and
an invasion fleet.

Before leaving Mirebeau, John had done his best to persuade
his mother to accompany him to Falaise. Her admiration for his
victory had made him selfish, and Eleanor found it necessary to

remind him that she was eighty years old, whipped raw and in need of peace and quiet.

"I know how much it means to you, a triumphal procession throughout the country, with me on your arm. But think of this, my lord. You will not be parading some young princess, unmarked by her experience. You'll be supporting a weary old woman, and the people you seek to impress may wonder why you let me be maltreated."

"Let you? Christ's eyes, do you think I let you?"

"I know you didn't, but before you put me on show would it not be better to let the swellings go down? Deal with your prisoners and, if there's no other way, prosecute the war; then, in a month or so, come and collect me. I shall not have forgotten your achievement, John. Allow me a month, and I'll tour Christendom with you, if that's what you wish."

He had no choice but to accept. He asked, "Where will you be, Fontevrault?"

"Yes, Fontevrault, it's my favorite retreat." With a smile she added, "Don't worry about me. I'll be safer there than I was here, at Mirebeau. For one thing, the abbey walls are higher."

John nodded sullenly. In a month's time his victory would be forgotten. Oh, the crowds would turn out to cheer the dowager queen. They always did. But how many of them would have breath to spare for him?

His attitude toward William Marshal was quite different. The warlord was another lodestone to the crowd, but John had no intention of sharing the glory with him. He'd heard how Marshal had crossed swords with Ralf of Exoudun, breaking the traitor's nose in the process, and if he'd heard it, so would everyone else.

". . . then the king came charging through the gate, well, there was nothing left but the stone, and he rode full-tilt into Hugh le Brun—just by chance. But the other Lusigan, Ralf, he was disarmed in a fight with William Marshal. First of all his sword was banged aside, and then the Arab went in—"

No, there was no place in the procession for the scene-stealing Earl of Pembroke.

When the carts had been assembled and the prisoners chained and shackled, the three trains set out from Mirebeau.

The one bound for Angers would go by way of Fontevrault, so that Eleanor could be delivered safe to the abbey.

The next, commanded by Marshal, was destined for Mortain, where some twenty of the captives would be lodged. But Marshal's journey would not finish there, for he was to conduct his remaining twenty-five prisoners to Barfleur, and thence across the Channel to England. And even that was not the end of it. The ship would dock at Portsmouth, or wherever the winds and currents allowed, and the prisoners would then be taken along the coast to Corfe Castle in Dorset.

With no one to praise him, John praised himself. How many times had the Arab expressed the desire to visit his family? Once a week for a year? Well, now his wish had been granted. He could take his wife to bed, romp with his children and boast to his heart's content of how he had disarmed the venomous Ralf of Exoudun. There was no need to hurry back to the court. He deserved a respite. Say until Christmas. Or better, until spring. His friends would miss him, of course, but it was enough to know that he *would* be back, with the warm weather.

So they went their ways; the dowager queen to Fontevrault and the ministrations of the nuns; Marshal to the small, heavily defended castle of Mortain, and then to Barfleur and a bout of seasickness; King John to Falaise, with Hugh and Ralf and Arthur riding in his wake, their wrists lashed to the pommel of their saddles. They had been spared the indignity of chains, but it was not compassion that had led John to put them on their horses. It was simply that, with all the dust rising from the path, no one would have recognized them if they'd been chained to the tail of a cart.

Among the European monarchs of the time, Philip Augustus remained the most equable, the most farsighted. He was not without a temper, and had more than once cleared the court, but he would rather his opponents were convinced than cowed. Nor was his vision unimpaired. Physically he was blind in one eye, but he could also fail to see reason.

The disaster of Mirebeau blinded him, and he panicked. In the month of August, he raised the siege of a dozen Angevin castles, including Arques and Driencourt, withdrew his troops and hovered on the borders of his kingdom, stunned by the brilliance, the *totality* of John's success.

He had met the Butter-Cutter; he *knew* the Angevin. He also knew the Lusignans, and the arrogant young Arthur, and he found it inconceivable that the one should have so easily outwitted the others. But the reports were consistent. Arthur and the brothers had been taken by surprise, disarmed without striking a blow, then led away, tied to their mounts. The inconceivable was true, and the credit belonged to Softsword.

The French had long suspected that the Angevins were the descendants of Melusine, one of Satan's many whores, and that the devil's powers passed with his seed from woman to woman. From Melusine through the female line to Eleanor of Aquitaine. . . . They had proof that Eleanor was possessed, for she had married Philip's father, King Louis, and twice turned into a bat before his very eyes. She was old now, and her powers were fading, but John was not old, and it did not stretch the imagination to see them huddled together, mother and son, glowing with the ghastly light of transfusion. It must have been done like that, with Eleanor bequeathing her evil powers to John and warning him to store them against the day when they would do the most good, the most harm. How else could one account for the hardening of his blade?

For years John had masqueraded as a weak and petulant prince —leathered and feathered, as someone had described him—aglow with jewels and rustling with silks. He had not dared risk his precious store of diabolism until, yes, until his mother lay trapped at Mirebeau, her enemies at the door.

And then the king had mouthed some special spell and flown in an instant from Le Mans to her side. The Lusignans had been frozen where they stood, unable to resist, unable to blink, petrified by the thinned-out powers of Melusine.

It must have been like that. Otherwise, the intelligent Philip of France would be forced to admit that he had underestimated and misjudged his high-heeled rival. But that was not possible, for one could not diminish the irreducible. It was magic, not the monarch.

The reports were spurred to Falaise. Throughout that month messengers arrived with news of another French retreat, another siege abandoned, another village spared. The enemy were withdrawing all along the front, and those few prisoners who had been taken spoke of nothing but the Angevin devil and his power. He could be wherever he chose at the click of a finger, and the French had already barred the gates of Paris. But little good it would do them, for John had only to click or clap and his army would alight in the very center of the city!

There had never been a more propitious moment in which to strike. Who cared if that joyless moderate William Marshal was bundled in bed at Pembroke? He had proved his worth in the past, but the Angevins did not need him now, for not even the Arab had struck such terror in the French. All they needed was John, or the rumor that John was about.

The news delighted him and, with his three special prisoners safely locked away in Falaise, he rode down to Le Mans to collect the Sparrowhawk. She had already sunned herself in the light of his victory, and now here he was, claiming her and drowning her in gifts, virile proof that he was as much a king as Richard had ever been, and far more a man.

The courtiers at Le Mans roared their approval. They came forward to petition him, not for favors, but merely to acknowledge the songs and poems they had commissioned in praise of their courageous king and his beautiful queen. Some mistakenly assumed that John was too proud to accept a gift and, instead, asked his permission to present Queen Isabelle with some trifle or other, usually priceless. He managed a smile, content with their admiration and his wife's intimate inventions.

The happy couple spent half the month at Le Mans, and half at Falaise. At no time did the English army move to consolidate its position, or take advantage of the French retreat. They believed what Philip had believed. King John possessed supernatural powers. He would land the French fish whenever it suited him. He'd wake up one morning and snap his fingers and Philip would be in chains, with a hook in his mouth. Mirebeau became the word of the moment, the rallying cry for England. Shout Mirebeau loud enough, and the enemy would flee.

However, by the end of August the King of France had come to terms with events. Reason prevailed and he accepted the dramatic reversal, and with it the loss of his three most powerful allies.

Hugh and Ralf could be replaced, though it would be difficult to find another pair with such a personal grudge against the Angevin. There were many who loathed him, but only the Lusignans felt cheated of their lands, their titles and, in Hugh's case, his betrothed.

As for Arthur of Brittany, he was irreplaceable, for no one else had such a claim to the English throne.

During Queen Eleanor's thirty-seven-year-long marriage to King Henry of England, she had borne her husband five sons—William, Henry, Richard, Geoffrey and John. Of these, only John was still alive. And of these, only Geoffrey had sired a son, Arthur of Brittany. By doing so, Geoffrey had resurrected the historic problem of inheritance. Who had the better claim to the throne, the younger brother, or the son of the older brother? If Richard had been a father, would England have looked to the Lionheart's whelp, or to the lupine John?

It was a problem that had never been satisfactorily resolved, and one that had given Philip Augustus the chance to make Arthur his protégé, his candidate for the crown of England. There were those who had supported John, and secured his coronation. But there were many who thought Arthur had the more direct claim, not least among them the people of Brittany and France. If John could be deposed, and Arthur crowned in his place, then the Bretons would be paramount at court, and the French given their due. It was Philip himself who had knighted the young Arthur and promised him his daughter in marriage. And, in return, Arthur had sworn that, on the day he was crowned, he would give the French king possession of Normandy and Touraine. Both men would prosper, and the world would be rid of the tottering Softsword.

It was an excellent plan, save that Arthur was now in chains at Falaise. . . .

Nevertheless, the long summer month was time enough for Philip to still his superstitions and regain his self-control. He no longer probed for weaknesses in the Angevin defense, but launched an all-out assault along the border, not only against his human enemies, but against the agent of the devil. There was nothing to fear, for Eleanor's offspring had failed to take the initiative, which meant his powers were sapped dry.

"Don't look for him in the clouds," Philip told them. "His wings have withered. Search him out on the ground if you want him. He's reverted to a wolf, and he'll take an arrow through the chest like the rest of them. There's nothing special about King John. Mirebeau was the first thing he ever did well. And the last."

The messenger had been given a purseful of coins and a head start. With these he was to travel from Mirebeau to Pembroke, where he would inform Isabel de Clare that her husband was on the way. An easy task, so long as his horses ran true, and he found a boat to take him across the Channel, and there were no storms on the water, and he safeguarded his money—his master's money —and did not allow himself to be waylaid by gamblers or women.

He did enjoy one serving girl en route, but his guilt was sufficient to bring him awake, terrified that he had overslept. There was no way of telling if night had just fallen, or if dawn was about to rise. The girl mewed in her sleep, then instinctively fumbled for the coins beside the bed. They were there and she sank back, leaving her nervous lover to creep downstairs, find his way to the stables and saddle his horse.

Three hours later he dismounted and huddled under a tree. It was still dark, if anything darker than when he had fled, and he was aware that he had undressed, made love to the girl, closed his eyes, opened them, dressed again and deserted her, all in the space of an hour. Poor value, he decided, but better that than to arrive late at Pembroke. The girl would understand, but not so William Marshal.

In the event, the emissary reached the castle several days ahead of the warlord. He had already heard about Isabel de Clare and, like many others, was in love with what he had heard.

At the age of nineteen she had married the forty-three-year-old William Marshal, and presented him with her dowry of lands and titles. The couple had not met until a few hours before the wedding; King Henry had promised her to Marshal as a reward for his long and loyal service, and the heiress had had no say in the matter. She might have wished for a younger man, but, equally, she might have been given a corpulent boor, who would then have squandered her inheritance and smothered her with his lard.

Fortunately, Marshal had done neither. He was almost twenty-five years her senior, yet he was less set in his ways than many men half his age. He had never been conventionally attractive. His nose was too thin, his expression too serious, even in repose. The outdoor life had marked him and left its scars, though he enjoyed both music and literature. His humor was as dry as his skin, his manners stiff and somewhat old-fashioned. He had never found it easy to trade in small talk, nor even to let his buttocks go numb after dinner, while the guests put the world to rights. Talk could be valuable—on occasion invaluable—but to hear the boasts and blatherings of wine-filled courtiers? No. When that happened he fidgeted in his chair.

If a woman wished her husband to snare the laughter and drown his friends in drink, then William Marshal was no prize catch. However, Isabel de Clare had never dreamed such dreams. She would marry whomsoever she was told to marry, but with luck he would be a man of authority and compassion.

The middle-aged Marshal was both and, within a few weeks of marriage, Isabel sympathized with those of her friends who were wed to callow, clear-skinned young knights. It seemed to her that she had gained the best of both worlds, for Marshal was not only mature, but still as lean and amorous as any strutting chevalier. He could sing and dance and recite the poems of Chrétien de Troyes. It was Marshal who had once knocked Richard Lionheart from his horse, Marshal who had been patronized by Eleanor of Aquitaine, Marshal who had served the kings of England longer than anyone else. And it was Marshal who had, supposedly, gained the favors of Eleanor's daughter, the beautiful Marie of Champagne. . . .

This last achievement was one Isabel preferred to forget. It had happened a long time ago—*if* it had happened at all—and it signified nothing, other than Marshal's undoubted popularity with women. She had known that before she married him, and she was still jealously pleased that women sought him out. Why not, so long as their expectations did not run high?

And now, thirteen years after Henry's champion had come to collect her from her lodgings in the Tower of London, Isabel de Clare was the mother of five healthy sons, and a daughter who squalled for attention. Perhaps because she was a stranger to court life, Isabel had retained her looks and gentleness of speech. It had taken her husband fifty years to become a hero of the West, but she had become a heroine of England in half the time.

She greeted the messenger from Mirebeau as though he belonged to her, then sat him in a corner, armed him with food and wine and questioned him until he sagged. He hesitated at first, torn between his enchantment with the chatelaine and his loyalty to Marshal. But it was not long before he was volunteering information, dwelling at length on the arrest of brother Ralf, rising up with fists clenched to show how the Arab—the Earl Marshal—how he had retreated, parried, then gone forward to break the bridge. He made a snapping sound with his tongue to show how Ralf's nose had broken under the pommel.

His audience loved it and queried it, to make him tell it again. He was not released from the corner until daylight flooded the room, and even then he was recounting anecdotes, and Isabel was mouthing encouragement, to keep them both awake.

In the days preceding Marshal's arrival, his wife spent a fortune on clothes. Not only for herself, but for her priests and the members of her household; robes and polished belts for the local clergy, boots and fresh-scraped gambesons for the sergeant and garrison of Pembroke. Even the smiths and farriers were given new aprons, though the craftsmen quickly reverted to their old, scorched clothes. A new apron was the mark of the apprentice, and most of the men had been in the smithy a good ten years.

She knew her husband would not approve of the extravagance, this man who had for so long saved his buckles and worn-out tunics. But he would appreciate the show. It was a fitting welcome for the hero, and Marshal was vain enough to enjoy it.

He came by way of Mortain, Barfleur and then, the weather permitting, Portsmouth. Even so, the voyage made him sick and he clung like a limpet to the bulwarks, the great Earl Marshal reduced to a vomiting wreck. He had made no secret of his weakness, and his friends were aware that he became bilious on the beach. But in this at least he'd had something in common with Richard Lionheart; both men had skirted puddles and turned green with the motion of the waves.

Philip Augustus was another poor sailor, though in his case the

English reveled in the knowledge that the fish was afraid of the sea. However well things went for him abroad, he had yet to conquer the Channel and his own queasy stomach.

At Portsmouth the warlord was helped ashore, and the detail waited until he had regained his color. Then, still unable to eat or drink, he led the prisoners and escort westward along the coast. He had spent the better part of August in the saddle, and wanted nothing more than to rejoin his wife and family and relax with the last of the summer. He knew he could leave the escort commander to see the prisoners safely to Corfe, whilst he, himself, rode on to Pembroke, and he was tempted to do so. King John would not care if he cut the corners from this particular mission. He would not care what the Arab did, so long as he stayed in England, leaving the monarch to take credit for Mirebeau.

There were, however, two things that prevented Marshal from hurrying home. The first and more important concerned the constable of Corfe, a man with a well-earned reputation for prejudice and cruelty. He had once before been given charge of French captives—eight knights taken in a border ambush—and of these eight, two had supposedly fallen to their deaths whilst trying to escape from the prison tower, another had been killed in a brawl with his fellow inmates, and yet another had died of self-imposed starvation. Four had survived to be ransomed, but they had emerged from Corfe scarred and skeletal, and were buried within the year.

The constable had denied all charges of brutality and appealed to his mentor, King John. The resultant investigation had dragged on for months, then absolved the constable of any premeditated crimes. In future, he was warned, he should keep a closer watch on his prisoners and fit a few more bars in the windows. He had taken the warning to heart and gone one better, bricking up every window and arrow loop in the tower.

Anxious though he was to see Isabel de Clare, Marshal was determined to meet the warden of Corfe and form his own opinion of the man. Otherwise, he too would stand condemned of prejudice.

The second thing that delayed his homecoming was more personal. The Lusignan captives had been enchanted to see him draped over the ship's rail and, since then, they'd been openly contemptuous of him. If he turned off now, short of the castle, they would assume he was too enfeebled to complete the journey. A nice revelation, that: the Angevin Arab, seasick and homesick. . . .

But he would not give them the satisfaction. Instead, he increased the pace and led the column on a final, jarring ride to Corfe. They reached the castle on the afternoon of August 23, and Marshal went ahead to meet its keeper.

The man's name was Saldon, and he had been warned to expect the prisoners. The warning had come directly from King John, and with it the information that the detail would be under the command of William Marshal. "Unless," the king wrote, "he has trotted nonstop to his marital bed." Elsewhere in the letter he referred to Marshal as "our stiff-necked earl," and advised Saldon to stand his ground. "The Lusignan knights will be your responsibility, lord constable, so you must treat them as you think best. Marshal may hold other views, but you are the master of your own house."

The letter coincided perfectly with Saldon's feelings. He had heard more than enough about the fifty-six-year-old warlord, and had long envied him his success. He had seen Marshal once, at court, and even then the constable had wondered how such a desiccated creature could have made himself the champion of three successive kings. *And* been granted the earldom of Pembroke and Striguil. *And* had them brought to him by the sought-after Isabel de Clare.

What was so special about the Arab that he had caused King Henry to elevate him to such windblown heights? What backstairs abilities did he possess that were denied to men like, well, Saldon for example? None that were apparent in the seamed Islamic face.

From Mirebeau, the Lusignan prisoners had been led, shackled and fettered, to Angers, Falaise, or Mortain. At this last fortress, Marshal had divided his contingent into two groups, twenty to be incarcerated at Mortain, twenty-five to continue on to England. Among the twenty were those with broken wrists and wrenched necks, and the warlord had taken the opportunity to release the others from their irons. When the second group of prisoners left

Mortain they were on horseback, as befitted their rank, and those who had given their parole were allowed to sit free in the saddle.

It was in this way that they crossed the outer bailey of Corfe Castle, the more intransigent captives roped in line, the rest bound only by their word.

One hundred and fifty yards separated the main gate from the keep, built directly against an inner curtain wall. A wooden bridge linked the keep's second-story entrance with a steep flight of steps, and Saldon waited there at the head of the flight, one foot tapping the outer edge of the bridge. Three of his knights stood at the base of the steps, watching the prisoners and escort follow Marshal across the yard. One of the knights muttered something and they laughed, then turned and looked up to include the constable in their joke. The one who had spoken said, "What if you were to tell him his orders have been changed, and he's to take the bastards to Nottingham? You could say the king had returned and was waiting for him in the north. That'd curdle his lust for Lady de Clare."

"It would," Saldon agreed, "but he's too near his kennel to be lured from it now." He nodded past them, and they turned back to see Marshal dismount and approach the keep.

As he did so, garrison guards began unseating the twenty-five prisoners and dragging them toward ring bolts in the wall. The Angevin escort stared at them, then attempted to intervene, roaring their indignation. "These men gave their word, most of them! They're not cattle at a market, and where do you think they can run to, here?" They moved forward, cursing, to find themselves within a spiked fence of spears. More guards emerged from the towers in the western wall, thickening the fence. They had obviously rehearsed the scene until they were pace perfect, and there was nothing the weary escort could do.

But Marshal was not yet fenced in. He turned at the shouts, saw what was happening, then lengthened his stride.

Saldon remained where he was, rapping a tattoo, while the trio of knights moved casually into line, as though to bar the way. They wanted to remind the Arab of his place—he was at Corfe now, not at Pembroke or prowling the court at Le Mans. This was Saldon's domain, in which his knights stood where they pleased. Once their visitor had been brought to a halt, acknowledging their power, they'd move aside. It was a petty display, but they, too, had heard of Marshal's high-flown ways, and they relished the chance to deflate him in public.

Near the wall, the Angevin escort were still bellowing at the garrison. Marshal waited until he was close enough to the knights to address them without shouting, then said, "You're blocking my path, messires. Move away, or I shall think you're out to arrest me. And you know I'll resist." The words were flat and unemphatic, but they left no room for doubt.

The trio hesitated, grinned without humor and let him come between them. Had they thought about it, they'd have realized their act had been performed a thousand times before. William Marshal was a popular target for bullish young knights, though he was not the only one. It happened to every warlord, every bishop and monarch, every man scented with success. The smell was attractive.

He went up the steps, dispensed with courtesy and pointed in the direction of the wall. "You have my escort at spear point. They are English and Angevin knights, and you've set Corfe against them."

"Yes, to discourage interference," Saldon retorted. "However, if you can assure me that your riders will hold their station, I'll withdraw the guards."

"You'll withdraw them anyway," Marshal told him, "or take the consequences."

The constable gazed at him, debating a challenge. Then he raised his arms, flagging his hands above his head. The fence moved and broke, and the escort immediately unsheathed their swords and settled their shields. The next time the garrison tried it, there'd be a few chopped posts.

"Well now," Saldon said, "that's done. It's a pity we've made such a bad start, Earl Marshal. Perhaps you misunderstood your orders. You've had charge of the prisoners for so long you're probably loath to part with them. But they are my responsibility now. Your mission ended when you brought them into the yard."

"Not so. It ends when I make them over to you, and I have not yet done that. You seem overanxious to air your reputation, lord constable, chaining them—"

"Reputation as what, Pembroke? As a loyal servant of King John?"

"As a jailer in whose cells the prisoners tend to die."

"Take care!" Saldon snarled. "No blame attaches to *me* for what occurred! Those other captives found their own way to the grave—"

"As will these if you leave them chained out in the sun."

With heavy patience, the constable said, "They'll be quartered in due time, don't concern yourself. But I can hardly lock them away without knowing who they are. The sooner you give me the lists, the sooner they'll be housed. And the sooner you'll be on your way to Pembroke." He managed to leer around the words, and Marshal half-expected a conspiratorial nudge. Christ's eyes, the man was an atrocity. Unable to resist the temptation, Saldon said, "We'll exchange papers, how's that?" He produced John's letter, handed it to Marshal, and took from him the list of prisoners, with their ranks and titles. While he glanced at the twenty-five names, the warlord read how John had described him to Saldon. "Our stiff-necked earl . . . The detail will be commanded by William Marshal, unless he has trotted nonstop to his marital bed. . . . Marshal may hold other views, but you are the master. . . ."

"He has an unkind turn of phrase, the king," Saldon commented. "Hmm?"

"He does," Marshal said, and let the parchment fall to the step. The smoothed-out scroll bore John's personal seal, and the brown wax splintered on the stone. Saldon blinked down at it, incredulous, while the warlord descended the narrow flight.

A few miles from Corfe he disbanded the escort, rewarding each of them with one of the horses that had carried the prisoners from Mortain, or its equivalent value in coins. Seven of the knights were landless, and four of them asked him if he would accept their oath of fealty. They would be his liege men, obedient to his wishes and loyal to the House of Pembroke. If later he granted them a fief, they would hold and defend it for him, as their suzerain. They had long wanted to serve him, and he could now judge how well they had acquitted themselves at Mirebeau and after.

"Oh, well enough, I'd say. But I should warn you, messires, I'm for home, so you're in for another hard ride."

It was not the kind of warning to deter them.

As he made his way north to Gloucester, then westward through the foothills of the Black Mountains, the scene at Corfe faded from his mind, to be replaced by images of Pembroke and of Isabel de Clare.

Even so, he was dogged by doubts. He had fulfilled his mission, and treated his prisoners with the respect due to their rank. The king had commanded him to deliver twenty-five to Corfe, and he had done so without loss or injury. Indeed, he himself had fared the worst, prey to seasickness.

But would he have entrusted the Lusignan captives to a man like Saldon if the castle had been in Anjou or Aquitaine? Was it coincidence that had placed Corfe within a few days' ride of Pembroke, or had John chosen it for the Arab's convenience? In short, had William Marshal delivered the prisoners, or merely rid himself of them en route to his marital bed?

The questions recurred, but went unanswered.

Throughout the final quarter of the year the French pressed their attack. If King John had ever possessed magical powers they were no longer in evidence, and Philip Augustus took full advantage of Softsword's lassitude. He could not understand why John had failed to follow up his success at Mirebeau, though the most encouraging explanation was that God sided with the French. He had seen Melusine's descendant swoop upon Mirebeau, and had thereafter raised His hand against the demon king.

There might be other, more mundane reasons for John's inactivity, but it suited Philip to dress his cause in the panoply of Christendom. Death to the English as the enemies of France! And death to the enemy as minions of the devil!

By late November the war had spread to several fronts, and a number of Angevin leaders had turned against their king. In Normandy, the fortresses of Arques and Driencourt were again beleaguered, and the French army had moved against Conches and Bonneville. In the west, Brittany was in open revolt, clamoring for the release of its prince, the fifteen-year-old Arthur. Maine,

Anjou and Touraine were now a battleground, many of the barons still loyal to the king, others ranged against him. Aquitaine and Gascony held firm in the south, though neither had yet come under attack.

In the three months that had elapsed since John's day of triumph, he had alienated his nobility, allowed the French to advance deep into his territories, and otherwise devoted his time and energy to the Sparrowhawk. It was as though he regretted his single, outstanding victory, regretted his short-lived reputation as a brilliant and courageous general, regretted the gifts and paeans of praise. Only Queen Isabelle had no regrets, loving the attention he lavished upon her.

The suzerains of Europe had been appalled by his treatment of the Lusignan prisoners—men of rank chained behind an oxcart— yet he had done nothing to placate them. Certain of his most loyal supporters had found themselves suddenly out of favor, charged with aggrandizement and self-seeking. The Bretons had appealed for the release of Arthur, but their appeals had been ignored. And all the while the king's chief adviser, William Marshal, remained on the other side of the Channel, barred from the court.

The French had believed that King John was in the devil's employ at Mirebeau. The English believed he was now.

And then a force more powerful than any army swept in and settled the country. Men hunched around their fires, the windows shuttered, the rooms partitioned with boiled-leather curtains. Outside, snow filled the fields and blocked the tracks, and the wind sent batteries of hail clattering against the mud-walled huts and ashlar castles. The war was not forgotten, but it could not be prosecuted chest-deep in snow. Instead, this was the time to boast of past achievements and plan for the future; to send luckless messengers struggling from one fortress to another; to take inventory of weapons, repair armor, compile lists of allies, potential defectors, known enemies. This was the waiting time, in which to air one's doubts and review decisions, the breathing space, where the threats and promises were visible to the eye.

It was during this bitter winter that Arthur of Brittany was transferred from his dungeon at Falaise to a similar prison at Rouen, John's new home.

He was, in many ways, a mirror image of the king. At fifteen, Arthur was as tall as his uncle, as addicted to jewelry and as venomous in his speech. He was never quite sure on which date he had been presented as a rival for the English throne—one would have to ask Philip Augustus—but he had been knighted by the French monarch, promised Philip's daughter in marriage, and had then paid homage for Anjou, Aquitaine, Maine and Brittany, should the French ever wrest them from the English.

If things went well, Arthur would one day be King of England. But until then he remained a child of France.

And now he was John's prisoner at Rouen, a wolf trapped by a wolf. It would seem unlikely that they would get along.

Nevertheless, the king had discussed the situation with Isabelle, and they had agreed to cosset the young man. He was, after all, a member of the family, and they could understand how he had been misguided by the Frenchman. They'd make friends with him and, in return for his fealty, offer him the dukedom of Brittany. If it was possible to make a captive feel at home, they'd do so, and perhaps he'd lose interest in the fish.

Before he was summoned to the assembly hall he was wined and dined, offered a bath and a choice of robes, and promised the attentions of a young lady, if the interview went well. In response to these courtesies, he ate to increase his strength, drank in moderation to warm his blood, then refused the bath, the clothes and the offer of company.

"I love these redolent garments," he said. "They have the stench of imprisonment, but they're the clothes I wore at Mirebeau, and I'm proud of them. As for your woman, I'll find my own in due course, and she will not be one of Softsword's rejects. God forbid, for I'd rather suffer injury than infection."

On this sour note he was herded none too gently into the hall.

The long chamber was decorated with the house standards of those who remained loyal to the king. Marshal was conspicuous by his absence, but even so there were sixty or seventy Angevin overlords, a wealth of knights and sufficient guards to form a frieze around the base of the walls. Uncharacteristically, the king and queen came forward to greet the prisoner.

"You've been whipped along a hard road," John told him, "but *grâce à Dieu*, you're with us now."

"So it appears," Arthur said.

"I gave orders for you to have fresh clothes; they weren't brought to you?"

"Brought and sent back," Arthur said.

John nodded. "Because you preferred your present garb. Yes, I can appreciate that. You're still effectively a prisoner, and you don't wish to discard your uniform until—"

"My lord king?"

"—you've been released from— What?"

"I wish to speak."

"Well, of course," John invited, "that's why you're here. You're a foolish young man who has been seduced by Philip's empty promises, but you can see now where it's led you. Or rather, misled you. Speak out, Arthur, there's no prohibition here. And go over by the fire if you're cold. Get the dungeon damp out of your bones."

Arthur looked at him, and stayed where he was. "What I have to say will not take long."

It was now the Sparrowhawk's turn to encourage. She was his senior by less than two years—a court comprised of children—yet she felt almost maternal toward this thin, misguided youth. "You have as long as you need, my dear Arthur. Understand, you have not been captured by your enemies so much as taken from those who would manipulate you. We have no real quarrel with you, or with Brittany. You're its rightful duke, and it's only the half-blind Augustus who poisons you with discontent." She nodded at the wisdom of her words and saw John nod alongside.

Arthur evinced a smile, drew a response from Isabelle, then promptly ignored her. Facing John, and making a target of his high-heeled boots and tentlike cloak, he said, "I'll take your blatherings from the beginning. I was not whipped along any road, though I *was* brought from Mirebeau, tied to the saddle. And in similar fashion from Falaise. And it was there, in that gaunt castle, that I was shackled to the cell wall and left to straddle a growing mound of excreta. Once a week it was shoveled away, this compost of stale bread and riddled meat, and even then I knew I was being treated better than my companions of lesser rank. Your smiles have faded, Majesties, why's that? Does it finally occur to you that I shall not be bought with pressed linen and the offer of a whore?

"Let me tell you how I *can* be purchased. By the knowledge that you've both been swept away—shoveled away. You, King, whose coronation must rank as England's greatest disaster, and you, Lady of Lusignan—"

In a last effort to be reasonable, John hurried, "Too far, Duke Arthur, that goes too far. Queen Isabelle was never the Lady of Lusignan, nor did she wish to be. I'm prepared to tolerate your outburst, but I'll have no one insult the Queen of England."

"Then," Arthur said, "you'll be very lonely, for she's a better object than a jester. You both are, outside these walls. A king on stilts, and a queen who rules from the bedchamber? God knows it; if any man is to keep his self-respect, he *has* to be your enemy."

He coughed into the cold air and did not resist when a group of guards and barons manhandled him from the chamber. He had said what he wanted to say. And, with luck, his cell would have been cleaned out in his absence.

The snow held them in thrall. January was more bitter than December, but the worst was left till last. In early February northern Europe was lashed by gales, tempted by an hour's sunlight, then swept by fresh falls of snow. Patrols floundered a few miles from home, their marks already obliterated. Emissaries died en route, trapped by the darkness and the numbing winds. It seemed that God no longer favored the French, but had imposed a curfew on the warring factions. They had displeased Him, and were frozen in their tracks.

It was now that Philip Augustus raised money for a monastery, while John kept company with priests and bishops, his purse for once stretched wide on behalf of the Church. He no longer yawned and chatted during Mass, and his courtiers left their dice at the chapel door.

Those extrovert clergymen who prayed and prophesied were well rewarded, as were the soothsayers who foresaw Philip die in agony, or John succumb to a poisoned roast, an arrow, an accidental fall. But the highest paid were those with a weather eye, who could assure their patrons of an imminent thaw and a bright blue sky. The French army could then continue its advance. The dilatory English troops could then resist. Both sides were ready and eager to reopen hostilities.

Concerned by Philip's autumn successes, William Marshal had penned a series of letters to King John. He had queried the Angevin's inactivity and forwarded a list of castles that were, in his opinion, vulnerable or of special strategic importance. By their very nature, most castles dominated their surroundings, but those on the eastern border of Normandy formed a bulwark against the French. If they were to fall—Arques and Driencourt, Conches and Bonneville and, heaven guard it, Château Gaillard—then Philip could lead his men to the very heart of the duchy.

By February, the warlord had dispatched five letters, but received no reply. He wrote a sixth, in which he sought the king's permission to return, then threw it on the fire. His pride forbade such a request. John had dismissed him, so John could recall him. Besides, Marshal was enjoying his first respite in more than two years, and he was loath to start the long struggle to Falaise, or Rouen, or wherever the king was now. The country was still snowbound, so the French would not yet have taken the field. And the Channel was still treacherous, something else to be borne in mind.

His wife steered clear of the problem. She was four months pregnant, and prayed that it would snow unabated until Midsummer Day. So long as the land lay buried and the sea continued to boil, Marshal might as well stay at home. She could not keep him against his will, any more than John could bar him from the court, but she was content to suffer the rigors of winter and grow big with his child. Their child. Their sixth son, perhaps, or their second daughter. It no longer mattered which, though her unspoken preference was for another girl, for Pembroke already dinned with the yelps of its future masters. Five male children in full cry and, thank God, the walls were still standing.

As for the situation abroad, she would neither encourage nor dissuade her husband in his views. If he felt it was right to go he would do so, regardless of John's silence or her own pleadings.

But until that sad, sunny day, she would share her happiness with him, and secretly entice down fresh falls of snow.

Three hundred miles to the southeast, at Rouen, the situation was less settled. Duke Arthur had been interviewed again, but with the same lack of success. No, he'd reiterated, he would not disavow Philip Augustus in exchange for Brittany. Nor would he pay homage to the so-called King of England. "However, I admire your impudence, uncle, offering me something that is already mine. I *am* Duke of Brittany, and recognized as such by everyone but you. Why not give me something I don't possess? Anjou, for example, or the crown that clings so precariously to your head? Philip was my age when he became king, and I'm quick to learn. Besides, your abdication would be such a popular event."

Once more he was hustled down to the dungeons, leaving John to decide whether firmer measures were called for.

Later, in the privacy of their quarters, the king and queen had turned their attentions to William Marshal. For the twentieth time John had upended an inlaid box and spread the warlord's winter letters about the table. For the twentieth time the Sparrowhawk had remarked on the spidery script, seeing it as an indication of Marshal's failing powers. "He's growing weak, though he's too proud to admit it, else he'd have dictated his dull warnings to a clerk. His fingers have stiffened, you can see. In another year or so they'll be nerveless, and then what use will he be, in battle or anywhere else?"

John managed a smile, anxious to humor her. He could not tell her now, in February, what he had failed to say in December —that he wanted Marshal back, stiff-fingered though he was, harsh and critical though he was. They would argue, of course, and the Earl of Pembroke would do nothing to hide his disdain for the jewel-laden monarch and the indolent Sparrowhawk. For her part, she would continue to see him as a dried-out relic, still feeding off his stale reputation, and she'd remember how he had ignored her during the first months of her reign. A rejected woman was a dangerous animal, but far less so than a disregarded queen.

As for John, he knew he would be torn between Marshal's obvious good sense and Isabelle's persuasions; torn between them and thus tempted to strike out blindly on his own. He was aware now that he had wasted the victory at Mirebeau. He should have treated the prisoners with dignity, dispensed with the parades and banquets, and—yes, kept the Arab nearby. Instead, he'd alienated many of his senior commanders and given fresh heart to the enemy; that and large areas of Angevin territory.

Mirebeau had been his first great triumph, and it had gone to his head. But he'd had the winter to think about it, and he was determined to learn from his mistakes. Unfortunately, his determination did not render him deaf to Isabelle.

Stirring the letters on the table, she said, "You've let the cold weather make you despondent, my lord. You don't say it outright, but I know you're ready to send for William Marshal. The French have gained some insignificant outposts, and a number of those men we thought trustworthy have turned against us. But the real problem is in your head, where you've worried things out of proportion. I agree we should have been more forceful after Mirebeau, but I do not look to the stiff-jointed Earl of Pembroke to redress the balance. I look to you. You've tricked the enemy before, and you'll do it again. But this time, when they think you incapable of furthering your success, you'll be on the way to Paris. I tell you, husband, no sooner will they have recovered from one defeat than they'll be reeling from fifty more."

Now that she had encouraged him, the young queen turned the coin. "What is France, anyway, but a petty kingdom squeezed between us and the German states? They are nothing, the French, and they'd do well to stay within their borders and thank God they've been granted what little space they have. I must say, sweet, it surprises me that you worry about them at all. Come the spring, you'll be on firm ground and playing them like the fish they are. You have already landed Arthur and the Lusignans; the rest are bound to follow, for they travel in shoals."

John admitted the possibility. Perhaps things *were* as the Sparrowhawk saw them; not as simple, of course, for one did not catch armored knights with a fishing line, but less gloomy than his own overcast views. The lost ground could be recaptured, the mistakes rectified and, as Isabelle had said, the balance redressed. But, most cheering of all, she looked to him to do it.

He said, "Your optimism is infectious, Sparrowhawk. Does it

extend to the Lusignans and my nephew of Brittany? If you could see the beginnings of a solution—"

"With regard to Hugh and Ralf, yes, but not Arthur. His mind is poisoned against us. If you threw that fish back he'd taint the whole river. He's more infectious than I." She yawned, shook her head, then treated him to a gentle, spreading smile. "I must retire, my lord, will you keep me company?" She watched him collect Marshal's letters and return them to the decorated box, and she noticed that on this, the twentieth occasion, the king made no attempt to stack or square the sheets. His wife took it as a favorable sign.

The snow thawed and ran into the rivers. The valleys remained spongy, though the patrols could once again ride the ridges and camp away from home. Reports were sent back to Rouen, but there was something odd about them, as though the patrol leaders had forgotten the object of their missions. Castles that should have been friendly to the Angevin cause were now listed as sympathetic to the French. Towns that had hitherto welcomed the passage of English knights had closed their gates to all who opposed Philip Augustus. The reports still contained estimates of the enemy's strength and deployment, but the greater part of the messages was taken up with the details of defection. Border fiefs that had been loyal to King Henry and King Richard had now gone over to the French. Barons who had fought shoulder to shoulder with Coeur de Lion in Sicily, Cyprus and the Holy Land were now seen in Paris, or Chartres, or Blois. Even new-made knights, their oath of allegiance still warm on their lips, were now disavowing King John in favor of King Philip.

It was clear that a new infection had spread through the Angevin possessions, and one that had apparently been carried by the snow.

John evaded the truth as long as possible. He insisted that each report be checked, then accused his spies of invention. Stabbing at names on the list, he said, "These men, for example. They both spent Christmas with us here at Rouen. And now you claim they've turned their cloaks! It's inconceivable. We played with their *children!* We gave them *presents!* Others on this paper, yes, I can see some who'd serve any master of the moment, but not these. Nor him, I know him. Nor these two, God's breath, I've slept in both their homes!"

The messengers flinched, but held firm. The reports were accurate, their word on it. Their lives, if need be. Everyone on the list was either in company with the French, or strengthening his house against the English.

Wisely, they did not mention the dozens of knights who had been seen, but not identified by name. If they were added to the list, the pages could be bound together to make a book.

And so it continued, the progress of the French army almost forgotten in the face of this greater threat from within. The infection was most widespread in the central territories of Maine, Anjou and Touraine, though the entire border of Normandy was now at risk. Aquitaine and Gascony were as yet untroubled; more than could be said for Poitou, hard-pressed by the allies of the captive Lusignan brothers.

However, it was the westernmost duchy of Brittany that inspired King John to murder.

Some men stood within the Angevin's circle of friendship, yet did not command his respect. They made good mealtime companions and could be relied upon for a scandalous story or a game of dice, but there it ended. They took no part in the war councils, but were merely expected to vote along with the king.

Others, like Marshal, were valued for their administrative abilities and the serious air they brought to the proceedings. Beyond that, they were encouraged to seek their own diversions, preferably outside the court.

There were a few who were both popular and revered, their advice heeded, their humor acclaimed. One such was William of Briouze, a stocky, pockmarked Norman whose ancestors had fought in the vanguard of the Conqueror and had been granted fiefs on both sides of the Channel. There had always been a William of Briouze, and he had always been favored by his king.

The present fifty-year-old suzerain was no exception, and it was he who brought Duke Arthur up from the dungeons for his third interview with John.

This time Queen Isabelle was absent, and the assembly hall deserted. There was no frieze of guards, no servants, no musicians, no dogs loping across the uneven tiled floor. This time uncle and nephew would be tête-à-tête, with only Briouze in attendance.

In an effort to induce an atmosphere of informality, the king himself had gone around the hall, extinguishing the torches in their brackets and snuffing all but a few of the thick tallow candles. There was now a pool of light at one end of the obligatory *table dormant*, and a dull red glow in the chimney alcove. A stone wine jar warmed beside the fire, whilst, on the table, three cut-glass goblets deflected the candlelight.

Dressed for the part, the king wore a plain gown, a drab leather belt and three unremarkable rings. He could not remember when he had last abandoned so much jewelry—most likely in preparation for the rescue ride to Mirebeau—and he was glad the hall had been placed off limits to his courtiers. If they saw him like this they would think he'd been reduced to penury. By tomorrow, Rouen would be alive with rumor. ". . . The king has sold his personal treasures to pay for the war. . . . England has been declared destitute. . . . There's to be a special tithe. . . . Half one's goods and chattels, three-fourths of one's coins. . . ."

Just as well he'd pinched the candles and put guards on the door. The plan was to soften his nephew, not panic his subjects.

He tested the warmth of the wine jar, grunted and set it on the table. As he did so the doors were swung open and Briouze ushered Arthur into the chamber.

"Come along into the light," John beckoned. "Warm yourselves with some of this; Vieux Cahors, if the vintner's to be believed. By the way, Briouze, did you see that my nephew was fed?"

The warlord waited until he had steered his charge along the hall, then said, "I regret, King, that the self-styled Duke of Brittany lacks co-ordination." He saw John frown and elaborated. "He threw some prime stew on the floor and remarked on the king's vomit masquerading as meat. It seemed pointless to serve him again."

John sucked his teeth, peered at the brilliant glasses, then looked up at his emaciated prisoner. "This won't do, Lord Arthur, starving yourself out of spite. I ordered an excellent meal for you this evening, fresh-killed today, and now you've wasted it. You tax my patience, but, if you've changed your mind, I expect we'll find something for you in the kitchens."

"Only you would know," Arthur murmured. "Is your vomit kept in store, or is it collected after each expulsion."

John nodded at Briouze, who clapped his hands on the young duke's shoulders, forcing him into a chair. "You're an unpleasant creature to keep around," the king told him. "And, as I say, you stretch my patience. So far we have had two profitless discussions, and after this I see no reason for a fourth."

His wrists manacled together, the dried blood visible on the backs of his hands, Arthur gestured in time with a shrug. "Personally, I see no reason for this one. Where are we, anyway, in some mysterious grotto? Or is England so poor that she can no longer afford a flame? Or is it you, uncle? Are you putting the cost of candles against your next gold ring?"

Behind him, Briouze said, "I'll make him more attentive." But John wagged a finger. "Not yet. First I want him to hear how Brittany has fared." He turned aside, filling the three glass goblets, then pushed two of them across the table. Briouze collected his, waited for John to drink, then copied him. Arthur ignored the remaining glass, as though it was intended for someone else.

"Brittany," John said, "yes, the sad state of Brittany." He rested his elbows on the table, making a roof for his glass, and went on, "You will not have heard, buried away in a dungeon, but the duchy to which you lay claim is in sorry repair. My troops have already taken Rennes and invested the city of Nantes, and it's only a matter of time before—"

The harshness of Arthur's laugh cut him short. "Rennes, you say. And Nantes. Taken or beleaguered. Oh, you purblind— My dear, purblind kinsman, your sight really has been ruined by these cheap candles. And not only your sight, but your mind as well. So Brittany's in a sorry state of repair, is it? And your troops are in Rennes?" He laughed again, and let it fade into a sigh. Then he emptied his goblet and held it up, twisting the glass so that the light cut fissures in his uncle's face.

"I don't know what you'll offer me today, but it should not be freedom. Rather, you should pay me a fortune to stay down there in the dungeons and tell you how the world turns. The sad state of Brittany? Is that what you've heard in this ill-lit nest? Well, Lord King of England, it's been a different story down below." He saw John frown, and turned in time to glimpse the warlord's bewilderment. Then he looked across the table again, his victory assured.

"What a silly trick, my lords. What an unworkable pretense. Did you really think I'd turn deaf in a dungeon? That the truth would not find its way belowground? Did you imagine you could snuff a few candles and, in this dishonest darkness, treat me to a lie? Your troops are nowhere near Rennes or Nantes! They are not even within the borders of Brittany! But hear what *I've* heard, though you know it already. The Bretons are within striking distance of Angers, and moving along the coast of Normandy toward Avranches. It's not *my* people who are in need of repair. It's yours, what few there are of them."

He came to his feet, catching Briouze off-balance. He was still holding his glass, and now he flicked it aside, sending it as far as his fettered wrists would allow. It shattered on the floor and splinters of glass flew back into the yellow pool. John pushed himself from his chair, his embarrassment fuel for his rage. Was it not enough that treason swept the countryside, or must it now find its way into Rouen, along the passageways of the castle and down to the dungeons? Arthur had learned the truth from someone—a servant, a jailer, a member of the garrison, a member of the court, a priest, why not? Someone had crept down there, put his lips to the spy-hole in the door and whispered the good news.

Angers . . . Avranches . . .

Briouze recovered his balance and stepped forward to restrain the prisoner. John was also moving forward, shouting at the warlord to let things be. Arthur had meanwhile withdrawn to the shadows, grinning in triumph, his blood-streaked hands raised to scratch his nose. He saw the king approach, lowered his arms and said, "It's no wonder the world knows what you do, uncle, before you do it. I am your most important prisoner, and yet even I receive daily reports of your plans. I daresay I could conduct the Bretons' campaign from my cell." He moved backward, farther away from the light, and it was only at the last instant that Briouze saw the wine jar in John's hand.

There was a mêlée of sound and movement. Arthur retreated, laughing at the king's discomfort, and John went after him, once more prey to the Angevin sickness. Briouze said, "No, King," realized he had pitched his voice short and roared, "King! Leave him be! *King!*"

"You should employ me," Arthur said. "Ensconce me down there with a chair and table, and some of your husbanded candles, and I could tell you—"

But by then John was swinging the jar. He did so with all his strength—the vestigial strength of Melusine's descendant?—and it shattered along with Arthur's skull. There was an instant's silence, and then the duke's body crashed to the floor, framed by the clatter of stone shards. There were other sounds, though these were mercifully forgotten—the noisome settling of the body, the last gargled cry of apprehension from Briouze, the ghastly sigh of achievement from King John. The sounds went together and died with the Duke of Brittany, and then there was a longer silence, broken only by the crackle of logs and the give of the uneven tiles.

Cautiously, as though infiltrating an enemy camp, Briouze moved alongside his king. The men had seen death before, dressed in every habit, but they had never been so relieved to find it cloaked by the dark. It lay there scarcely visible, a faint gleam around the wrists.

Few men behave rationally in the aftermath of murder. John skirted the corpse and began edging the shards of stone against the wall. Briouze said, "Leave him be," then realized his advice was too late. He started toward the door—to alert the guards, to summon a physician?—then turned abruptly on his heel and went back to review the body. John appeared from the shadows and thrust a goblet into his hand, but the glass was empty and anyway the jar was gone. Somberly, the king said, "We must find out who gave him the information, eh, Marshal? You know how to go about it and—I mean Briouze. You know what to do."

The warlord looked at him for a moment, then slowly shook his head. "No, King, you meant what you said. You meant Marshal. I, too, wish he were here, wish he'd been here to prevent—" And then a despairing lift of his hand.

John suddenly started to shake. It was forbidden to touch the monarch, and it was anyway something he abhorred. But now Briouze caught him by the upper arm, and John clutched him in return. For the first time, they acknowledged the enormity of their act.

"We have killed your nephew," Briouze intoned. "We have committed a mortal sin and are consigned into Hell. Our flesh will be scraped away, and every raw part turned in the fire. But even before that, when the world learns what we have done—"

"When the world learns," John echoed dully.

"You must send for Marshal."

"When the world learns of it, then—" He swung his head away, his eyes vacant. He may have glimpsed the corpse, or seen nothing, but when he faced Briouze again his expression had changed. "If the world learns of it," he said. "*If* it learns."

"We must recall Marshal and—"

"Yes, we will, but first listen to me. Think on this. The world need *not* learn of it, not yet."

"Conceal the body? But—"

"Wait!" He remembered something Isabelle had said. *If you threw that fish back . . . If you threw that fish back . . .*

And why not?

He wrenched himself free, his voice distorted by fear and guilt and complicity. "Listen to me, Briouze. There is a way." He turned toward the eastern end of the hall, pointing beyond the pool of light. "You see that window? It's no more than twenty feet from the Seine. The river flows fast enough there. It'll take the body downstream, maybe to the sea. Bodies float for a while, don't they? And then they sink, and that's an end of it. Like men washed overboard, who ever finds them?" He stared at Briouze, stared and nodded, willing the man to agree. "Well, are you with me in this, or not?"

He had already decided that if Briouze rejected his appeal he would run for the door, pull it open and scream that the warlord had murdered Arthur of Brittany. And he might do it yet. . . . The temptation was growing. . . .

"Yes, I am with you. We are already condemned by Heaven, so — Yes, let's get on with it."

It was a slow and grisly task. They went down on their knees to scour the floor with rushes, which they then heaped on the fire. Briouze sacrificed his cloak, so that Arthur's blood would not drip a trail across the tiles. Then they dragged the corpse into the window alcove, the young duke's head bound with its makeshift turban. John opened the shutters and waited to lift the body over the sill. He was overcome by another brief paroxysm, shuddering at the realization that he must spend the next few moments in the moonlit aperture, in full view of Almighty God. The King of England seen as a murderer, his nephew as victim.

Eventually, he managed to control himself and flapped a hand to send Briouze on his way.

And now a fresh terror afflicted the king. What if Briouze summoned the guards and they ran in to find their monarch crouched in the window, sharing the view with the lifeless Duke of Brittany?

The warlord was passing the pool of light when John hissed, "My Lord William? When this is done— A month from now, and you'll be raised to the highest estate. That was always my intention. I have always seen you as the most deserving of men."

Looking back, Briouze could not separate the king from the shadows. The horror of what he had done—what he had failed to prevent—had tilted his senses, and he heard himself say, "As my lord king desires." Then he nodded courteously in the direction of the moonlit window and went on along the hall.

Outside, he told the guards that King John and Duke Arthur were still deep in discussion. "They may well be reconciled before the night's out, and there have already been tears of remorse. None of us need witness such a scene, it's too private. Stand away out of sight somewhere. Down at the foot of the stairs, that'll do."

The guards understood. This was a family matter, and they'd all been faced with comparable problems: truculent children, interfering relatives, that sort of thing. Nice to know, though, that it happened to kings and princes.

They clattered off along the passage and down the steps, while Briouze made his way outside, then around to the river wall. On the way he stopped, afflicted by the same spasms that had already gripped the king. He found it necessary to squat in the darkness before groping his way along the talus of the wall. The shame of that act would outlive the murder itself, and the memory of it would, in time, cost him everything he possessed. He was inalienably loyal to the king, and could excuse anything John did. He was a Norman warlord, one of a line, and inured to death. It happened, brought pleasure or regret to others, and was then forgotten. But what he would not forget, nor forgive, was his own weakness, the need for sudden physical relief. It made him no better than a fearful child, and the darkness made it worse.

Nevertheless, he found his way to the window, reached up to tap the hilt of his dagger against the stone, then accepted the bundle that was pushed out over the sill. The conspirators kept silent, and Briouze dragged the turbaned corpse across the damp grass to the Seine. The body went in with a quiet splash, disappeared and then rolled to the surface a few yards downriver.

A moment later the current edged it aside, as though rejecting so dangerous a passenger, and it disappeared again under the lee of the bank. Briouze started after it, then saw it drift obstinately into the mainstream and float away into the darkness. He waited, but there were no warning shouts, no flares of light on the bank. Duke Arthur had gone from the castle unnoticed.

Briouze turned and peered up at the window, hoping to see his king. What they had done they had done together. Briouze had witnessed the death; it was only right that John should have witnessed the departure. But the window was already shuttered against Heaven and the moon.

Lost Cause
May–September 1203

There had been no news for several weeks, and now, on the same morning two messengers entered the yard at Pembroke. The first had visited the castle before, in February, and would continue to call every three months or so, for as long as Earl Marshal remained there. Dignified with the title of *courrier*, the man was in Marshal's employ, his eyes and ears in Normandy. There were other *courriers*—a harsher term was spies—and their reports enabled the warlord to keep abreast of events on the other side of the Channel. He had *courriers* in most of the continental territories, but this morning's caller was the best situated, an accepted member of the court at Rouen.

Encouraged to cast his net wide, his reports consisted of proven facts, rumors and sheer guesswork. Nothing linked them, unless, like today, it was a thread of pessimism. Whatever the news, it was bad.

There had been more defections, more defeats, more names added to the list. A flight of angels had been seen circling above Paris. The city of Le Mans and the fortress of Vaudreuil were rumored to be on the verge of surrender. King John and Queen Isabelle had closeted themselves in their private chambers and, so far as the *courrier* could tell, the Angevin defense was in the hands of individual commanders. If a baron wished to take the field against the French, he did so. If not, he stayed within his own borders or, more likely than not, allied himself with the enemy.

Oh, yes, and one other thing. Every prisoner had been removed from the dungeons at Rouen and dispersed throughout the country. But stranger than that, the jailers and their families had also been transferred; not to another Norman stronghold, but to a castle in southern Aquitaine. And, strangest of all, no one had seen hide nor hair of Duke Arthur since the first days of April.

Of course, he might have been sent back to Falaise, to rejoin Hugh and Ralf, or even to England for safekeeping. But it was odd that he had vanished without trace. Almost as though he had been—buried?

There was now a definite pattern to the war, if it could be called a war. Philip Augustus was threatening the chain of border fortresses in Normandy, and with every expectation of snapping the links. Maine, Anjou and Touraine were in turmoil, neighbor turned against neighbor, or merely sitting it out, whilst in the west the Bretons were poised to strike at Angers, Avranches and an ever increasing number of towns and castles. In short, Normandy was now cut off, and John was upstairs with the Sparrowhawk.

It was time Marshal reentered the fray. Indeed, it was long past time, but his pride would still not allow him to ask permission of the king. He had been banished—no, that was too strong a word—excluded then from both the court and the continent, and all because John had wished to take sole credit for Mirebeau.

Mirebeau . . . Great God, how that victory had dwindled, changed shape, then reared up to spawn an endless stream of defeats. It was surely the costliest triumph ever achieved by an English king, for it had convinced Softsword that he was all the things he was not.

If Philip Augustus had any sense he'd engineer another Mirebeau, then wait for the Angevin empire to collapse. And what if he lost a further two hundred knights and nobles, and a second pair as hotheaded as the Lusignans? He had already made up the numbers in turncloaks.

Enraged by this latest series of disasters, the Earl of Pembroke urged himself to swallow the bitter lees of his pride. Whether or not John would admit it, the king had need of him. Christ see it, *Normandy* had need of him! *And* the rest of the schismatic territories. They all needed him, or someone like him, to raise their spirits and stiffen their spines. The French might think themselves at war, but the English clearly did not. Left without a leader, they seemed content to fence off their own petty holdings, barricade their doors and hope for the best. But the best would very soon become the worst. The empire would be lost, and on its heels would come a full-scale invasion of England. And who, by then, would be left to patrol the shores? A few hired mercenaries and the garrison of Pembroke?

He would leave for Rouen within the week and, if necessary, force his way into the royal bedchamber and haul the dilatory king . . .

No. He could not leave yet. Not when his wife was almost eight months pregnant. Not when the news of his departure might upset her enough to lose her grip on the child. He would wait until she had given birth. Then he would do what he could to save the Angevin empire.

But the second messenger of the morning destroyed his plans. The man was not a *courrier,* or, if he was, he was paid by King John, for the letter he brought bore the king's brown wax seal. The last time Marshal had handled such a seal was at Corfe, where he'd dropped it on the steps.

The letter did not quite constitute a summons, not quite an invitation, not quite an apology. It was if anything a request, formal and polite and out of character. It addressed, "Our respected friend and champion the Earl Marshal of Pembroke and Striguil," then went on:

> *You must know, Earl Marshal, that the French have been blessed by a series of fortunate victories, whilst we ourselves are plagued by the treason of little men.*
>
> *Your presence here would add immeasurably to our determination, and with you at our side we shall quickly rid ourselves of the intruder. Be with us as soon as you can, in the knowledge that whatever advice you give will be taken to heart.*
>
> *We send warm greetings to the Lady Isabel, but would remind you that you are missed at court, and missed by England.*

If the letter had not already convinced him, he was swayed by the final phrase. King John had at last admitted the truth. England did need her senior warlord—her stiff-necked earl—and not ensconced at Pembroke, but at Rouen, or wherever the battle was to be joined.

It would be hard on his wife, for he had, in a way, overstayed his welcome. Had he set out three months ago she would have had time to adjust, time to resign herself to another lonely birth. God willing, this would be their seventh healthy child. But, of the six she had already borne him, only two had been placed wet and squalling in his arms. Far from home, he had heard about the others from emissaries, *courriers*.

Visitors to Pembroke were invariably surprised at the chatelaine's freedom of speech. William Marshal was as arrogant as a lion, as vain as a peacock in display and, with anyone else, as touchy as a baited bear. Yet, during the latter years of his marriage he had allowed—indeed almost encouraged—the Lady Isabel to dispute with him, as though her woman's head encased the mind of a man. They found it unsettling, the lords and ladies who called by, then dismissed it as the Arab's infatuation with the pale-haired de Clare.

In their own homes things were different. The wife was required to comfort her husband, administer the estates in his absence, and otherwise devote herself to the everyday business of the castle and the welfare of her children. It was understood that her thoughts were inconsequential, and that her opinions would merely reflect those of her husband. How else could they be expected to live together, if not in complete harmony?

There were a few exceptions, a few men who invited their wives' views, a few women who aired them uninvited. The dowager Queen Eleanor, now in retirement at Fontevrault; the Sparrowhawk, presumably in bed at Rouen; and Isabel de Clare, who had taken the news calmly and urged Marshal not to delay his departure.

"The letter is untimely, we're agreed on that, and it's unjust that you should miss the advent of your child. But you've been absent from court too long, my lord, not least because of your mutual pride, yours and the king's. Now that he *has* called you, you'd best rejoin him, before the entire empire becomes a hunting ground for France."

"That's curtly put," he said. "Do you blame me for the situation? You call it mutual pride, but what more could I have done? How many letters have I dispatched since last autumn? Ten? A dozen? A dozen letters sent to court and placed in his hands. And not a single reply, until today. Now, tell me, lady, what was I supposed to do, beg at the gates?"

She rested her hands across her belly, her fingers entwined. "It would not have come to that, and you know it. Beg at the gates? No, for they'd have been wrenched open the instant you appeared. Your arrival would have done more to hearten the army than anything so far. It still might, if there are enough men left to form an army. But don't you see where your pride has placed you? No one will advance unless you are there to lead them. Every contingent will ask for you. You, William Marshal! They will all want you! And the more you are drawn into combat, the greater the risk that—"

"What?" he smiled. "That I'll be damaged? My sweet Isabel, do you think I'll be harmed by the *French?* Oh, thirty years ago, perhaps, when I handled a sword like a thresher's flail. But not now."

Holding himself erect and scowling dramatically to make light of his boast, he said, "Bear in mind if you will—it was this proud creature who knocked Richard Lionheart from his horse. And I daresay the patch of ground still bears the imprint of his buttocks."

She realized he was trying to cheer her, and did not remind him that his skirmish with King Richard had taken place thirteen years before, when he had been in the prime of his life. True, he was still one of the paramount champions of the West, witness his dealings with Ralf of Exoudun, when he'd disarmed the troublemaker with practiced ease. But even so, even with his skill and experience and peerless authority, he was almost fifty-seven years of age and by any standards old for battle. The enemy would be hard put to bring down William Marshal. But it was not inconceivable, for they had already caused an empire to stumble.

In spite of the rumors, King John had not spent all his time in bed with the Sparrowhawk. He too had his *couriers*, legions of them, and they apprised him of events in England and—as true spies—in France, Flanders and the German states. His clerks had also been kept busy, writing at his dictation to the English nobility and the money-hungry mercenaries throughout Europe who had not yet allied themselves with Philip Augustus.

John's appeals were attractively worded, though they did not dispose of the two outstanding problems. The royal treasury was as low as an ebbed tide, and mercenaries by definition worked for reward. If they could not be paid, they could not be hired. Or worse, if they were recruited with a promise and it failed to materialize in the form of coins or booty, they were liable to turn on their masters—in this case King John and his few remaining suzerains.

In England, the nobility were no less concerned about money; not how much they would receive, but how much they would be asked to raise. A few of them owned fiefs on both sides of the Channel, but the majority were established in England and Wales, and loath to contribute to the support of places they had never even seen. What were Argentan, Alençon, Arques and Angers to the lords of Ashdown or Abergavenny? The continental possessions were part of the kingdom, yes, in a way, but there was nothing to be gained by sending a flotilla of ships to the relief of Normandy. It was not cowardice, no one could accuse them of that. It was plain good sense, good husbandry. What use were a thousand knights if, when they reached Normandy, they found half the castles overrun and the other half barred against them, or deserted, or garrisoned by starving troops? Why send a relief force into lands that were already sympathetic to the French, or, to put it more bluntly, averse to King John?

Few of the barons bothered to answer his appeals. Those who did suggested the king return to England to explain his indolence and account for his eviction of William Marshal. Come home, they said, and we'll hear what you have to say. After that we'll discuss sorties abroad.

Isabel de Clare's tribute to her husband ran close to the truth. The gates of the city were not wrenched open, but his arrival sent riders spurring from Rouen like discovered deer.

He was accompanied by the four knights who had sworn fealty to him after the delivery of the prisoners to Corfe, and these, plus the thirty he had summoned from his estates at Pembroke and Chepstow, found themselves the object of an adoring crowd and a welcoming court. The object, though not the centerpiece. That position was reserved for Marshal, come back to save the kingdom.

With understandable discourtesy, the warlord had omitted to give advance warning of his arrival, so King John had been forced to change in a hurry, and was now fretting over the absence of a ring. It was in one of the jewel cases in his chambers, but short of unlocking every box and delving through them . . . Well, no matter; he'd found the correct boots, the trappings of office and, so long as he could resist clamping his hand to his head . . .

Queen Isabelle stood beside him on the castle steps, not merely fretting, but openly annoyed. "He's been away eight months or more. Why must we rush to greet him now? Tomorrow would have been soon enough, and by then I could have—"

"Just stand and listen," John snapped. "The city's in eruption. Look, they're invading the castle even now, look at them streaming in. Their hero has returned, don't you understand? Theirs and ours, my lady, for that's how we'll receive him. You've done well, I grant you, raising me with one hand, whilst depressing him with the other. But from now on—"

"What did you say?" She glared at him, aghast. "What's this, that I'm a puppeteer, playing you both on strings? Oh, no, lord King of England, oh, no. *You* sent him off and kept him off, then milked me for support. You've enjoyed the sweetest period of your life, and why? Because I was here and he was not. But you arranged it, in the same way that you arranged my abduction. The strings are tied around your fingers, John"—and in spiteful conclusion—"what room there is between the rings."

The king rounded on her, appalled by her accusation. But before he could speak, he glimpsed the crowd squeeze back from the gate arch and turned to watch Marshal ride in, followed by his bewildered, petal-strewn troop.

Well, John thought, none of them will go short of a woman for the next few nights.

He glanced again at Isabelle, but she was still rigid with anger, and he decided to ignore her. There was no sure way of foretelling her behavior, but please heaven she kept off the subject of manipulated toys.

He descended the steps, crossed the yard with commendable enthusiasm and grasped the headstall of Marshal's horse. The animal was tired and irritable and reared back, pulling the king off-balance. His fingers were securely hooked around the cheek-band, his rings pressing against the horse's muzzle.

John gazed up at the warlord, waiting for Marshal to humiliate him. The slightest tug on the reins and the damned palfrey would draw farther back, leaving him suspended from the bridle.

Like a puppet . . . Yes, and how the Sparrowhawk would love that. . . .

Marshal leaned forward, as though bowing in the saddle. Then, as his head dipped toward the king he murmured, *"Calme-toi, cheval, calme-toi."* He felt the animal respond and said, "Slip free, Sire, that's the way. Now catch him farther from his face. He's impressed enough, without being asked to kiss your hand."

The entanglement had gone unnoticed, and the crowd bellowed at this reconciliation of monarch and magnate. When had they ever seen King John play the ostler? When had they ever seen Earl Marshal bow so deep? They'd heard that the two men were estranged, but, whatever their disagreement, this was the way it should end, each man humbling himself before the other. Only great men would do that. But better than anything, they'd done it in public and not charged a penny.

Outside the walls, other crowds heard the roar and yelled in chorus. It would be some time before they learned why they had opened their lungs, but they'd seen Marshal go by and that was enough. The fortunate few hundred in the yard would tell them later what had happened, and no doubt embroider their stories in the expectation of ale. King John, helping the Arab from the saddle . . . Marshal kneeling before his king . . . The two of them going off, arm in arm, whilst the warlord's horse reared up, pawing the air, a certain sign of victory. . . .

Praise God that Marshal was back. Now there'd be some action, and some red grass on the hills.

For the next few days the court at Rouen was in almost permanent session. The barons had shown guarded enthusiasm for Mar-

shal's return, though the majority of them believed he had left it
too late. It was easy enough for the townsfolk to stamp and cheer;
all they knew was that the Earl of Pembroke had come back to
rally the army and stop the rot. It was all they wanted to know,
though, in the circumstances, it was as well that they remained in
ignorance. A little more knowledge, and they'd probably surrender
Rouen to the French.

Marshal also had things to learn. He was aware that the situation was desperate, but it was not until he reached the court that
he was told the worst of it.

King John had released the Lusignans.

Incredible though it was, he had accepted their parole, in return for which they had promised to ride directly to their fiefs, set
about raising their ransoms, then trot back and deliver them in
person. Apart from this single jaunt to Rouen, or wherever John
was at the time, the lords of Lusignan and Exoudun would sit out
the war. His two most dangerous enemies, dedicated not only to
the downfall of the Angevin empire, but to the personal ruin of
John Softsword, and he was expected to believe—*had* believed—
that they would stay at home, twiddling their thumbs. And why
not, when he had their word on it?

Even before he had assimilated this ominous news, Marshal was
informed that Queen Isabelle's father, Audemar of Angoulême,
had finally succumbed to his wasting paralysis. The death of Taillefer, the Iron-Cutter, was a loss in itself, for he had been one of
the most honorable of Christian nobles. However, the loss was
aggravated by the knowledge that Angoulême shared its northern
border with Lusignan.

Count Audemar's lands had been inherited by the Sparrowhawk, his sole offspring, but the only way she could secure them
now was by force of arms, for that entire region had turned against
the Crown. Of course, the situation would be made easier if Hugh
of Lusignan kept his word and remained impartial, seated beside
the fire, filling doeskin bags with coins. . . .

The third item of news came as no surprise to the warlord.
Hugh le Brun had not raised his ransom, but had once again declared war, this time in alliance with Angoulême. Both he and
brother Ralf might yet make the jaunt to Rouen, though if they
did so, it would be with cavalry, not coins.

Marshal's arrival—his return, albeit overdue—was not enough in itself to stem the tide. Nevertheless, it gave many of those in the outposts and border strongholds pause for thought, and encouraged them to make contact with the Arab. As a result, the court was inundated with messages of welcome, requests for help, estimates of enemy strength in the district, assurances of support, threats of defection, accusations leveled at neighbors, eyewitness account of fiery angels, foul-smelling demons, ravens that blanched into doves, and a swarm of bats that had, in an hour, stripped the leaves from a forest five miles square.

King John masked his embarrassment, for he had never been asked to weather such a storm of parchment. Indeed, during the past months he'd had the greatest difficulty in extracting information from any of these now-eager correspondents, and his mask hardened as he saw that the letters were addressed exclusively to Marshal, not even as a courtesy to the King of England. However, he decided to make the best of it. So long as a reliable picture emerged, it did not matter who'd commissioned it.

The senior commanders were reintroduced to hard work. The pockmarked William of Briouze concentrated his efforts on the army, assessing the complement of nobles, knights and squires, of sergeants and archers and common foot soldiers, of smiths and fletchers and farriers, physicians and engineers, coopers and wheelwrights and those members of the clergy who were prepared to fight. To these he added the mercenaries and musicians and camp followers, both male and female. The army would have its own butchers, bakers, hangmen, prostitutes, its own seamstresses and tentmakers, its tailors and cordwainers, its bridge-builders and miners and poachers, its unacknowledged sodomites and, in case the clergy failed to inspire the troops, its soothsayers and palmists.

Twice a day Briouze pounded the table and strode off, his head dinning with figures. This was no job for a soldier.

He began to invent the numbers, cowing his team of clerks until they arrived at totals that would satisfy King John and Earl Marshal. Under their pens, the Angevin force swelled to a respectable size, strong enough, it was believed, to stop the French in their tracks.

Then a single flake of good news arrived with the bad. The chatelaine of Pembroke had given birth to a daughter, and both ladies were well.

The courtiers seized the chance to celebrate, if only for an hour, and the king took Marshal aside and presented him with a heavy silver buckle—not for himself, but for the child. It was an exceptionally valuable piece and the warlord was surprised that John would part with it, especially in these straitened times. Nevertheless, he accepted it on behalf of his daughter, promising to safeguard it until her tenth birthday. "She will then be instructed that it is a gift from the King and Queen of England. Apropos, I must convey my thanks to Queen Isabelle."

"There's no need," John dismissed. "I'll tell her it was well received."

"And so shall I at the first opportunity."

"I said there's no need! Just leave it be, will you?" He blinked at the intensity of his words and hurriedly hooked on a smile. "Understand, my lord, the queen is not yet aware that I have, how shall I put it, marked the occasion? It would be better if— Yes, you tell your Isabel, and leave me to tell mine."

"As you wish," Marshal nodded. "It remains anyway a fine present and one that will be treasured by my house."

"That's it," John said. "And who knows? I might fasten the buckle in person, ten years from now."

The warlord neither described nor displayed the gift to his compeers, but locked it in his field chest, prior to sending it on to his wife. Later that day he returned to his narrow, sparsely furnished chamber to discover that the chest had been broken open and the buckle taken. Nothing else was missing, and the contents of the box had not been disturbed.

He had already composed a letter to Isabel de Clare, in which he'd recounted the king's clandestine behavior. He now destroyed the sheet and wrote again, this time omitting all mention of the gift. Nor did he report the theft to John, for he did not think the king was involved. Well, yes, he was, but indirectly.

The parchment blizzard continued to sweep the court. The mass of information from the outlying baronies showed that King

Philip had not only probed deep into Angevin territory, but had deployed his forces in such a way that Normandy was now almost completely encircled. French ships patrolled the coastal waters, an ominous warning that the Norman ports would soon be blockaded.

The patient, half-blind monarch had also moved contingents of his army along the north bank of the Loire. Their intention was to link up with the Bretons in the west, and they were already able to wave across the river at the men of Lusignan and Angoulême.

The mighty Angevin empire that had once extended unbroken from the shores of the Channel to the Spanish border was about to be cut and cut again. Normandy was shrinking like wet leather in the sun. The last vestige of unity had disappeared from Maine, Anjou and Touraine. And, all the while, the French nation stretched and expanded and reached for the English throat.

At Rouen, the harassed commanders heard a thousand things they did not wish to hear. But one item of news was denied them —the whereabouts or fate of John's nephew, Arthur of Brittany. Try as they might, they could swallow nothing more substantial than rumors, and were left hungering for more. The king would not be drawn on the subject, not even by so skilled an interrogator as William Marshal.

"Don't press me, my lord. Just take my word for it, he's safe and secure. No, he does not yet side with us, though he will eventually, I'm sure of it. And when he does I shall return him to his duchy, and those misguided subjects will be welcomed back into our ranks. But don't worry, Marshal, I shan't release my nephew as I did the Lusignans. I've learned that lesson. Indeed, Arthur will be kept hidden as long as necessary, and in a place where none of us will be tempted by his blandishments. It's a matter of time, that's all."

Perhaps so, Marshal thought, but time until what? Until the young man emerges contrite from his secret dungeon, or until our worst suspicions are confirmed?

By midyear the French were feeling the first buffets of Angevin resistance. Marshal, Briouze and others led their men south or east, engaging the enemy in a series of border skirmishes. There were no clear-cut victories, no abject defeats, though Philip's troops moved more cautiously, reminding themselves that there was, after all, someone to fight.

However, as the summer lengthened it became apparent that the figures Briouze had submitted to the war council at Rouen were largely fictitious. A castle that was supposed to produce thirty accoutered knights could, in reality, field less than a dozen. A district from which two hundred able-bodied men might be recruited was devoid of all but infants and the infirm. The thousands that Briouze had listed as available were nowhere to be seen.

Philip Augustus had made his own assessment of Angevin strength, and now, whenever his troops crossed swords with the enemy, they were expected to estimate the numbers and report them to the king. In this way he was able to check his forecast against the facts, a task that became more pleasurable by the hour.

It was clear that the English were as thin on the ground as coins in a street. Earl Marshal's return had come too late and, if that knife-nosed warlord could not assemble an army, then no one could.

This had been Philip's greatest worry, until now. He had met Marshal several times over the years, and he shared with Europe an abiding respect for, what did they call him, the Saracen, the Arab? Yes, the Arab, in some ways the mainstay of the Angevin empire. He must be aging now, the man who'd bolstered King Henry, King Richard and, against all odds, King John. If he was not yet sixty, he was close enough to touch it. And still dangerous, still unseated, still the one who prowled the ramparts of England, the one his countrymen expected to see when they looked up at the walls. And did he still make a point of touring whichever castle he was in, once in the morning, once at night? Doubtless he did, the way a watchdog sniffs its boundaries.

Pleased though he was by the reports that reached him, Philip Augustus felt some compassion for the Arab. Had John not dismissed him after Mirebeau, things might have been different. *Dieu sait*, they would most certainly have been different, for Marshal would not have let the French intrude unchallenged, nor released the Lusignan brothers, nor allowed young Arthur to disappear without trace. He might never have rid the empire of its disaffection with Softsword, but he would not have let it crumble so easily, nor so fast.

But John *had* dismissed him, allowing Philip to seize the initiative. Unfortunate for Marshal, but a blessing for France.

And now Philip was determined to retain his advantage, aware from the estimates he'd received that the Arab had stayed away too long. His patience finally rewarded, the Frenchman led his troops against Vaudreuil, Bonneville, Conches, Alençon and Le Mans. He encouraged the Bretons to launch a full-scale assault upon Angers and Avranches. He sent word to Ralf of Exoudun and Hugh of Lusignan, singling out targets for them in Touraine and Poitou. He issued more than sixty copies of a speech in which he detailed the strengths, or rather the weaknesses, of the enemy, indicating where his allies could best press their attack.

They obeyed him to the letter and, one by one, with dreadful inevitability, the fortress-fence of eastern Normandy cracked and collapsed. Elsewhere, Le Mans and Angers surrendered without a fight. Avranches resisted for a week, then hauled down its flag. The smaller outposts were starved into submission, the larger towns weakened from within by civilians who saw little profit in death.

It was as though God or Satan had leaned forward and crumpled the empire in His fist. A few fields and castles, a few rivers and valleys were spared, but most were caught by the curled fingers, the curved talons. Whoever one held responsible, the effect was the same; Normandy and Maine and Anjou were crushed, Poitou and Touraine savaged, the empire disfigured beyond repair.

And yet Rouen survived. French patrols reined in beyond arrow shot of the walls, made their calculations, then withdrew. John and his commanders watched for the enemy banners, the swaying siege machines, but they did not materialize. It was as though Philip intended to insult them into submission by ignoring them altogether.

Then they learned that their most powerful neighbor had also survived. Château Gaillard, a few miles upstream, the fortress built and christened by Richard Lionheart, his Insolent Castle.

It stood on a three-hundred-foot-high rock, dominating an entire loop of the River Seine. When the Lionheart had first set eyes on it he had seen it for what it was and heard it cry out to be crowned. In the months that followed, the enemy patrols had watched from a distance as the walls and towers and corrugated keep rose above the rock. They had reported on its progress, and when Philip Augustus had tired of hearing about it, he had issued a direct challenge to the Lionheart.

"My scouts tell me that when your building is completed, it may well prove impregnable. I think not. I think I would take it, even if it were fashioned from hammered iron."

Rising to the challenge, Richard had replied, "I find you too optimistic, for I could defend it, even if it were made from patted butter."

It was a nice exchange, though it had never been put to the test. And for good reason, since the castle boasted three independent baileys, twelve towers, a deep central ditch and quarters for eight hundred men. The causeway across the ditch could be destroyed at the first sign of trouble and, perched on its near-vertical rock, the fortress was only accessible from the south.

To attack Château Gaillard, one would first have to advance along the narrow southern approach, braving the hail of arrows, crossbow bolts and slingshots that would sweep the unprotected ridge. Then avoid the inextinguishable Greek fire tipped from the walls. Then smash an entry below the gatehouse. Then seize the outermost bailey and its flanking towers. Then bridge the central ditch, another target for oil and missiles. Then force a passage through the next gateway and secure the second bailey and its turrets. And still be faced by a further five towers and the corrugated keep.

It was not for nothing that Coeur de Lion had taken pride in his Insolent Castle.

However, before the last of the oxblood mortar had hardened, King Richard had been killed below the walls of a far less significant castle, and it had been left to William Marshal to oversee the completion of the border stronghold.

Delighted to hear that the enemy had bypassed Château Gaillard, John said, "It will outlast us all, my brother's monument.

The French fish is showing good sense, for he'd never subdue it."
He shook his head, in keeping with his conviction.

Three weeks later, an urgent message arrived from Roger Lacy, the long-time castellan of Château Gaillard, advising John and Marshal that the fortress was under attack, and that King Philip himself was directing operations.

The word that now came most readily to John's lips was not Gaillard, but Mirebeau. He told his commanders, "This is our best chance yet to land the fish. It can't be done without risk, for we shall have to leave Rouen undermanned for a while. But it's a risk worth taking, and we might even better the success of Mirebeau. Think of it, messires! Gaillard relieved, and King Philip here, before us, squinting with his one good eye!"

The threats and promises were interleaved with more sober discussions. The almost daily reports from Roger Lacy made it clear that the French now occupied both banks of the Seine below Gaillard. Moreover, they had laid a barrier across the tidal river in order to prevent any rescue craft reaching the castle. It was, according to Roger Lacy, "like a wall in the water," and he obviously did not expect help from that direction.

The Angevin commanders studied the reports; yet, as with Mirebeau, it was King John who voiced the most imaginative scheme. "What the castellan said about the barrier shows he's impressed by it. And if he assumes we'll be frightened off, so will the French. It must be a formidable structure, but that might work in our favor, for it's the weak spots that are most heavily guarded."

"I have one or two friends in that district," Marshal said. "They'll tell us what we need to know."

Within two days the Angevins had their answer. The barrier was, indeed, like a wooden wall, for the French had lashed together several hundred barrels, then attached planks to both sides of the pontoon. More boards had been laid on top of the barrels, so that it served as both a wall and a bridge. However, there was a second, more substantial bridge upstream, and it was this that carried the weight of enemy traffic. Marshal's spies had watched for most of a morning, but no one had crossed the barrier. It was guarded, they said, by less than a dozen men, and these watchdogs were already looking bored with their work.

"Then that's where we'll strike," John decided. "We will launch a two-pronged attack, by land and by river. I shall lead a flotilla against the barrier, whilst you, Marshal, will take a force wide of the castle and attack the French from the rear. If we do this right, my troops will be off-loading supplies and weapons for Gaillard, whilst yours are trampling a few pretty tents. And, God willing, you'll bring us back the French fish for supper."

After that, the king devoted himself to his ship-borne assault. He retired to his chambers, where he discussed the plan with Queen Isabelle. These were like the old days for John, the days preceding Mirebeau. He would not be rescuing Eleanor this time, nor leading his chevaliers on a wild, half-naked ride across country. But there were similarities, not least that both ideas had been his.

In his absence, the defense of Rouen would be entrusted to William Briouze, the man who had helped him dispose of Duke Arthur. Briouze was not at all pleased to be left behind, and said so, but the king silenced his objections with a further gift of land.

"I'm a man of my word," John told him, unblinking. "I promised to raise you to the highest estate, and you have already received properties in Glamorgan and Limerick. Now you have a further triangle of castles; Grosmont and Skenfrith and the White Castle at Llantilio." He smiled and added, "Much more of it, and you'll be in competition with the Crown."

Briouze denied it and bowed and went off to arrange the skeletal defense of the city. He now owned more fortresses and manors than he would ever find time to visit, yet the king's largesse could not obliterate the memory of what they had done together on that clear, moonlit night, five months before.

Sooner or later the world would learn that John had murdered his nephew, and that the king's accomplice had squatted in the darkness, his body infected with fear. The truth would emerge because, when the shame became unbearable, William Briouze would make his confession.

By the end of August the relief force was ready, the flotilla loaded and manned, the cavalry assembled. King John commanded seventy small river craft, each containing as many oarsmen, soldiers and provisions as the vessel could hold without wallowing. On the north bank, Marshal had mustered almost a hundred knights, then supplemented the contingent with a further sixty mounted archers. He was disappointed by the lack of response, though he prided himself that no other warlord could have raised even this make-do troop.

Among his knights were all but three of the thirty-four who had accompanied him from Pembroke. They looked wan and haggard, as well they might, for the reality of the past few months had exceeded their most extravagant dreams.

On their arrival at Rouen, they had found themselves acclaimed as heroes. The crowd had, at first, directed its approval at Marshal, but he had then disappeared into the castle with John and the Sparrowhawk, leaving the citizens to visit their gratitude upon his knights.

Merchants had jostled each other in their eagerness to give these fine young men free rein in their stores. They had invited the knights to dine, and afterward trumpeted the beauty of their daughters or, failing that, their wives. The surrounding villages had vied for the privilege of entertaining Marshal's bemused companions, and the churches had been filled by the assurance that an Angevin hero would attend the service. Each day brought fresh excursions, each evening a new host at table, each night a different bedmate. Since the people could not get close enough to their savior, they would make life as pleasant as possible for his disciples.

The knights had reached Rouen in June, and it was now the last day of August and they had had enough. They assembled before the Arab, thirty-one of them, and blearily explained why the other three would not be present at the relief of Château Gaillard.

Two of the three were dead, one murdered by a man who had regretted offering his daughter, the other drowned when he had fallen drunk into a millrace. The last of the trio had simply disappeared, no doubt following the ripples of his unearned fame. He would probably seduce his way to Gascony or the Spanish border, marry the prettiest girl in the district and settle down. No one would accuse him of desertion, or ask what he had done to merit such adulation; it was enough that he had come to live with them and be their champion, this man who had served under the great William Marshal.

At midday the cavalry set out for the beleaguered castle, whilst the flotilla moved upstream toward the wall in the water.

Firmly established on both banks of the Seine and assured that the Angevin empire was already in ruins, the French perimeter guards were less than alert. Those unfortunate few who patrolled the eastern camp below Gaillard heard the crack of sun-dried briers, turned toward the sound and were almost immediately trampled by the charging palfreys.

The camp erupted in confusion as Marshal's men spurred forward, his knights unsheathing their swords as they rode clear of the undergrowth, his archers drawing and notching their arrows in a single fluid movement. They loosed their shafts at any likely target, and although most of the arrows missed their mark, the French were completely nonplussed.

The attack had been timed for dusk, when soldiers turn toward their camp fires and the welcome smell of food. Many of them had already disarmed and shed their sweat-soaked gambesons, and they were now caught unprotected, their only weapon a dice cup or a leather flask. They ran for the nearest tent, the nearest stack of spears, but Marshal's horsemen swept through the camp, charging down soldiers and shelters alike.

. . . By now the river craft should have reached the barrier. . . .

An arrow whicked through the gathering darkness and cut Marshal to the jawbone. He yelped with surprise and felt the air bite at the wound. *What was it I told Isabel? Do you think I'll be harmed by the French?*

The cavalry plunged on, flattening the camp, then turned in the direction of the river, intent on taking the upstream bridge.

. . . John's men would have seized the barrier, and the axes would be out, chopping at the roped barrels. . . .

Blood dripped from Marshal's jaw and it hurt him to speak. But orders had to be given, and he couched the wound in his hand, as though nursing a bad tooth. "Get across the bridge! Hold it till I say!"

Darkness closed in like a third, impartial force. The riders had skirted wide of the castle and it now loomed beside them,

overlooking both the barrier and the bridge. Marshal rode to the
river's edge and gazed downstream, but he could not distinguish
the barrier. Just as well, he thought. There's enough to do here.

The first of his knights had already hacked their way across the
bridge, and were fanning out on the west bank. Before long the
enemy would counterattack in force, and Marshal roared at his
incendiary detail to prepare the firebombs. They were crude
but effective; leather sacks filled with pitch and inflammable oils,
the drawstrings pulled tight around a stub of soaked material.
Thrown correctly, the leather would split on impact and the
glutinous pitch ooze out, burning fiercely.

The men shouted that they were ready, and the warlord spurred
forward across the bridge to recall his knights. Each moment
brought more Frenchmen from the darkness, more arrows whir-
ring through the air. Several shafts hit the bridge and, on the
east bank, men and horses were going down.

No longer favoring his injured jaw, Marshal yelled at the
knights to withdraw. They came back two to a horse, or on foot,
some dragged along by their companions, others left to fend
for themselves. Marshal waited until only the dead and dying
were left on the western bank, then turned to follow the survivors. As he did so an arrow embedded itself below his left knee.
He felt no immediate pain, but the velocity of the shaft was
enough to hurl him half out of the saddle. He snatched blindly
at the pommel, dragged himself upright and hacked his right leg
against his horse.

By the time he had regained the eastern bank the pain had
risen like floodwater through his body. Unable to speak, he made
a feeble, indecisive gesture, but it was enough for the incendiary
detail. They had brought tinderboxes with them and now they
scratched sparks onto the fuses and hurled their bombs as far
as possible along the bridge. The first sack exploded obediently
as it touched the wood, and the flames leaped up as though
they themselves had been burned.

No longer in control, the warlord hung in the saddle, his
gloved fingers curled around the arrow. Common sense told him
to wait until the barb could be removed and the wound cau-
terized and dressed. But he was also aware that he would not

cover more than a mile with the broad tip buried in his leg. By then, the razor-sharp edges would have severed the limb.

The western end of the bridge was now a mass of flames. The French were ranged along the far bank, exchanging arrows and slingshots with the Angevin raiders across the river. Time favored the besiegers, and they had already dragged two light catapults from their western camp. The first cloud of flints flew overhead, smashing against the base of Gaillard, but the next took its toll of the riders. They waited for Marshal to order the retreat, heard nothing and began to withdraw. They did not know that their commander had been wounded, only that they had achieved their object and were overstaying their welcome. If things had gone as well downstream, King John would have off-loaded his supplies, embraced Roger Lacy, then started for home. With both the bridge and the barrier destroyed, the French would be stranded on the western bank, whilst the garrison of Château Gaillard would settle down, replenished, in their impregnable fortress.

The riders streamed away into the darkness, skirting the base of the rock.

Abandoned for the moment, the half-conscious warlord closed his fist around the shaft. He again remembered his boast to Isabel de Clare. *Do you think I'll be harmed by the French? Oh, no, my lady.* The memory brought a weak, ugly smile and, mouthing her name, he pulled the arrow from his leg.

It was a necessary but reckless act; necessary if he was to ride, but reckless in that it robbed him of his senses. The arrow fell to the grass and he slumped forward over the saddle horn, his wound bleeding profusely. Made nervous by the sparks that blew from the burning bridge, his palfrey moved away, then stood quiet and patient, awaiting the touch of his heels.

The two knights had ridden off in the wrong direction, to find their way barred by the earthworks that supported the southern approach to Gaillard. Hurriedly retracing their steps, they all but collided with the silent rider. Their blurted challenge brought no reply and they both swung wide, ready to cut at the lean, bowed figure. Then, their faces reddened by the firelight, one of them said, "Hold back! Oh, sweet God, it's him, I came from Pembroke with him, it's Earl Marshal!"

With simple disbelief, his companion hissed, "How can it be? This man's dead. It can't be Marshal."

They sheathed their swords, edged closer and peered at the warlord.

"It *is* him!"

"He's been cut on the face."

"And here, somewhere on the leg. Wait, steady him in the saddle." He leaned forward and, as though guilty of *lèse majesté*, prodded tentatively at Marshal's shoulder. He made no sound, though his body jerked against the pommel. It was answer enough.

The rescuers did not wait to bind his leg, but led him east and north and west around the base of Château Gaillard. On the way they passed a dozen of their compeers, some dying in silence, others with sufficient strength to plead for help. The knights ignored them, not daring to stop until they were well clear of the castle. Then, in the light of a full, cloudless moon, they fastened Marshal's wrists to his saddle horn and tied a leather bootlace savagely tight around his knee, just above the arrow wound. The stream of blood narrowed to a trickle and they led him onward, in the direction of Rouen.

Some way short of the city he recovered his senses. In a voice thickened by pain, he said, "Is this your retribution for Mirebeau? Because your men were led away at the carts' tail, you rope me like a felon? Then you lose your advantage, messires, and behave as badly as we."

The knights realized that he was confused and, while one of them untied his wrists, the other said, "You're safe, my lord. We're not the French. We are your men, and we're almost at Rouen."

Marshal had time enough to say, "My blood's drained out. I must not be seen like this. The Cistercians . . . Take me to their infirmary. . . ." Then he fell senseless again, and the knights retied his wrists.

Obedient to his command, they avoided the castle and delivered him to the austere Cistercian monastery that abutted the

west wall of the city. The white-robed monks showed themselves
to be practiced and professional, though they asked several times
if their dark-skinned patient was really William Marshal, Earl of
Pembroke and Striguil. The knights assured them he was, then
watched in weary admiration as the monks drugged him with
mandragora and cleaned and stitched his wounds. Only later
did it occur to the onlookers that, if the Cistercians saved
Marshal's leg and possibly his life, they would expect something
more tangible than a grunt of gratitude from their patient. Another monastery, perhaps, this one to be situated on his lands. Or
a covenant, guaranteeing their Order one-twentieth of his income
for life. Something that would jog his memory each time he put
his left foot on the ground.

In the week that followed, the Earl of Pembroke was left to the
ministrations of the monks. He was too ill to receive visitors, too
heavily drugged to discern more than the white-clad shapes of
his physicians. The arrow cut on his jaw was healing, though it
would leave a long, ugly scar. But the leg wound was more
serious, for it had become infected and the monks feared that
they might yet have to amputate the limb. Meanwhile, they fed
their patient on a thin, monastic diet, and continued to drain
the poison from his wound. Throughout the week he lay silent,
for the most part asleep, yet sometimes with his eyes half-open,
seeing nothing but the blur of candlelight or the sliding progress
of the sun.

Those visitors who called at the monastery were told that
Earl Marshal could not be disturbed and sent away. However, it
was from them that the monks learned of events in the castles
of Rouen and Gaillard, and they decided to keep the truth from
the warlord.

They stationed two of their burliest brethren at the entrance
to the infirmary, while the abbot himself took charge of all
letters and messages of goodwill. He had not realized until now
that the patient was so popular or in so much demand, and he
told his monks to do their best for the master of Pembroke and
Striguil.

A worldly man, the abbot acknowledged that Marshal's death
would not only be a tragedy for England, but also for the

Cistercian Order. The monastery at Rouen would become notorious as the place where he had died, and there would be no question of founding another community on his lands. After all, his widow Isabel de Clare was unlikely to thank them for having failed to save her husband.

Excusing the guards and physicians, the abbot ordered the other monks to attend a nightlong vigil, and decorated the chapel with the candles left over from Lammas.

Exactly seven days after Marshal had been carried into the austere infirmary, he was awoken by the sound of scuffling in the passageway outside his cell. Confused by the fumes of mandragora, he imagined that the monastery had been invaded by would-be assassins. Groping at the wall behind his head, he wrenched down a simple stone cross. As chalk and plaster littered the pillow, he hauled himself upright, wincing with pain, then clasped both hands around the solid granite shaft. He raised the cross high, not for comfort *in extremis*, but as the only available weapon. Swung or thrown correctly, the religious artefact would cave a man's skull.

There were further sounds, a loud gasp of indignation, a yell for help, and then the door was pushed open and the pock-marked William Briouze shouldered his way into the cell. He did not immediately recognize the scarred, emaciated figure, and hesitated before accepting that it was, indeed, Earl Marshal. He had expected to find the warlord thinner than usual, but not pared down to the bone.

"Lie back," he growled. "You're in no danger from Briouze." Then he closed the door and advanced to the foot of the bed.

Struggling to come alert, Marshal peered at him and let the cross sink slowly to the plain woolen coverlet. "Well, well," he mouthed, "here's a treat. Our governor turned vandal."

"It was the only way," Briouze said bluntly. "The monks believe they own you. This is my fifth attempt to see you, and I was tired of being refused."

Marshal gestured at the cross and said, "Lift it off me, will you? My leg's sufficiently painful, without having it crushed." He sank back as Briouze removed the polished stone, then asked,

"What was that all about, outside? God forbid that you cut your way in here."

"No, I just eased two of them aside, that's all."

Marshal managed to twitch a smile. "I can imagine. But why this—easy visit, my lord governor? Did you think I was malingering?"

Briouze shook his head. "We know the extent of your injuries, Marshal, and we pray you'll recover. But we have heard nothing from you, and it was decided— I decided to collect your views in person."

"Views on what, William?" His mind slowed by the mandragora, he made a visor of his hand and massaged his temples. He heard Briouze say, "On the fifty letters you've been sent," and he pushed his hand up over his skull.

"Sent, maybe, but not received. You say you've heard nothing from me, but equally, I've heard nothing from you. Not a single word, let alone the contents of fifty letters."

With a snarl of exasperation, Briouze glared at the door. "Much as I thought. Those damned monks have kept everything from you! They'd do better working for the French!" His voice had risen to a bellow, and he was tempted to go in search of the abbot. And this time, if anyone stood in his way, he'd do more than ease them aside.

Still fighting the effects of the drug, Marshal asked, "Why would they intercept the letters, William?" Then, in answer to his own query, "Unless they knew the contents would distress and weaken me. Is that it, my lord governor? Is the news so bad that the monks thought to protect me from it?"

Briouze turned to face him again. "It seems we are both unprepared, Earl Marshal. All of us at the castle, we accepted that you were too weak to write, or even dictate your replies, or, at the worst, unable to read the letters with your own eyes. But we were sure they would be read to you, and that you would have learned about—things."

"I'm sorry," Marshal said, "but you will have to teach me."

Having forced his way into the monastery, the visitor now felt trapped. He made a last, feeble attempt to delay the moment— "I've no desire to worsen your condition"—then nodded reluctantly as Marshal said, "You won't. Just say your piece, William, and say it straight out. Remember, I'm fifty letters behind."

Briouze cleared his throat, set his feet flat on the boards as though to ride a blow, then said, "The first thing you should know . . . The attack on Gaillard, it failed. . . . The king's fleet never reached the barrier. In truth, they did not get halfway there." Seeing Marshal stir, he hurried on, "Your part in the raid was successful, everyone speaks well of it, but it was not enough. If King John had gained the barrier and destroyed it, the French force would have been divided. But, as it was, the enemy simply moved down from the bridge and used the barrier as a crossing."

Marshal was pushing himself upright. Briouze did not know whether to help him, or stand his ground. In the end he stayed where he was, assembling his answer to the next, inevitable question.

"They never reached the barrier? Why not, my lord governor, why not? The river was clear between Rouen and Gaillard. They could not have failed to reach it!"

"Calm yourself, Marshal. Yes, the river was clear, but it's also tidal and—" He shrugged with embarrassment, aware that what he had to say next would not only sound tragic, but comical. "It's tidal, the Seine, but the king did not take that into account. The night of the attack, there was a full moon, when the water's pulled down to the sea. But no one thought to study the tides, and the current proved too strong for the oarsmen. They made some headway at first, but by the time they'd covered half the distance they were exhausted. After that, they drifted back downstream with only the helmsmen to steer them. From what we can gather, eight of the vessels tipped over in the river, and at least ten more were swept past their moorings and went on to founder in the estuary. By all accounts, King John lost—"

"The devil gut King John! How many were lost from *my* contingent? How many knights died in the French camp or at the bridge, and for *nothing!* Tell me that, Briouze! List *my* casualties for a change!"

Without warning, the latch was lifted and the door pushed open. The abbot entered, followed by the monks whom Briouze had eased aside. One was still massaging his bruised chest, while the other favored an elbow.

"I was in the garden," the abbot apologized, "else I'd have been here—"

"Not now!" Marshal snapped. "Not for a while!"

"But you should know that this man assaulted both Brother—"

"And will again," Briouze assured him. "Leave us be."

Marshal nodded sourly. "Yes, Abbot, leave us be. Go back to your garden. Or better, unearth the letters you've been keeping from me." His face drawn by pain and emotion, he watched the monks bluster and retreat. Briouze laid a hand flat against the door and pushed it shut, then glanced anxiously at his compeer.

For the moment, Marshal's strength was expended, and he did not repeat his demands. Instead, he leaned back against the wall, his eyes closed, his head and shoulders still speckled with chalk and plaster.

"So the attack failed, eh, William? And the supplies? Were any of them off-loaded?"

"I regret, they were not."

"Then Gaillard is still besieged."

Briouze nodded, realized that Marshal's eyes were closed, and said, "Yes, and short of salt and arrows."

"Does the king plan another rescue attempt?"

There was a silence.

"Well, does he?" He waited for Briouze to speak, then opened his eyes in time to see confusion add its ravages to the pockmarked face. The continued silence brought Marshal forward and, as he peered at his discomforted visitor, he realized that there was worse news to come.

"What is it, William? *Was* there another attempt, another failure?"

"No, my lord, and there won't be, for the king left us this morning."

Marshal frowned, as though defeated by the complexity of the words. "King John has left us? He's left Rouen?"

"He's left Normandy. He's on his way to England."

Still dulled by the drug and the knowledge that his knights had died for nothing, Marshal repeated what he heard. "He has left Normandy, for England. And Queen Isabelle, has she gone with him?"

"She has, with him and the remnants of the treasury. In my

opinion, we shall not see either of them again on this side of the Channel."

There was another silence, broken only by the creak of the boards beneath Briouze's feet. Marshal had sunk back on the dusty pillow, his eyes open, his gaze held by a patch of sunlight high on the wall. To his bemused mind it looked like the fore-castle of a galley, or a half-fallen tower, and it served as the inspiration for his words.

"I should not be surprised at what you've told me, for our high-heeled monarch has been at the mercy of the currents all his life. . . . Thank you for visiting me, William Briouze. . . . Now, with your permission, I'll lie here and listen as the walls of Normandy crash to the ground. . . ."

Briouze found himself bowing to his compeer. Then he left the cell and made his way through the monastery and onto the cobbled street, emerging near the west gate of the city. Once there, he thought of going back to tell Marshal about the murder. But he was not yet ready. Not quite.

6

❧•☙

Ebb of England. . .
September–December 1203

Had the Sparrowhawk been truly a bird of prey, she would have savaged her husband before he had ever left Normandy.

The royal party had zigzagged across the duchy, riding south from Rouen to the riverside castle of Bonneville and thence northwest toward Lisieux. The king and queen were escorted by less than twenty knights, together with a dozen household servants, each of whom bore responsibility for a packhorse or a saddled palfrey. The riders were aware that Philip's spies would have reported their departure from the city and that French patrols would be scouring the countryside. As a result, King John had left the bulk of his entourage at Bonneville, packed his seals and jewelry into nondescript panniers and issued his diminished force with plain, hooded cloaks, the uniform of the wayfarer. Nothing could guarantee their safety, but dressed in their unremarkable garb, they were more likely to pass for merchants than monarchs in disguise. During the first week, their anonymity was further protected by bad weather, and they managed to reach Lisieux without being challenged.

On the road, John and Isabelle kept silent, sometimes riding abreast, more often apart. The fate of the river-borne assault on Château Gaillard had left the king vexed and dispirited, and he hunched in the saddle, lashed by the late summer rains and swamped with self-pity.

His dreams of a second Mirebeau had been literally washed away. He had not dared visit the stricken William Marshal, but had instead convinced himself that he should return to England and organize a full-scale invasion of his lost territories. The decision was reasonable enough—if a year overdue—but the method showed the weakness of the Angevin condition. The king and queen had not so much departed the city as fled from it, cloaking their identities and staying clear of the well-trodden paths. With large areas of the duchy in enemy hands, or at least sympathetic to the French, the rain-soaked group could not tell which of the suzerains would reaffirm his loyalty, or which would claim them with a Judas kiss. Ever cautious, the king insisted that his escort stand guard throughout the night, ten men to a watch, and that the party ride on before dawn. Then, once out of sight of the manor or castle, the travelers changed direction, veering again at midday. These evasive tactics left them unchallenged, though from time to time they found themselves huddled amongst the dripping trees, whilst one of the servants went off to ask the way.

Throughout the latter weeks of September, the royal party continued its slow, erratic progress toward the coast and Barfleur. The rain that had helped conceal them gave way to the final heatwave of summer, and they removed their hoods in favor of broad-brimmed hats. The knights were forced to discard their helmets, burying them in a thicket, but not before they had secured John's irritable assurance that they'd be recompensed for the loss. As for Queen Isabelle, she had refused to cut or plait her hair, and it was decided that in the event of her being challenged, she would identify herself as the daughter of the eldest wayfarer.

John pleaded with her to show proper humility.

"Say as little as possible, and for God's sake don't argue with them. It's unlikely they'll recognize you, unless any of them saw service with the Lusignans, but a highborn manner will certainly arouse their suspicions. You are supposed to be a merchant's daughter, and that's the impression to give."

The Sparrowhawk responded with a shrug. "Timidity is an unnatural state," she told him, "though I daresay it comes more readily to some than others. What will you be, my lord, when they question you? An apprentice in a smithy? Or does such work have too much fire and noise about it?"

"Just play the part," John snapped, "and we might all get back to England." He noticed that his fellow travelers had moved away, deaf and blind to the exchange. Studiously avoiding his gaze, they resettled their hats, murmured amongst themselves, stretched and yawned or lifted their buttocks from the sweaty saddles. They had been on the road—more accurately off the roads—for twenty-three days, and they were well aware of the growing dissent between king and queen.

It had started at Rouen, the night John had returned wet and shaken from the near-comic disaster on the Seine. Those knights who had stayed behind to help Briouze garrison the city had been horrified by the news, but were even more disturbed by its effect on the king. He had arrived back in tears, blaming first the oarsmen who had failed to combat the current, then the local boat owners and fishermen for denying him such crucial information. Within an hour he had fabricated a conspiracy. The attack was never meant to succeed, for all those who knew the ways of the river were in the pay of the French.

Several of the more senior knights remembered his brother, Richard Lionheart, and they were hard put to hide their disgust for the present monarch. Would that Richard were alive, they thought; a man born to victory, yet made implacable by defeat. There'd be no tears or laying of blame from the Lionheart. He'd simply tell his oarsmen to rest, salvage what remained of the flotilla, then wait for the tide to turn. But he was dead and gone, his place taken, though no one would say filled; by the sniveling Softsword.

A number of the barons reminded him that he had planned the attack in secret, closeted in his private chambers with Queen Isabelle. He had intended to repeat his triumph at Mirebeau, but this time, greedy for acclaim, he had clutched the plans to his chest. He could blame whomsoever he liked, but he could not evade responsibility for the fiasco. King Richard would not have done so. But then King Richard would have tested the tide.

Later that night, John had turned to Isabelle for comfort, and been immediately rebuffed.

The young queen had never forgiven him for recalling William Marshal to Rouen, nor for the fulsomeness of his welcome. Trotting across the castle yard like a common ostler, and catching at the harness of the horse . . . Pleasing to the crowd, perhaps, but scarcely the actions of a king. . . .

Nor had her respect for him been restored by the blizzard of letters that had then swept into the castle, all of them addressed to the beloved and wondrous Earl of Pembroke. John had allowed his authority to be usurped by an arid old man, and the entire court had seen how Marshal's popularity outweighed that of their chosen king. Isabelle thought it a miracle that her husband had not offered to open each letter as it arrived, then, kneeling, present it for Marshal's scrutiny.

There remained a third, more personal grievance, and one she made no attempt to allay. She had never mentioned it to John, fearing an onset of his Angevin sickness, but she nursed it and looked forward to the day when she would ride through the gates of Pembroke. Then, and only then, would she produce the heavy silver buckle that the king had presented to Marshal as a gift for his newborn daughter, the buckle that Isabelle had promptly stolen from the warlord's box. She would show it to John, and to the Arab, and to her namesake, Isabel de Clare. And then she would throw it to the ground and let whoever wanted it stoop and wipe it clean. King John was not the most sensitive of husbands, but even he would sense her disapproval. In future, if he had jewelry to spare, he could give it to his wife, not to the squalling offspring of his knife-nosed tormentor. The Arab was already rich in popularity, rich in power, rich in paternity. Neither he nor his spawn had need of silver buckles from the king. . . .

Sufficiently critical of John's attitude toward Marshal, the Sparrowhawk had been in no mood to console her tear-and-river-worn husband.

"Regard it as a lesson," she told him, "and learn from it. The attack on Mirebeau was well prepared, but you never really put your mind to the problems of Gaillard. You imagined—"

"I?" he howled. "Why am I singled out? You were with me when I planned it, when we planned it, and I never heard you speak of currents or the size of the moon!"

"But I did, my lord. Quite early on. I said it was essential that you take your fleet to the barrier with the flow of the tide, gain control at the change, then return with the ebb. I'll share your distress, and not for the first time, but you are unfair to blame me for advice you overlooked. Oh, don't glare so, husband. You were immersed in the memories of Mirebeau, and you chose not to heed my words. In truth, you probably never even heard them." She waited until the first furrows of doubt had been plowed, then said, "You listened to no one, my lord, or am I mistaken? Did you ask around? Did you approach Briouze or Marshal, or the captain of your craft? I don't believe you did."

The intensity of his gaze had become blurred, his certainty torn at the hem. He stared at her, but he was no longer sure of what she had or had not said. Perhaps she *had* mentioned something about tides and the pull of the moon. Perhaps, in passing, she *had* spoken of the ebb and the change and the flow. He did not remember it, but it was possible, and the possibility sapped his strength. Never a Lionheart, the wolf sank weeping to the floor.

Isabelle looked down at him, the man who had snatched her from Hugh le Brun in the valley below Moncontour. The man who had married her and made her Queen of England. The man who had amused her with his cruel wit, aroused her with his sexual prowess, startled her with the brilliance of his tactics at Mirebeau.

The same man who was cowed by William Marshal. The same man who had murdered his nephew and let Normandy leak like oil between his fingers. The man who had found a silver buckle for Marshal's brat. The man who now sobbed beside the bed, so unsure of himself that he could not even tell when his wife was lying.

She laid an unfeeling hand on his head, felt him shiver and relax, then left him crouched against the coverlet whilst she thought how best to resurrect him.

He had sunk to a piteous level, no doubt of that. England would not survive another year unless its leadership was strengthened, and, if John did not soon reestablish his authority at court and in the country, he might find himself deposed, or worse. How many men, Isabelle wondered, were even now thumbing a knife blade, or leaning forward in some dim-lit tavern, hissing assassination?

The glory of Mirebeau had faded and vanished, and the French no longer peered at the sky in search of Melusine's descendant. By morning Philip Augustus would have learned of the attempt to succor Gaillard, and of the fleet that had been so ignominiously washed away. He would know then that John's earlier triumph had been exceptional, and he would probably unfold the blanket with which to smother the Angevin empire. What better time to advance than on the heels of England's self-inflicted disaster?

The Sparrowhawk decided that she and her husband must leave Rouen at the first opportunity. All year the barons in England had been caterwauling for the king's return, and there was nothing to be gained by staying on here. The way things were going, the city would be in French hands within a month, and Isabelle did not intend to surrender either her liberty or her crown.

She knew of too many queens and princesses who had been relegated to the drab chambers of some minor castle and, for perhaps the first time in her life, she felt a pang of sympathy for her predecessor, the luckless Berengaria of Navarre.

Once married to King Richard, Berengaria had been widowed and forgotten, ignored by John and the court, befriended only by her mother-in-law, the aged Eleanor of Aquitaine. Isabelle had seen some of the letters Berengaria had written to John, plaintive reminders that he had yet to return her dowry—of which, in fact, little was left—or pay the annuity he had promised her. She was living in a small castle near Toulouse, again supported by Eleanor, a sad and lonely woman who signed her letters with the heartbreaking title, "once humble Queen of England."

It was not a future to which the Sparrowhawk aspired.

She struggled with the problem of John's resurrection, then her frown vanished in a yelp of laughter, and she glanced down to make sure the sound had not awakened the king. He slept on, hunched beside the bed, mercifully unaware that his wife had decided to implement the teachings of his tormentor, William Marshal.

Had he known, he might well have pleaded with the warlord

for further instruction. It would have been a hard and painful tutelage, but nowhere near as miserable as the treatment to be afforded by his sixteen-year-old wife. She was, after all, a predator, determined to save her nest.

From Lisieux they circled south, then west, then north, to come level with Caen. Each day seemed longer, their progress more erratic, the forests more infested with flies. Their hands blistered in the sun, and the blisters became sores, and they no longer resembled merchants so much as penitents, bound to encompass the world.

Each evening they struggled to sit erect, then retired to their allotted quarters, the escort reacting blearily to the slightest chink or flare, John and Isabelle bickering until neither could remember the last spoken phrase. Already dulled by his defeat at Gaillard—halfway to Gaillard—the king wept and foundered, while his wife jarred him with her elbow, demanding to know what he would tell the waiting barons, how he would behave when he reached the shingle of England?

And there was always the dawn, and the clumsy, uncertain departure of these imitation merchants. Twenty-three days . . . Twenty-four . . . Twenty-five. . . . And then the first chill of October clung like ague to their skins.

They changed direction, swung back and changed again. Habit directed their steps, and one of the more resilient knights made a joke about sailing from Normandy to England, via Spain. But the joke died in the air, and the riders continued to thread their way along the valleys, or force a path between the trees. John and Isabelle kept apart, the king terrified of her questions, the queen aware that he was lost for an answer. Instead, they set their minds on reaching the port of Barfleur. If they did that, they would at least have shared an arduous journey, and, God willing, the subsequent voyage home.

A final squabble at the port. And then, for no better reason than that King John controlled the purse strings, they boarded a fishing vessel, its decks still slippery with scales.

The crossing was mercifully smooth, and the royal party landed somewhere west of Dover, sometime in early October. Neither the date nor the destination were recorded, for the King of England was not at all sure that he would be welcome on the step.

The guards stood in the shadow of the gate arch, their gaze taken by a young woman who was leading a mule past the barbican. She ignored their lascivious invitations and the explicit jerk of their bodies, and guided the animal along one of the narrow, sunless alleys that led to the central market.

The men exchanged a few more ribald comments, then glanced left and right in search of another likely victim. Market day was the best for such diversions; it brought the girls in from the nearby farms and villages, and helped alleviate the boredom of guard duty.

They watched an elderly couple pull a handcart along the street. The sides of the cart were draped with plain woolen shifts and a selection of leatherwork, untooled belts and straps and laces. As the couple drew level with the barbican, a tunic fell between the cart and one of the solid wheels, wrapping itself around the axle. The guards watched, expressionless, as the couple struggled to free the ruined garment, but they made no effort to help.

Eventually the man and his wife managed to unwind the cloth and continued on their way, grumbling quietly to each other. The torn tunic might have fetched as much as three pence, the price of a young lamb or a gallon of the cheapest wine. If they were lucky, they might still get a penny for it—"A bargain purchase, with winter coming on!"

A cripple emerged from one of the alleys and stood, his eyes lowered against the sun. When he had accustomed himself to the glare he hobbled across the street, almost in the direction of the arch. The guards had already noticed, then ignored him, expecting him to limp past, another useless mouth to be fed from Rouen's dwindling stores. They hoped he would not stop and plague them with the stupid questions so loved of civilians. "Is our Lord Briouze at home today? Is it permitted to enter the yard? Do you know, I've lived in Rouen all my life, yet I've never ventured inside the castle walls? Can I fetch you something, *surveillants*? Some ale, or fruit; or what you will? We must keep our soldiers in good fettle, isn't that so?" Always the same questions, the same overfriendly smiles.

And now the cripple had stopped in front of the barbican and was tapping toward them on an ashwood crutch.

One of the guards moved forward, holding his spear like a quarterstaff. Idly barring the man's path, he said, "That'll do. This isn't the way to anywhere."

"No? Then the keep has been resited since I was last here. Let me into the shade, soldier, and then one of you can find Lord Briouze—"

"Stay still, old man, we're not decoration."

"—and tell him the Arab is out."

The second guard materialized from the shadows. He squinted at the thin, lop-shouldered cripple, felt the juices dry in his mouth and without a word edged his companion relentlessly against the wall. Marshal nodded and limped forward, sparing the men their embarrassment. He had been in the Cistercian monastery for the better part of three weeks, and he acknowledged that both he and the garrison had changed. In fact, he thought himself fortunate to have been recognized at all, for he bore little resemblance to the warlord who'd led the charge against the camp and bridge at Gaillard.

Reeking of fish and still disguised as merchants, John and Isabelle led their party westward along the coast. During the voyage from Barfleur they had drawn up a list of those men—clerics and barons—on whom they could rely for support and a guarded tongue. There were at least fifty, though many of the fiefs and bishoprics were in the north, or too close to a town. The zigzag flight across Normandy had been arduous enough, and neither the king nor his Sparrowhawk were prepared to undertake another long journey, with its attendant risk of recognition. In a few weeks' time they would let England know they were home, and confront their barons, friendly or otherwise. But, for the present, they sought nothing more than a traveler's rest—a sanctuary from their subjects.

They chose Corfe Castle, the isolated fortress to which Marshal had so reluctantly delivered the twenty-five Lusignan prisoners. An unpleasant habitat for the French knights, but ideal for the

King and Queen of England. They would be made welcome at Corfe and greeted with open arms by John's ardent supporter, Constable Saldon. He would tell them what they needed to know, and then together they would plan how best to approach the court.

It would not be easy, this confrontation between a prodigal king and his stay-at-home peers. John would maintain that, had they responded to his call, Mirebeau would have been but the first of a hundred Angevin victories, and the French would now be huddled within their borders, a ruined nation. As it was, the nobility of England stood accused of inertia, even cowardice.

And then in turn, the barons would claim that their king had allowed the advantage of Mirebeau to evaporate. How many months had he spent parading through his territories, the child queen on his arm? Why had he dismissed William Marshal, his most experienced commander? Why had he released the Lusignan brothers, yet seemingly buried alive his nephew, Arthur of Brittany? And as for the celebrated call to arms, it had come a year too late. In truth, it was the King of England who stood accused of inertia, even cowardice.

No, it would not be an easy meeting. But at least, John thought, he had time to prepare for it, and could count on the support of Saldon and the increasingly militant Sparrowhawk. Foolhardy the barons who would go against them.

The habit of a lifetime kept Marshal on his feet. Too restless a man to stay long on a bench or in a chair, he forced himself to limp and hobble about the castle, dragged himself upstairs and down, set himself distance targets—a third-story room, a section of wall, a corner tower—then made his way there, gasping and grunting. With each successive pilgrimage he let his weight rest a little longer on his injured leg, and lifted the crutch more often from the ground.

The garrison at Rouen saw him misjudge his step, saw the stick slip from under him, saw his good leg shudder and jerk. Time after time they watched him crash against a wall, or merely lean against it, his mouth open, his face shiny with sweat. They were not foolish enough to help him, nor pretend he had passed unseen. Indeed, after the first few days, they showed an undisguised interest in his progress, and a number of them dared to shout encouragement. The warlord rarely responded, conserving his energy for the next ten paces, the final flight of steps.

He did not expect a miracle, and none was performed. It took several weeks, several hundred circuits of the yard before he could dispense with the crutch and move unsupported, his left leg swinging in a clumsy arc, the knee joint stiff as wood.

He started to ride again; a less grueling pastime this, for it required no special effort once he had gained the saddle. However, he had first to mount a block, guide his foot into a low-slung stirrup, and then, for an instant, place all his weight on the injured leg. The resulting growl of pain embarrassed him, but even as he twisted into the saddle he drew comfort from the fact that the leg was still alive. Another month, six months, a year if necessary, and he would mount unaided and in silence.

He owed it to the Cistercians, who had sponged the poison from his wound and stopped short of amputation. He owed it to Briouze and the garrison of Rouen, and to those knights who had accompanied him from Pembroke, ridden with him to Gaillard, then chosen to stay on in the city in which their overlord lay stricken. He owed it to his wife, Isabel de Clare, the young woman to whom he had boasted, "You think I'll be harmed by the *French?*" A stupid boast, belied by the ugly scar on his jaw and by the knowledge that however many miles he walked and rode, he would never again break into a run. Nevertheless, he would one day return home, dismount without fuss, then stride to the door. Isabel might frown at the scar and his odd, rolling gait, but she was not to flinch, and his arrival was not to be greeted with tears.

And he owed it to himself as the Earl of Pembroke and Striguil, as the unquestioned leader of—what were they now? A dwindling army? A patchwork force? An abandoned rearguard? Most likely the latter, but even so they had looked to Marshal for guidance, and expected him to lead them without growling.

Briouze continued to run the defense of the city and organize the patrols, though both men heard their reports and studied the letters that arrived from every corner of the duchy.

Whether written or recited, the news was unrelievedly grim. The French were swarming across the borders, encircling this castle and that, no longer opposed, but merely accepting the surrender of their disenchanted foes. King Philip's Breton allies were also driving deep into Normandy, whilst the Lusignan brothers wrought havoc in Touraine and Poitou. It was no longer correct to speak of the English possessions, or the Angevin territories, for they only existed as regions, fiefs, the occasional stubborn fortress.

But the worst news emanated from Rouen's neighbor, the beleaguered Château Gaillard.

Crouched on its shiplike rock, it dominated not only the loop of the river, but the nearby village of Les Andelys. The huddle of houses had stood there long before King Richard had chosen the site for his Insolent Castle, but the villagers had welcomed this unexpected source of employment, this ready market for their produce, this impregnable refuge. When the first garrison had been raised, a quarter of its number had come from Les Andelys and the surrounding district.

From time to time, the castellan, Roger Lacy, had found it necessary to hang a local-born thief, and there had been the unpleasant incident of the knight accused of raping a girl from the village. Tht knight had vehemently denied the charge, but Lacy had thought it advisable to strip him of his horse and armor and send him on his way. The shameful punishment had satisfied the villagers, and they had been further impressed by the castellan's vow that, if the girl gave birth to a male child, he would honor it as his own.

In short, Gaillard and Les Andelys were well suited to each other, which made the present news all the more distressing.

The speed of the French invasion, and the ferocity with which they had attacked the outlying farmsteads had sent the villagers streaming along the southern approach and into the first of the three great baileys. Roger Lacy had admitted them, convinced that the enemy would soon withdraw, or that King John would send an army to the relief of his brother's Insolent Castle.

But the French stayed put, whilst John's flotilla had been washed downstream. . . .

Throughout July and August, more peasants had deserted their fields, more villagers their homes. The enemy made no attempt to prevent them entering the castle, and it was not until the relief force had failed that Lacy realized he had been outwitted. The

French had razed the farms for a purpose, and not merely to rid the world of a few more Normans. By doing so, they had caused panic in the district and sent the occupants of Les Andelys scurrying up the hill. It was a harsh observation, but the castellan remarked that Gaillard might as well be plagued by rats, for both refugees and rodents need to eat.

And so the message he sent to Marshal and Briouze:

> We have heard of our king's furtive departure, for England, and we appeal to you to save us. There are now four hundred civilians within these walls, a number far in excess of the garrison. The daily ration is a half-filled bowl of barley mash, an inch of salted eel and, so far, thank God, an ample supply of water. But, by the time this letter reaches you, there will be no more fish, save what little has been put by for the soldiers. A choice must be made, my lords; to halve the rations, such as they are, or evict those who make the least contribution to our defense.
>
> In the name of God and England, restore us, before we are forced to lighten the load.

By that he meant the aged and infirm, the infants and children. Not that it mattered, for the warlords at Rouen were helpless. There had been too much falling away of support, and it was doubtful if the city itself could withstand an all-out assault. Marshal and Briouze had been left to do the best they could for Rouen. Roger Lacy must do as much for Gaillard.

The story Saldon had to tell brought a nod of commiseration from King John and an impassive stare from the Sparrowhawk.

The royal couple had been three days at Corfe, most of it spent sleeping or, in John's case, wallowing in a bathtub. Their fish-tainted clothes had been burned, the saddlebags unpacked, the queen's gowns pressed and hung from wall bars. One of the satchels had contained three pairs of boots—property of the king—and these had been cleaned and polished, then braced with iron trees.

Although Saldon himself was a bachelor, several of his knights were married, and the ladies of Corfe presented Isabelle with a chestful of girdles, linen stockings, pelissons and a variety of headgear. Just in time, someone remembered that King John was also a lover of finery, and a second chest was filled with cloaks and tunics and a pointed Phrygian cap decorated with ostrich feathers. The gifts were well received, and the couple paraded for each other before making their first appearance in the hall.

The baths and fresh clothes had a remarkable effect upon the king. For the first time since his fleet had been swept away by the current, he regained his bearing and looked optimistically to the future. Isabelle watched him, pleased that he could once again strut and smile, yet aware that England needed more than a high-heeled peacock. She had not forgotten the decision she'd made at Rouen. She would see her husband through the eyes of William Marshal, and judge him accordingly.

It did not occur to her that she was unequal to the task. She had neither Marshal's experience of the world nor his natural sense of probity. She had always disliked him, done everything in her power to loosen his grip on John, even stolen the silver buckle intended for his child. She might mimic him for a while, but so could any other sixteen-year-old who fashioned a mask depicting a knifelike nose and a scar on the jaw.

Nevertheless, the king and queen made a fine entrance into the hall, John's reddish hair visible beneath the brim of his cap, Isabelle's unblemished features framed by a silk barbette. The ends of the band were concealed by a flat-topped fillet, its sides sewn with colorless glass beads. The light from the fire and torches and candles was mirrored in the headdress, and it seemed that England was wealthy again, with jewels to spare.

Saldon had invited his closest companions to join him in honor of the royal couple, but had warned them to keep their tongues for the food. "When the king and queen wish to proclaim their presence, they'll do so. Meanwhile, we shall entertain them and turn mute at the gates. Corfe is privileged to have been chosen as their refuge, and I know that none of us would care to see that privilege abused." He had glanced from knight to lady, recruiting their assurances, his smile pillowing his words. Declare the king's whereabouts, he had suggested, and you risk a charge of treason. But, more perilous than that, you will earn yourselves the enmity of Corfe and its master.

Knowing Saldon as they did, it was the latter threat that had set them nodding. . . .

The meal went well, the entire assembly captivated by the Sparrowhawk and heartened by John's appraisal of the war. He admitted to a few reversals, then discounted them as the normal give-and-take of conflict.

"The problem abroad is one of leaves and branches. But the roots are buried here, in England, where we are denied our proper support. It's nothing to surrender a weak-walled castle, or cede a stretch of riverbank. We shall recapture everything we've lost, but we shall not do so until the English nobility stir themselves and cross the Channel. France is a pitiable nation, and if we stand disgraced at all, it's because we have not yet whipped them home. Their impudence has gone unpunished too long, and it's time we made them smart. And we will, my friends, just as soon as I have laid the stick to a few English hides."

The talk of chastisement brought appreciative comments from the guests. The king was right; the French *were* in need of a thrashing—and it would not come amiss if a few homemade nobles danced from their chairs. However, the occupants of Corfe had no wish to be included, and they pounded the benches as Saldon said, "You know the reason that prevented us from joining you, lord king. A twenty-five-fold reason, at the start."

John frowned momentarily, and it was left to Isabelle to remind him of the Lusignan prisoners, delivered to Corfe by the Arab. "Yes," he nodded. "The creatures who would have burned my mother at Mirebeau. I remember." Then, pointing with the peak of his cap, he asked, "Did anyone furnish their ransom, or are they still here, chewing your food?"

The guests fell silent, some glancing at the constable, others reaching for a wineglass or wiping their mouths with their hands. Saldon stared at the table, then looked up sharply at John.

"The answer must be no and no. The lords of Lusignan and Exoudun—brothers, aren't they?—well, they made no offer to buy back the prisoners, so they have only themselves to blame."

"Blame for what?"

"For the desperation that led the captives to break free."

"Are you saying they escaped? From a place like this!"

"No, lord king, I'm saying they tried. They overpowered the

guards in the prison tower, seized their weapons and made a sortie across the yard. Whether by accident or design, they emerged at a time when I and most of my knights were absent, and we returned to find them in possession of the keep. Once there, or rather here, for they made their quarters in this very hall, they defied all attempts at recapture. Your frown deepens, though I don't see why it should." He held John's gaze, daring him to find fault with what had been said, then heard Isabelle murmur, "It's understandable that the prisoners forced their way in here. Your guards would not have anticipated an attack from *within* the castle and, with you and your knights away, the garrison must necessarily have been depleted. Go on with your story, Constable."

Saldon nodded, aware that he had hitherto been addressing the wrong person.

"They made their nest in here and, as I've said, resisted all attempts at recapture. The storerooms below where we sit contained enough food for a year, besides which the prisoners held two of my knights and eight men-at-arms, all of them taken in the attack." He sighed, milking sympathy from the queen. "The tables had been turned on us. It was we who had to forage for food, we who had to sleep in the vacant prison tower. A galling experience and one we imagined to be endless."

Nudging him along, Isabelle said, "How was it resolved?"

"How, my lady? By poison." Jabbing a finger at the floor, Saldon explained, "There's a well down there, fed from a stream beyond the north wall. Few people know about it, about the link between the river and the well, for it remains the weakness of Corfe. If our enemies learned that we relied on a visible stream, they too could poison the supply." A brief smile, to be shared by king and queen, and then he went on, "We ourselves had forgotten about it, and the prisoners sat here for a month, reigning supreme. Then we remembered our own vulnerability and spiced the water."

"A sensible move," John nodded, "yet you say they're no longer chewing your food. Is this because they're too ill to—"

"The story is not finished," Saldon told him. "I did not say they surrendered."

"But without water—"

"Without water they had nothing to drink. Save wine, which only makes a man thirsty for water."

"So they held fast, here in this room?"

"Yes, my lord king, that's just what they did. They held fast, sipping wine and, as you put it, chewing the food, until the last casks were empty."

Again premature, the king said, "And it was only then that they surrendered?"

Saldon saw the queen rest a hand on John's arm, a gentle reminder to be patient. "Get to the crux," she said. "Did they emerge, or not, master Saldon?"

"No, my lady, not for the better part of a week."

"Surviving without water, or even wine?"

"Some of them, yes, and some dying in the keep."

John queried, "And how many—"

"Three, my lord king."

"And of the ten they held hostage?"

"Two, a knight and an archer."

A nod from John, and an impassive stare from the Sparrowhawk. "It's an acceptable loss," the king commiserated. "Five from, what was it, thirty-five?"

And now Saldon frowned as he told them they misunderstood. "I do not mean five were lost, I mean five emerged. The rest were poisoned, what else did you suppose?"

True to his word, Roger Lacy evicted the weaklings from Gaillard. The decision aged him beyond his years, and he went through the great southern bailey leaden-footed, nodding at an old man here, a group of scampering children there. His guards herded them together, the work made easy by the mothers who ran to join their enfeebled husbands, their squalling offspring.

As soon as the women had declared themselves they were fenced in by the guards, then jostled forward to the gate. It took a while to catch the more truant children, who saw the whole thing as a game, and to conduct the aged civilians across the windswept yard. But at last it was done, and the castellan climbed to the barbican tower and told the refugees from Les Andelys and the surrounding district that Gaillard could no longer feed them and must therefore expel them from the castle.

The shrieks and groans set the children howling, and the guards stood silent, scarcely defending themselves against the clawing women and the clumsy blows of old men. Roger Lacy looked down at them, his sight mercifully blurred, his tears running cold in the air. He could do no more than gesture at the gate guards, then murmur over and over, "God preserve them, God preserve them."

The well-balanced gates were swung open and almost four hundred civilians driven out onto the narrow southern approach. It was November now, and the wind keened across the ridge. The castellan forced himself to drive his knuckles into his eyes, then turn about and watch the results of his handiwork. The old and young, the weak and world-weary, the playful children and stumbling infants, all filing away down the zigzag path, bound for their nearby homes or distant farmsteads, and the bleak prospect of winter.

The snake writhed away down the hill, a reptile that fed like a rat and could be cut into human form. . . .

And then one of the wall guards hurried alongside Lacy and said, "Look down there, my lord. You see those soldiers on the hill? You see those Frenchmen? I don't think they're going to let them pass. I think the people are being sent back! They're being returned, my lord! Do you see that? They're being returned!"

And so they were, as the second half of the trap sprang shut.

The French had terrorized the farmsteads, panicked the villagers, driven them into the castle—like rats, as Lacy had said, like rats to eat the food—and now the enemy would not let them leave. They were the castellan's problem, Gaillard's concern, England's civilian allies, and the French wanted nothing to do with them. Lacy had taken them in, so Lacy could keep them. And the longer they stayed, the more they would eat, and the sooner the Insolent Castle would submit. If it was such a fine place, this towering monument to Richard Lionheart, then it could surely find bed and board for the families of those who had helped construct it. If not, Lacy and his garrison could join the zigzag line.

He peered southward, saw the enemy—sensibly beyond arrow range—halt and turn the refugees, threatening them with clubs and the butt end of their spears. Oh, yes, he thought, you'll buffet and bruise them, but you'll leave them alive, and with their appetites intact. They're of value to you, as rats who'll gnaw us to the stem.

He turned to the wall guard. "Tell me, do you know any of those people?"

"No, Sire, except to kick a path through when they clutter the yard. We're well rid of them, I'd say. They've turned the place into a midden. When the weather was warmer, the stench—"

"That'll do. However, now you've declared your feelings, I've an errand you'll enjoy. Go down to the gate and tell the guards to settle the bar."

"To close it? They're to close it?"

"Yes," Lacy said, "they're to close it. Against all comers. Go on and tell them." He watched the man hurry away, then turned to lean against the crenellated battlements. The refugees were already filing back toward Gaillard.

By the end of November, the supplies of ink and wax were exhausted. As were the king's clerks, and those supplied by Saldon. As was John himself, complaining that his head dinned with names and titles, while his wrist ached from pressing the seals. He had dictated more than a hundred letters, though so far only one had been dispatched.

This had been addressed to the elderly Archbishop of Canterbury, Hubert Walter. A tall, dour man, who matched William Marshal in both age and stature, Hubert Walter had held office as Dean of York, Bishop of Salisbury, and later as Richard Lionheart's justiciar. From there he had risen still higher in Church and State, and had been England's senior prelate for more than a decade. It was Hubert Walter who had crowned John and Isabelle and, even though the old man bore an unnerving resemblance to Marshal, the king had need of him. Walter knew the things John wished to learn; how much was in the treasury, how wide the gap between monarch and magnates, how best to finance an invasion of the lost territories.

In his letter to the archbishop, he had expressed his desire to spend Christmas at Canterbury, though he warned Isabelle she'd be in for a dull few days. "I once described Walter as 'the spire to Marshal's turret,' so you know what to expect. His own humor is unfathomable, and I never saw anyone else make him smile."

"Spare yourself a thought," she told him. "Remember you've a birthday due. Of all the days to be born, Christmas Eve. And of all the places to celebrate it, in the archbishop's palace." She shook her head in time with John's drawn-out groan.

The unsent letters had been divided into two piles, the larger destined for those barons who had refused to join their king in Normandy. John made no reference to their inertia, but greeted each man as "our beloved and faithful subject," inviting him to attend a council at Oxford, "on the first day of the blessed new year, in the fifth year of our reign." He praised the barons for having kept the peace during his absence, then concluded, "We shall recompense you for the costs of your journey, both with coin and the warmth of our affection. Be with us if you will, so that we may embrace each other and the cause of England."

He was not entirely satisfied with the final line, but Isabelle had lost patience after the umpteenth draft. "You have so far stood shoulder to shoulder with them, kissed and embraced them, invited them to join you for the sake of Christendom, the cause of England, the downfall of our foes. Make a decision, my lord, and stick to it."

"But the phrasing's important."

"No, it's not. The barons will not be sweetened by a kiss or a hug. All they need to know is that we shall receive them at Oxford on the first day of the year. The kissing can wait."

The second group of letters was addressed to those nobles who had, in some way or other, responded to John's pleas for help. A mere handful had made the crossing to Normandy, and then only to reconnoiter and return, whilst the others had contented themselves with a donation to the war chest. Even so, the king singled them out as "our very special friends," and assured them that "no man who ever served us went unnoticed."

It was an extravagant claim, but with the mass of his barons set firmly against him he was forced to woo those who had not yet hardened.

The skins, poles and cords had been thrown down from the ramparts, and there was no more to be done. The refugees had used the material to make shelters, but they could not stop the rain flooding the hillside, nor prevent the wind from shredding the fabric.

Roger Lacy had already paraded his garrison and announced that under no circumstances were they to throw food or clothing to the evicted civilians. "You will find it hard to resist their cries, particularly those of the women and children, but it may help to remember this. Each crumb you dispense will prolong their agony and weaken our resistance. If the French see we are feeding the civilians, they will not allow them to leave. On the other hand, the enemy are not monsters and must face that hillside day after day. They will not let the infants die there, though they'd like us to believe it. It's a test of resolve. We must be monsters, at least for a while, or we shall lose Gaillard. But the French are not rationed in anything and, when they realize we are deaf to the civilians, they'll let them pass.

"That said, I must warn you; any man who aids them will be judged as a traitor. Be he workman or common soldier, he'll be hanged from the barbican tower. Be he priest or sergeant, he'll have his hands severed at the wrist. Be he knight or nobleman, he'll be stripped naked, branded over the heart and sent out from the castle. The French will recognize him for what he is and treat him accordingly. Now go back to your posts, and pray God we're soon relieved."

The French continued to bombard the castle with arrows, crossbow bolts, missiles and the putrescent carcasses of sheep and goats—a noisome reminder that meat was plentiful outside the walls.

The defenders burned the carcasses, or threw them back, though they were more selective with their arrows and had already dismantled a stone outbuilding, using the blocks as missiles for their catapults.

The civilians clung precariously to the hillside. A group of them made a feeble attempt to scale the castle wall, then fell back under the garrison's pitiless gaze. Their injuries were appalling, and their screams forced the watch guards to move away.

Another misguided civilian assembled a dozen of the more presentable women and sent them down the rocky slope to plead with the French. They were collected by a patrol, escorted to the enemy lines, then raped and murdered, their bodies thrown into the river. By the time the rain had chilled to sleet, the last of the infants had died, and the survivors were chewing the roots of thorn bushes, or bludgeoning each other for possession of an ants' nest. Above them, the garrison existed on its diet of barley mash, whilst below, the enemy courted the remaining women with fresh-caught fish or a steaming disk of bread.

Roger Lacy no longer walked the walls. He had been trapped into taking the civilians, trapped when he'd evicted them, and was now trapped by the enemy's refusal to let them leave. The long-time friendship between Gaillard and Les Andelys had been reduced to mutual torment, the casual everyday greetings turned to shrieks and invective, the civilians pleading for mercy, the soldiers snarling rejection.

The French had not yet found a way to assault the castle, though their shafts and quarrels had filled the infirmary. The defenders had not yet found a way to raise the siege, though they too had inflicted heavy casualties on the besiegers. And between them, their bodies flayed by wind and hail, their blood poisoned by the grubbed-out roots and verminous river rats, were the refugees from Les Andelys, the unwanted friends of Gaillard. Of the four hundred who had been evicted from the castle, almost half were dead or dying, and the first snow had yet to fall.

7

Christmas at Canterbury made nonsense of the king's predictions. He had warned Isabelle to expect a dull time, then arrived to find the archbishop's palace ablaze with candlelight, the air filled with the plangent sounds of lute and dulcimer.

Hubert Walter had invited a number of his friends to attend the festivities, though he had only asked those who were in sympathy with the monarchs. As a result, John and Isabelle were accorded a rapturous welcome, and the queen leaned close to hiss, "An echoing vault, wasn't that your forecast, husband? Just you and I and the prelate, peering at each other through the gloom? Then who are these others, if not figments of the imagination?"

Before leaving Corfe he had advised her to eat her fill, assuring her that she'd be licking the plates at Canterbury. "One look at Walter shows you he lives on air and prayer. I swear his bones rattled during our coronation." It was an unmemorable joke, though Isabelle reminded him of it as the palace servants brought the chickens, hares, partridges, rabbits, peacocks, pork and venison to the table. There should have been swans, Walter apologized.

And so it continued, the king stupefied by the prelate's hospitality, the boundless variety of diversions, the wines and delicacies that weighted the boards. John's birthday was celebrated with a morning's hunt, during which the diplomatic Walter arranged for a captured boar to be caged in the forest, then hamstrung and sent blundering across the king's path. With a roar of surprise, John drove his spear deep into the animal's neck, then wheeled in triumph as the archers loosed their shafts. Word of his success preceded him home, and he returned to find Queen Isabelle waiting to lead the applause.

Four days later the archbishop gave John a silver clasp, in the shape of a tusky boar. He did not bother to tell the king that the brooch had been cast a full week before the hunt.

Throughout their stay at Canterbury, the royal couple devoted the afternoons to serious discussion. Whatever the topic—the inertia of the nobility, the situation abroad, the need for an invasion fleet—the talk led back along well-trodden paths to the Exchequer and its empty coffers. Officials arrived to plead their case, and it was decided to levy an immediate tax on income and possessions. Both Henry and Richard had employed this method to finance their wars, though even the officials blanched at the figure John proposed.

"My father asked for a thirteenth part of the country's wealth, and my brother exacted a tenth. But our present condition is far more serious. Henry held the French at the border, and Richard did his fighting in Cyprus and Palestine, whereas we face the enemy almost on our doorstep. If the people of England are to be roused from their torpor, they must be made to feel the pinch."

The officials murmured agreement, but he waited for Walter's cautious nod of assent before adding, "I want one-seventh of the value of all goods and chattels. We are not yet taking their property, only their movable possessions, so they'll have no great cause to squeal. On the contrary, it's the first real demand we've made on them in years." Jabbing a finger at the officials, he asked, "How much will it yield, assuming there's no wholesale deceit?"

"It's hard to say, my lord king, but it should be somewhat in excess of a hundred thousand pounds. And if one adds to this the rents and port duties—"

"Which we will," John nodded, "those and a few other things I have in mind." He noticed that neither the officials nor the archbishop had mentioned a subscription from the Church, but he let it pass for the moment. He'd wait until they were ready to leave for Oxford, then inform Walter that if the laity could produce one hundred thousand pounds, so could the clergy.

The king and queen enjoyed the festivities, though they thought

Walter foolish to have paraded his wealth. There should have been swans, indeed!

On the other side of the Channel, bad weather hobbled the war. The fields around Rouen lost their identity as snow blanketed the land, and the patrols were called in, their work done better by the watch guards in the towers. There was no sign of the French, though they were known to be encamped less than ten miles from the city, with their largest force encircling Château Gaillard.

Ironically, the garrison at Rouen had also grown in strength, a last refuge for the suzerains, knights and men-at-arms who had been driven from their own threatened fortresses. They arrived looking grim and weary, expecting to be accused of cowardice, then bowed with relief as Marshal and Briouze commended their good sense. "You've shown courage to have held out this long, messires, and we'd rather have you with us than rotting in a French dungeon. No doubt you did what you could to slight your castles before you left?"

Most of them nodded and described how they'd set fire to anything that would burn, prized corbels from the roofs and stairways, wrecked the catapults, fouled the water supply and, in some cases, set traps for the new occupants.

A few of the warlords objected to the question, unwilling to admit that they had suffered anything more than a temporary reversal. "The king is even now raising an army in England. Come the first fine weather, they'll make the crossing and we'll be in our homes again by Easter."

"Pray God you're right," Marshal told them, "though I'd rather the French did not receive their gifts intact."

More men found their way into the city. More snow drifted over the roofs and ramparts, dragging a final curtain across the year. The common soldiers were kept busy chipping ice from the wall walks, or greasing the chains and ratchets that worked the defensive siege machines. Twice a day the barbican detail lowered and raised the portcullis, smearing more grease on the winches and clearing the snow from the murder holes above the gate. Palfreys and destriers were exercised in the main bailey, whilst the archers took turns to practice at the butts.

The garrison had all heard of the refugees' plight at Gaillard, and a group of chivalrous young knights sought Marshal's permission to rescue them. "We'll follow the route you took, my lord, get behind the enemy lines and—"

"How many do you represent?" he asked courteously. "Apart from you ten, how many are there?"

"We have not yet started to recruit, Earl Marshal. We wanted to secure your permission before announcing—"

"I'm sorry to interrupt again, but you put too fine a point on your hopes. Do your recruiting first, and then, when you've raised a sizable force, we'll discuss it further. But be warned. The people on that hillside below Gaillard are peasants and villagers. They are not of your station, nor even sergeants or mercenaries."

"They are nevertheless our people," one of the knights retorted. "Ours and God's."

"So they are," Marshal nodded, "though I doubt if that simple truth will impress the garrison. However, you must put it to the test."

Three days later the chevaliers abandoned their scheme. It had been greeted with raucous laughter, withering stares, even outbursts of anger. "You ask us to ride through a wasteland of snow in order to drag these civilians from their perch? You want the Angevin nobility to risk life and limb for a huddle of farmers and snout-nosed serfs? Why not make a crusade of it, and we'll save all the dogs and foxes on the way? Be your age, messires. Cudgel your brains."

The Williams Marshal and Briouze had now held joint command of Rouen for three months. It had seemed an unlikely alliance at first—the austere and critical Earl of Pembroke standing side by side with King John's favored accomplice—but it had worked out well. Briouze was the official governor of the city, though, as his admiration for Marshal increased, he conferred more readily with his stiff-legged compeer.

But there was still one subject on which Briouze would not be drawn; the whereabouts of the king's nephew, Arthur of Brittany.

Time and again he had thought of sharing his agony with Marshal, but had always stepped back from the brink. Scarcely a day passed without the memory grating like a fractured bone, and he had lost count of the bodies that had wallowed on the surface of his dreams. So real were they and so vivid the recollection of his own disgrace, squatting by the wall, that he had twice awoken in a soiled bed.

He had to steel himself to enter the assembly hall, and he kept clear of the far window and the stretch of riverbank beyond. He could no longer hold a stone wine jar without seeing his hand tremble, and he raged at anyone, servant or suzerain, who broke a vessel at table.

The barons were impressed by his anger. Briouze had obviously come to regard Rouen as his adopted home, and wished to conserve the dishes.

At Oxford, the year had ended in misery and panic. There were less than twelve hundred dwellings within the walls, yet the castellan had received orders to make a quarter of them available for the visitors. He discussed the problem with the burgesses, and it was decided to vacate the houses nearest to the castle, then work outward, street by street. It was as impartial a method as any, though there were ugly scenes as the soldiers dragged the more stubborn occupants from their homes. Those who had friends in other parts of the city moved in with them, whilst the less fortunate were billeted on strangers.

The task was almost finished when the first snow-flecked riders clattered in. And after that it seemed as if the procession would never end.

Witness the arrivals . . . William of Wrotham, Keeper of the Ports . . . Reginald of Cornhill, Chamberlain of London and custodian of the mint . . . Ranulf, Earl of Chester, one of the most powerful barons in the land . . . Geoffrey fitz Peter, Justiciar and Earl of Essex.

These were followed by William de Ferrers, Earl of Derby . . . William de Warren, Earl of Surrey . . . William de Redvers, Earl of Devon . . . William d'Albini, Earl of Arundel . . . Robert de Beaumont, Earl of Leicester . . . Roger Bigot, Earl of Norfolk . . . the earls of Warwick and Huntingdon.

In their wake came the bishops of Winchester and Norwich . . . militant barons such as Robert FitzWalter, William de Mowbray, Saher de Quency . . . then a group of King John's loyal seneschals and free-lances, among them Gerard d'Athies, Engelard de Cigogné, Peter Stoke and the unswerving Constable Saldon.

All these arrived, and five times their number, each with his consort of knights, squires, mounted archers, common mercenaries, priests and household servants. This was the nation's response to its prodigal king . . .

. . . who had by now fallen out with his Christmas host.

Patient to the last, Archbishop Walter had explained that John's second demand for one hundred thousand pounds, this time from the Church, was excessive and unreasonable. "We will pay what we can, but it will be nowhere near the arbitrary figure the officials suggested. We are not wealthy, my lord."

"But I say you are, Walter, and I've the documents to prove it. Let's see, now; what shall we take as an example? Winchester?"

The archbishop stayed silent. It had been a rhetorical question.

"Winchester," John repeated. "Held by Godfrey de Lucy, I believe. One of the more profitable Church estates, and yielding an annual income of not less than three thousand pounds. Added to which, the good bishop owns and has earnings from the castles of Taunton, Farham, Wolvesey and somewhere else, I forget. And how many similar estates are there? How many other episcopal baronies throughout the country?"

"I don't carry such knowledge in my head. I'd have to check."

"Don't bother, I've already done so. There are thirty-nine or forty." An ominous pause, before he added, "Including your own see of Canterbury, which you'll agree comes close to Winchester in land and revenue." The king was too small to clap Walter on the shoulder, so he squeezed his arm and said, "Don't look so mournful. I'm not going to steal the altar cloths. I'm merely showing you that your fears are groundless. With forty bishoprics and God knows how many parish churches and priories? Of course you can afford it. You raised the money for Henry and Richard, so why not for me?"

"It would not be for you," the archbishop corrected sourly. "If it was done at all, it would be for England."

During the ride from Canterbury to Oxford, the weather matched their mood. John and Isabelle traveled ahead with their entourage, while Hubert Walter and his consort lagged a mile behind. They shared the same overnight quarters, but there was no more laughter or music, no extravagance of any kind. Frugality was the watchword now, and neither king nor churchman would be seen squandering England's money.

The seventeen-year-old Sparrowhawk was delighted with her husband. Not only had he stood firm under Walter's forbidding gaze, but had researched his case and kept a bridle on his temper. It was John and not the prelate who knew the revenue of Winchester, the names of the castles, the number of profitable sees. And there was more to come, for his study of the documents had unearthed some interesting facts about the nobility. They would balk and bluster, that was to be expected, but they'd find their king uncomfortably well versed in their affairs. John Softsword, maybe. But no less John Shrewdhead.

The council lasted a week and was, by common consent, as exhausting as a seven-day war. Prayers were said, and Hubert Walter invoked God's blessing on their endeavors. Formal greetings were exchanged, some of the barons kneeling in homage to the king, others muttering pointedly to their friends as John welcomed them by name.

It was a necessary ritual, but no sooner had the king invited the minor barons to swear fealty than the first barked questions were loosed.

"We hear there are more Frenchmen outside France than in it, and that the best work goes to their masons, building prisons to house our leaders. Is it true we've lost half the Norman nobility?"

"Why did you not return to us before now, King? Were you too busy ceding territory to the invaders? Have you already made a treaty with Philip Augustus? We've heard it's so."

"Where's the Earl of Pembroke these days? You banished him to England when he should have been in Normandy, and now he's absent from this all-important council. We know you dislike him, King, but at least his words ring true. And come to that, where's the Duke of Brittany? There've been some fine tales told about *his* disappearance. Walled up alive, that's a popular version."

"Stoned to death at Falaise!"

"Stoned to death, yes, but in Rouen itself! Is that the truth of it, my lord king? *Could* you produce him, alive?"

And so it had gone, whilst John yelled rebuttal. No, there were
not more Frenchmen. No, there was not a treaty. No, he was not
purposely keeping Marshal at a distance. No, Duke Arthur had
not been walled away, and would be released at the proper time.
No to their accusations, but yes to his!

Yes to the lack of support they'd given him throughout the war.
Yes to the French advances, and small wonder when the bulk of
the English leadership lolled at home.

His hand flying to his head to fiddle with the plain gold coronet,
he snapped, "You are in no position to demand an accounting,
for you never incurred any costs! Oh, yes, I grant that ten or
twenty of you made the crossing. But you were back here on the
next tide! And you think—do you think that gives you the right
to weep for your Norman friends? You *should* weep, messires, but for shame.

"You believe I'm a poor leader"—to which there was a howl of
assent—"well, perhaps so, but how can any man lead when his
own nobility stay away and grow fat? What prowess can a rider
show, if his horses all refuse?"

"If that's the case," someone shouted, "it'd be the rider that's at
fault, not the mounts!"

"And the remedy?" John countered. "A change of rider, is that
it? A new leader for the army? Or would you go the whole way
and dethrone your king? Would you dare that, my lords, and
turn our war with France into bloody anarchy at home? How
Philip would love you for it. Before he robbed you of everything
you have." He unhooked his fingers and let his hand fall to his
side. Then he waited, staring at them, knowing the impetus had
been checked.

There were a few inaudible comments, but no one answered
his challenge. They told themselves he had overstepped the
mark, a favorite ruse of the Angevin kings. He hoped to silence
their criticism with his talk of anarchy and then, having raised
the specter, stand alongside it and offer them the choice. It was
a despicable trick, and one that evaded the real problems, but
they were forced to admit that even a flawed king such as Softsword was better than no king at all. Besides which, John would
harden his blade at the first sign of rebellion. He was unpopular,

but by no means friendless, and there were a number of foreign princes, a host of mercenaries, who'd rally to his support.

The only sure way to dethrone King John was to kill him, and it had not yet come to that.

From then on he pressed his advantage. Armed with the information he had collected at Canterbury, he set out to gratify his friends, woo those who were uncommitted and isolate the rest. He held a series of meetings at which he dangled the bait of reward and advancement. The Earl of Surrey was won over by the promise of Stamford Castle, the Earl of Arundel by the immediate gift of L'Aigle in Normandy—for which he'd have to cross the Channel—and the Earl of Huntingdon by the cancellation of a debt his father had owed Richard Lionheart. In return, these and other interested nobles pledged their support to the king and agreed to contribute to the war chest.

By midweek he was able to tell Isabelle that he had purchased half the court. "Most of them have an eye for reason," he said sarcastically, "it's just that their patriotism needs the spice of profit. I tell them it's their duty to defend the realm, and they sit unblinking; then I let slip that there's a vacant fief in Kent or Anjou and they come forward to kiss my hand and blather on about the imminent destruction of our enemies. Ours, they say, theirs and mine, as though we'd been fighting shoulder to shoulder since the war began."

"And those who are not so—reasonable? How do you deal with them?"

"As we planned, my sweet. I ask them how much it cost to get here, and reimburse them from my own pocket. Then, whilst they're reaching for the coins, I remind them that however important they might think themselves at home, they are still tenants of the Crown. They hold their lands on condition that they make available a certain number of knights for military service, an obligation they have so far failed to honor. I let them know that *we* know the exact number of knights enfeoffed to them, and charge them accordingly. I list their manors and castles, assess one-twentieth of their value and add it to the bill. And then, since they seem so happy to handle money, I impose the one-seventh tax on their goods and chattels."

"And arrive at a punitive sum," the queen remarked. "Good. It's time they were milked. But how do you know they'll pay? These men are a law unto themselves."

"Oh, they'll pay," John assured her. "They may need further encouragement, but sooner or later—"

"What kind of encouragement?"

"The kind husbands and fathers find irresistible."

Isabelle nodded. "You mean you'll take their wives and children hostage."

"Into the protection of the court," John amended. "They will be our guests for a while."

The sound of a trumpet, its strident blast flattened by the rain. Then more clarion calls, and a roar that spread through the eastern camp and was taken up by all those who encircled the castle. Before long a fanfare and a jubilant chorus and the steady pounding of mailed fists on shields.

The noise was enough to bring the garrison of Château Gaillard to the walls. Weak and haggard, the defenders urged themselves up the steps and sank gasping against the battlements. Sections of the wall walk had been torn away by French missiles, and it was no longer possible to man the entire perimeter. But the inner steps were still intact, all but one of the towers still inhabitable, the fortifications still unbreached. The siege had now lasted for more than five months, yet the castle remained as impregnable as ever.

Roger Lacy found a vantage point above the river and peered out between the fractured merlons. The rain impeded his view, and he could see no farther than the flat stretch of meadow beyond the far bank. But even as he watched, a group of heavily armored French knights emerged from the downpour and indicated that they wished to parlay.

Dragging damp air into his chest, the castellan shouted to his archers to hold fast, then clambered to his feet and raised a hand in response. One of the Frenchmen saw him, pointed him out to the others, then trotted dangerously close to the riverbank. Braving the rain, he squinted up at the battlements and shouted, "Can . . . me, Lord . . ."

Lacy shook his head, swept a hand across his body in a negative gesture, then cupped both hands around his mouth. The knight copied him and tried again. "Can you hear me, my Lord Lacy?"

"I hear you."

"And the trumpets?"

"Even them."

"Do you know why?"

Lacy ignored the question and wiped his face with a slimy leather glove. There could be any number of reasons for the fanfare; the arrival of reinforcements, the completion of a siege machine, the news of another French victory, anything that would bring fresh heart to the besiegers. So long as there were trumpeters there would be fanfares, though it was true the enemy had roared louder than ever before.

Suddenly exasperated, Lacy shouted into the rain, "Why then? Why such a bleat?"

"As a welcome," the knight taunted. "Can you guess who for?"

The castellan uncurled his hands and waited. Yes, he thought, now that the snow has gone and the roads are passable. Yes, I can guess who it's for, though pray God I'm wrong.

But he was not wrong, and the Frenchman delighted in telling him that the trumpets had sounded a welcome for Philip Augustus. "The king is prepared to accept your surrender, and will impose no special hardships upon you. Unlike John of England, King Philip treats his enemies with honor." He broke off, his throat raw from shouting, and Lacy leaned forward to jab a finger at the hillside below the wall.

"Before any talk of surrender, tell your king about *those* poor wretches! Let him first treat *them* with honor. Four hundred were sent out from here, and you have a fine view of the survivors. At the last count less than thirty. And do you still say he'll impose no special hardships? We'll believe that when the hillside's been cleared." He waved his hand in dismissal, then coughed his way down the treacherous steps to the yard.

King Philip had been present, though not in the eastern camp, during John and Marshal's abortive attempt to restock the castle. But he had left before the refugees were evicted, and was perplexed to hear that his commanders had refused to let them pass. "What have you achieved?" he asked them, his good eye bleak with contempt. "What advantage does it bring to starve women and children?"

"We thought Lacy would waste his food on them, or take them back inside."

"And when he did not? When a week had passed? A month? A hundred days? How long *did* you allow him?"

"We set no date on it." They shrugged. "The locals have always looked to the castle for work and refuge, so why not this time? It's Lacy's responsibility, not ours."

"Not as his enemies, perhaps, but surely as my friends. If the world remembers me at all, I would not like to be credited with this."

The commanders worshiped their half-blind monarch, but even so they rejected his criticism. "And what if twice the number of refugees had existed? Were we to feed them all, then let them roam at will behind our lines? With due respect, lord king, we'd employ any method if it would hasten the downfall of that— that monument to the sodomite they called the Lionheart."

"Nevertheless," Philip told them, "we will not allow any more of these unfortunates to die. Ask the castellan to disarm his archers, whilst we lead the remnants from the hillside. Who knows, they may tell us of a weak spot in the walls."

But the civilians had nothing to say. Only twenty-two of the evicted four hundred left the rocks, and the physicians pronounced half of them sick unto death. As for the dozen who would live, their gibberings and unrelated movements showed they were mad. Several of them had eaten their own fingers, though only as a last resort. Until the snow had thawed there had been enough stringy corpses, preserved by the cold.

The soldiers who led them from the slope were not so tongue-tied, and their story was passed from sergeant to knight, from warlord to the king. When Philip heard it he removed his casque, unlaced the hood of his link-mail hauberk, peeled back the woolen lining and knelt bare-headed in the rain, the water glistening on his bald pate.

His prayer was short and succinct. "Almighty God," he implored, "make it so, make it true." Then he hurried into his pavilion, toweled himself dry and sent for the soldiers from whom the story had originated. If it *was* so, if it *was* true, a weakness did exist within the walls of Château Gaillard.

The army was alerted. Archers and crossbowmen made ready to let fly at the battlements and window slits, their shafts supported by a steady barrage from the catapults. Other machines were dragged to the southern end of the rock and set up beside the approach path. Their task would be to batter away at the prow of the shiplike castle and, if possible, damage the gate. With them went grappling hooks, scaling ladders and a large detachment of foot soldiers. Fifty mounted knights milled about at the far end of the zigzag path. Some while later, they were joined by the commanders of the southern and eastern camps, their rain-soaked pennants visible from the barbican.

By midafternoon the last catapult had been wound and the light was beginning to fade. His feelings concealed beneath his mask of amused skepticism, Philip Augustus signaled to the trumpeters. The blast vaulted the river and echoed among the rocks, an overture for the missiles. Then, as the sounds were thinned and flattened by the rain, the air grew heavy with the weight of flints and arrows and bales of blazing straw.

Inside the castle, the garrison moved away from the windows or ducked behind the merlons. They had watched the enemy deploy, and now prepared to repulse an attack from the south. The French had tried similar tactics before and failed, so Roger Lacy was not unduly concerned. The besiegers were obviously putting on a show for their king, if only to prove to him that Château Gaillard was indeed impregnable.

On the other side of the Seine, and beyond the range of any retaliatory missiles, King Philip turned his attention to the six men on whom success or failure would depend. They were all young and, understandably, they shivered in the wet, for they wore nothing but woolen shifts and pliable, rabbit-skin shoes. That and a belt, from which was suspended a leather bag containing broad iron pegs. In addition, two of the men carried hammers, but the six were otherwise unarmed.

"Do you think you can find the place?" Philip asked. "Even in the dark?"

"We can, King. It's just over there, behind that outcrop. You can't see it— I mean, nobody can see it from here, but—"

"Very well. The boat's waiting, so you'd better get started. And may God protect you." He accorded them a deep nod and they backed away, not sure how far they need retreat before turning. The king frowned to speed them along, and they wheeled and ran.

Accompanied by his bodyguard, who promptly ringed him with shields, he followed the six toward the bank and watched the pitch-blackened craft angle across the river. It went unspotted, though a defender loosed an arrow at random, missing Philip and his guards by less than ten feet.

It was close enough for his protectors. They crowded in on him, their shields raised, obstructing his view. He moved his head from side to side for a last glimpse of the craft, but he knew better than to remonstrate with the guards. They would tell him what they always told him; arrows and cats, they've respect for no one.

Meanwhile, the boat had grounded itself, and the men were scuttling up the slope. It was almost dark now, and they were anyway too involved in their task to be deterred by the grisly litter of bodies and bones. Finding their own paths amongst the rocks, they reached the outcrop, edged between the natural feature and the base of the wall, and grinned at what they found.

The outflow of a disused latrine.

As his one concession to the refugees, Roger Lacy had prohibited his garrison from using the garderobe situated directly above the slope. So the shaft was dry and, of greater importance to the invaders, long forgotten.

They could not tell if the latrine had been merely boarded over, or sealed with a slab of rock, and they could only guess at the height of the shaft. Thirty feet, perhaps, and thus level with the wall walk. Nor did they know whether the garderobe was linked to other rooms, or just an isolated cell. If the latter, they would probably emerge on the ramparts and be cut down where they stood. And their bodies added to the rubble with which the defenders would block the shaft.

A grunt of assent, and the first man wriggled through the aperture and stood upright in the darkness. The shaft was a few inches wider than his shoulders, and he was able to crouch down, feel for a joint in the ashlar blocks, then hammer in the first foothold. He balanced on it to fix the next iron peg, climbed again and repeated the process. The air was still foul and, although he could see nothing, he paused to wipe the sweat from his eyes. Then he hammered in the next broad spike, not caring that the sound reverberated through the shaft. It was an unavoidable hazard, and the quicker they all got to the top, the better.

A second man inched his way inside, cursing viciously as he tore his scalp on a peg. Then he too began to climb. The others followed, passing their stocks of pegs upward, from hand to hand. The leader paused again, spat directly against the wall, then went back to work. His companions found their next foothold, and the next. . . .

Blazing straw arched above the battlements and exploded on impact. The rain favored the defenders, and they saved their strength for the fireballs that fell against the gate. In truth, there was little wood left in Château Gaillard, save for the beams and joists and defensive gates.

And the boards that covered the latrine.

The leader hissed at his companions, and they braced themselves for the final climb. Then, without further hesitation, he shoved upward with the palm of his hand and was astonished to feel the unnailed board lift and crash to the side. Lacy's men must be an obedient lot, he thought, and used his shoulders to scatter the planks.

There was no light in the garderobe, but as the invaders emerged from the shaft they discovered an archway and a passage beyond. It was not in their character to invade a castle unarmed, so whilst the first and second men imagined their hammers as clubs, the rest made daggers of the spikes.

They reached a door and listened. But they could hear nothing, so the leader felt for the latch, lifted it and eased the door open. They entered a storeroom, the long dry chamber illuminated by a single, cruciform window. Rats scurried behind empty barrels and squeaked in protest as the invaders crossed the room. Another door, which also yielded and was pulled open to reveal a spiral staircase, curving both upward and down. The leader's whispered message was passed back to the last two men in line. Then, leaving them where they were, he led the others up the steps.

They passed a larger window and discovered that it overlooked a curtain wall and part of the middle bailey. The leader cursed with pleasure and continued to climb. A dozen steps more and they reached the head of the flight, to face a final studded door. Again they listened, tested the latch, made the hinges creak.

"Aah, Jesus of Mercy, what better goal than this?" The room was deserted, though two thick candles burned on the distant altar. The invaders had found their way into Roger Lacy's private chapel.

The leader grinned at his men, moved back to the head of the stairs and, crouching forward, bellowed at those below. "We have taken it! Here, use this and let them know!" He sent his hammer ricocheting down the steps, snatched at something one of his companions offered him and realized it was a heavy girandole. Perfect. A man could make a nice loud din by thrashing a silver candleholder against the stair post.

In the upper chamber, the invaders were wreaking havoc, hurling the carved pews from end to end of the chapel, screaming commands, howling encouragement. The leader joined them, whilst fifty feet below, members of the garrison stared at the tower and heard the sounds of a full-scale assault.

The shock unnerved them. The deprivations of winter and the ever thinning diet of barley mash had already left them weak and edgy, and the realization that the enemy had gained the tower—*and were destroying Lacy's chapel!*—was too much to bear. They panicked and fled for the inner bailey. They deserted the barbican and its flanking towers, evacuated the walls, withdrew from the bridge that linked the middle and outer yards. The contagion spread to the hard core of knights and, last of all, to the castellan himself.

Men yelled at him to hurry before the French made the sortie from the tower, and two of his knights caught hold of him, hustling him toward the narrow central bridge. Still in the southern bailey he wrenched himself free and stood blinking amid the pools of rainwater, the hissing wreckage of fireballs, the snapped and angled shafts of a thousand arrows. Then, when the yard was empty of all living defenders, he unbuckled his sword

belt and let the strap and weapon fall to the mud. He would
join his garrison in the keep and tell them that the siege was not
yet over. But he would accept his own personal defeat here,
within sight of the gate he had just abandoned.

After that it was a matter of time. So anxious were the defenders
to gain the safety of the keep that they left the central bridge intact. The invaders waited until the last of the garrison had fled,
then emerged from the chapel tower. Risking death from the
flints and arrows that still riddled the open ground, they dashed
across the bridge and lifted the massive gate bars from their rests.
Then they cavorted in the entranceway, identifying themselves in
their shifts and rabbit-skin shoes.

An hour later, Philip's army had taken possession of all but the
innermost yard and the corrugated keep. Siege machines had been
brought up the zigzag path and were already at work, using the
stones of Gaillard against itself.

On February 27 French miners began tunneling into the base of
the keep, shoring the tunnel as they went. By March 4 they were
deep enough in for their purpose and withdrew, having first
smeared the props with pitch and set them alight. That same
evening the weakened tunnel collapsed, bringing down a wedge-
shaped section of the wall. An assault force of knights and nobles
waited until dawn, then hacked their way into the breach.

On March 6, 1204, the castle that Richard Lionheart had
claimed he could defend if it were made of butter, the castle that
King John had said would outlast them all, this finest of border
châteaux, surrendered to Philip Augustus.

It had been built to stand forever, insolent and impregnable,
and was now not quite seven years old.

At Rouen, it was as though the twin had died. Marshal and
Briouze each reacted in his own way, the older man limping off
to the privacy of his quarters, Briouze threatening to lead the entire garrison of the city—*now!*—and trap the French king—*now!*—
within the walls of his new-won fortress.

But he did not implement his threat, aware that the garrison
lacked everything necessary for an attack. Where the catapults and
mangonels, the supplies of shafts and quarrels, the tents and

hoardings? And more than that, where the fighting spirit of these military refugees? Most of them had abandoned their own castles and sought sanctuary at Rouen, and what little determination was left had been channeled into the defense of the city. The garrison did not want to attack, whatever the prize. They were conditioned by too many defeats, too many shameful memories. Let the French come to them and they'd fight the enemy toe-to-toe. But they were no longer interested in sniffing out a battle.

When they had recovered from the shock, the joint commanders made ready to withstand the greater impact of a full-scale assault. It could come at any time, for less than ten miles separated Rouen from its fallen twin. A break in the weather; that seemed the most likely portent.

So the warlords were intrigued when ten days of clear spring skies failed to reveal the French army on the hills. But they were far more mystified by the reports that began to come in. King Philip had garrisoned Château Gaillard, and the army was striking camp. . . . It was on the move, though not directly toward Rouen. . . . It was traveling due west, and well beyond sight of the city. . . .

"They're circling," Briouze commented. "They'll get around behind us, so Philip can tell them we stand between them and their homeland. That's what he'll do. He'll encourage his troops to destroy us on their way back to France."

Marshal had nothing better to offer, and they waited to hear that the enemy had turned north and crossed the Seine. When that happened the alarm bells would be rung.

But the patrols reported otherwise. The army had reached Brionne, fifteen miles from the city, and was continuing westward. Then it had turned, not toward Rouen, but in the direction of Argentan, a further fifty miles to the south.

"It seems," Marshal said, "that King Philip has an aversion for this place. It's the second time he's ignored us."

"But why, when we had his breath on our necks? I mean no discourtesy, though I doubt that even your reputation—"

"No," Marshal agreed dryly, "not even mine would terrify a king and his army. But I think I see what he's about." He reached down to massage his stiffened leg. It ached constantly these days, and he had taken to sleeping with a heated stone against his knee. A poor substitute he acknowledged for Isabel de Clare.

"Yes, I can guess at his plan. And if I'm right, we shall one day surrender the city without a blow being struck."

"Not whilst I command it!" Briouze retorted. "And I did not expect to hear you, of all men—"

"Nor did I, William, not until today. But think on this. We've been left alone for a reason, isolated if you will, ignored in favor of weaker citadels and less stubborn forts. But what's to happen when all Normandy has fallen to the French, as I fear it must? Rouen will be left, with the enemy camped in the fields, and our grain barrels hollow to the fist. We are a magnified version of Gaillard and, although Roger Lacy managed to evict *his* civilians, we can hardly expel the thousands from here. King Philip has no need to force us out. Our appetites will do the job for him."

"Unless King John brings an English army to our aid."

Marshal nodded, but only out of affection for Briouze.

The story was told of a rider whose horse trod on a sharp stone, reared and threw him. The dazed man picked himself up, examined the animal's hoof and was kicked in the head for his troubles. As he staggered backward he tripped over the coping of a bridge and fell into the river. He was about to drown when he felt firm ground beneath his feet. But the ground was really the back of a great fish, which swallowed him. The moral: that misfortune loves company.

It was to prove true for the Earl of Pembroke. Château Gaillard had fallen, the fate of Rouen was as good as sealed, and now he received the heartbreaking news that his friend and patroness, the dowager Queen Eleanor, lay dying at Fontevrault.

It might perhaps be a welcome release, for the woman who had once been Queen of France and later Queen of England was eighty-two years old, far beyond the normal span.

She and Marshal had exchanged many letters over the years, but the note that was brought to him at Rouen had been written by a clerk. Nevertheless, the tone was unmistakably hers.

> *I hear that Richard's Insolent Castle has lost its smile. It was the last enduring monument to my son, though I am not*

stricken by the loss. You could not save it, my dear Marshal, so I have long accepted that it could not be saved.

The mothers and sisters of this Order are too bright-eyed for my liking, and it pleases them to blame my illness on the winter. I know they are wrong, but we humor each other and chirrup like birds in a tree.

I shall not ask John to visit me. He has not done so since he, and you, rescued me from Mirebeau, and he would only come in order to apprize my wealth. He shall have it, less what I have set aside for the Abbey, and I pray that he spends it on something other than boots. Did you know he once owned twenty-seven pairs, and that each was higher in the heel? I have often wondered what difference it would have made to things, had he matched his elder brother in height and stature. Most likely none, for they had nothing in common but the color of their hair.

The defense of Rouen must be your paramount concern, William Marshal, though I admit I listen for your footsteps. Are you as lean and foreign-skinned as ever, or have you grown pale with the worries of our shrinking kingdom? I hope not, for you looked well as the only Arab at court.

If there is no risk in a visit to Fontevrault, come and see me. But if you cannot leave, hide the truth. Say you will be here before long, and I shall keep my ears pricked and have the wine put by.

I ask God's blessing on you, Marshal, as I have always done. And you must do as much for me.

She signed herself simply "Aliénor d'Aquitaine."

The warlord discussed the request with Briouze, who agreed that he should not only hasten to Queen Eleanor, but go on from Fontevrault to England. "The king himself may not be inspired by your presence, Earl Marshal, but with luck you'll rally the barons. Tell them that Rouen can hold out for—how long did we say?"

"Two months, under siege."

"For two months, and that they'll have the chance to rout the entire French army." With a grim smile, Briouze added, "The irony is that although King John will listen more readily to me, the barons won't listen to him. One day, perhaps, and for the sake of Rouen it had better be soon, we shall all pay heed to each other. Meantime, do what you can to enliven our peers."

They bade farewell and embraced, and Marshal left his pock-marked companion to hold the citadel, as Roger Lacy had once held its twin.

Of the thirty or so knights who had ridden from Pembroke a year before, eighteen had survived to keep him company on the journey south. They were lightly armed, and planned to run from the first signs of trouble. Their target was the Abbey of Fontevrault, not a skirmish with a French patrol.

But they were halted anyway, within a few miles of Mortagne, and the escort remained at a discreet distance while their suzerain heard what the lone messenger had to say. The man handed him something, then turned and rode back the way he had come, leaving Marshal to dismount and limp from the path, his face buried in his hands. He was gone a long time and, when he returned, the escort noticed that he had discarded his spurs in favor of another pair, these of silver.

The riders turned westward, toward Barfleur and England. Toward the court of King John and the earldom of Pembroke. Toward their families, and away from the lands in which they and not the French were called enemy.

And in England they discovered that the barriers were up. John and Isabelle were in mourning for Eleanor, though it was rumored that they used onions to embroider their grief. True or not, they were inconsolable, and refused to attend any further councils of war. The Archbishop of Canterbury, Hubert Walter, was gravely ill, and so, deprived of the leaders of Church and State, the majority of the barons had returned to their fiefs.

Those few who could be cornered told much the same tale; whether friend or critic of the king, they insisted that the situation had changed with the fall of Château Gaillard. Before that, yes, they had been willing to join an army of liberation, and help drive the French out of all the overseas dominions. But now things were different. If Château Gaillard could be taken, then the French must be invincible, and it made better sense to defend the island itself than risk annihilation in some Norman wasteland.

"There'll be an invasion, Marshal, no question of that. But it will have Philip's flag at the masthead."

"And the people of Rouen? Will you send a message of hope to them?"

"I'd tell them to join us here, that'd be my message. In the greatest natural stronghold in the West. Let's see the French make a ladder long enough to reach the top of an English cliff!"

"A good point," Marshal said bitterly, "though it did not quite deter Duke William, the man they called the Conqueror."

But his efforts were to no avail. The castle gates had been bolted, the windows shut tight. Let the French come to them, and they'd fight the enemy toe-to-toe. . . . That again, and this time on the very doorstep. . . .

On June 24 William Briouze surrendered the citadel of Rouen, as Marshal had said, without a blow being struck. On the other side of Normandy, Falaise capitulated.

Six weeks later, the French king accepted the keys of Poitiers. The rest of the county was already in the capable hands of the Lusignan brothers, Hugh's brown hair streaked with gray, Ralf's nose disjointed where Marshal had crushed it at Mirebeau.

Tours fell. And, in the summer of 1205, the fortresses of Loches and Chinon and all of Touraine.

The Loire valley now played host to France. Anjou and Maine were overrun, and it only remained for the French army to link up with their allies in Brittany. They did so the following spring, though were unable to tell the Bretons what they most wanted to know—the whereabouts of their liege lord, the arrogant young Arthur. It was a mystery, and it needed to be solved.

Meanwhile, England crouched on the cliff-top, honing its blade and watching for the fish.

8

WOLF AT THE DOOR
July 1208–August 1213

If the weather was fine, as today, Marshal and his family spent the last hours of daylight outside the walls of Pembroke. More often than not they left their horses in the stables and strolled alongside the estuary, or walked the three miles over the hills to visit their neighbors in the great coastal fortress of Manorbier.

Its castellan, Gerard de Barri, was just eighteen days younger than Marshal, and at sixty-three never tired of deferring to "my more experienced friend." In return, Marshal enjoyed prefacing a story with the reminder that "this was probably before your time." Harmless banter between men who had known each other for twenty years, and liked what they knew. Fortunately, Isabel de Clare got along well with the Lady Nesta, and the children of Pembroke with the offspring of Manorbier.

Situated in the most westerly shire of England, and all but severed from it by the restless principality of Wales, the two families were at a remove from the intrigues of court. Nevertheless, both men made regular visits to Oxford or Canterbury or Windsor, gave their advice if it was asked for, then returned home at the first opportunity. The heavyset Gerard de Barri had once been secretary and tutor to the young Prince John, but it was Marshal who remained in demand. Four or five times a year he was summoned by the king, and on each occasion he found John more nervous, more overbearing, more suspicious of those around him. And with good cause, for he was making enemies as assiduously as a baker makes loaves.

Two years had passed since the fall of the overseas dominions, and in that time the king had managed to alienate the majority of his barons, scandalize the court and engage in a personal vendetta with the head of the Christian Church, Pope Innocent III.

The planned invasion of the lost territories had foundered for lack of support, and the nobility were still anchored to their fiefs, embittered by the taxes that had been levied upon them. They were convinced that the king's demands were fraudulent. What he really wanted was to impoverish them; to force them to sell their lands, then come begging to the court, tugging at his sleeve.

The Church had more dramatic reasons for concern, for thanks to King John they had just been put out of business.

The problem had arisen with the death of Marshal's contemporary, Hubert Walter. The monks of Canterbury, privileged to choose the next archbishop, had elected their prior, a rotund and easygoing man named Reginald.

But King John had other ideas, and foisted his own candidate, John de Grey, Bishop of Norwich.

Both men hurried to Rome to seek the blessing of the young Pope, only to find that Innocent III also had someone in mind. An Englishman, to be sure, but one who had studied in Paris and preached throughout Italy. His name was Stephen Langton, and he counted the Pope as his most intimate friend.

The dispute had dragged on for almost three years. King John had scorned Reginald as "that fat favorite of Canterbury," and denied all knowledge of Langton. The Pope had also brushed aside the corpulent prior and rejected John de Grey as "the king's key to the offertory boxes of England."

The dispute had turned rancorous. John sent a group of his loyal barons to evict the monks of Canterbury and seize its considerable treasury. The action was dangerously akin to his father's treatment of Thomas Becket, though the monks had the good sense to leave without a fight.

Pope Innocent was aghast. He'd had dealings with John before, and had reprimanded him a dozen times at least for his malevolence toward the English clergy. He warned John to desist, or risk the sanctions that only Rome could impose. John laughed in the emissary's face and issued a warning of his own.

"I know little of your Pope, and care less. Added to which, I know nothing of his nominee, save that Langton did all his learning in France, our enemy's land, and all his teaching in Rome. On the day we seek an *outsider* as primate of England, we shall let you know. Until then, Langton would be advised to stay away."

Later, with mock astonishment, he told his companions, "Word's getting around. Now all the foreigners are trying to invade us!"

But his comments brought no smile to the lips of the papacy, and they issued the first terrible sanction against England. Unless John submitted, and allowed Stephen Langton to occupy his rightful place as Archbishop of Canterbury, the kingdom would be denied religious protection. In short, the Pope would proclaim an interdict and bar the people from their God.

It had been the prime topic of conversation at Pembroke and Manorbier, for the interdict was now three months old, and the people of the isolated shire went in terror of their souls.

The churchyards were in impeccable condition, for they had now become the aisle and the altar. But the doors were locked, the candles snuffed, the relics draped as though to hide them from the shame.

The bells had been removed from the towers, or swaddled to stop them ringing in the breeze, and the bell ropes coiled and stored. Mass was no longer celebrated, nor prayers chanted for the dead. This alone committed the soul to an eternal voyage, lost in a limbo between earth and the final judgment. But worse, in practical terms, the dead could no longer be buried in consecrated ground, and the gravediggers could be seen at work on the open hillsides, whilst the mourners stood weeping, watched from a distance by their impotent priests.

Lovers could be married, either in the churchyard or, if it was raining, huddled on the porch. Their newborn could be baptized, and confession could be heard, the sinner kneeling at one side of a tree, the priest at the other. But it was a pathetic substitute, shouting one's sins against the wind.

There were, however, renegades, both at Pembroke and Manorbier. Not that William Marshal and Gerard de Barri were more or less religious than the common folk, but simply because the services could be conducted in their private chapels, out of sight and hearing of papal spies.

It was a cruel thing to ask, but if a local villager could give fair warning that his mother or father was about to die, the warlords would arrange for him to bring the body to their castle, and say a Mass for them. It was risky, though the people of Pembroke were a tight-lipped lot, and they arrived with the corpses in a hay cart, or concealed beneath a careful spread of fruit.

Beyond that, there was nothing Pembroke or Manorbier could do, for they would not admit the common dead to their family plots. The people would just have to trust in God and pray that He would take to His bosom the souls that floated up from the valleys and hills.

Whenever Marshal or Gerard attended the court, they asked if the king was prepared to receive Stephen Langton as Archbishop of Canterbury. The answer was always the same; not until he bore a perfect likeness to John de Grey, and signed himself thus.

The Wolf and the Sparrowhawk were drifting apart. It was not a sudden thing, though on reflection it was inevitable. They had changed, John more than Isabelle, and it was only odd that the change had come so late.

At the age of twenty-two, Richard Lionheart's landless younger brother had married his cousin Hadwisa—and lived to regret it. He had treated his wife appallingly, insulted and abandoned her and then, ten years later, run to her for help. Understandably, Hadwisa had shown him the door, and by the convenient device of consanguinity the marriage had been annulled.

His first wife had known him at his worst, or at least at his most callow. She had seen him cowed by his brother, cowed by Marshal, cowed by anyone who spoke above a whisper. She was glad to be rid of him, and he likewise looked back on the marriage with a mixture of embarrassment and regret.

And then, somewhat less callow and with Richard dead and buried, John had abducted the child Isabelle, heiress of Angoulême, and made her his wife and queen. And the same thing had occurred.

The uncertain prince, husband of Hadwisa, had become an uncertain king, husband of Isabelle. The Sparrowhawk had treasured him for his wit, his clever asides, his performance in bed. But, as his enemies had multiplied and his fortunes diminished, she had begun to worry about her own security. Her light laugh was held in check, and she did what she could—what she believed Marshal would have done—to instill in him a sense of responsibility.

But she was too inexperienced for the job, and his spiteful gibes had been replaced with honeyed words and acts of extreme cruelty. He smiled where he would once have sneered, then sent his cronies to take hostages, bully the clergy, impose his will on the people of England. He, too, mistook harshness for strength of purpose, largesse for generosity of spirit. He withstood criticism better, but he did not learn from it.

And in his free moments he indulged his appetite for other women.

Queen Isabelle was now twenty-one years of age, the mother of a son, Henry, and physically in her prime. She should, by rights, have held greater appeal for her husband than ever before, but she had ample proof of his disenchantment. The proof was named Suzanne, and then Clementina, and then Avise, the dowager Countess of Aumale. Just three of his many mistresses, all of whom were accorded his fullest, if short-lived affection. God's fist, Isabelle thought, I have actually *met* these whores! The thick-hipped Suzanne, who will doubtless bear him a bastard or two. And the mincing Clementina, stupid enough to imagine she'll be advanced by virtue of her outstretched legs. If virtue's the term. And the pretty-mannered Avise, who dares to put her hand on my arm and talk to me as an equal, because we're both titled and because she knows we have both been enjoyed by John. The comradeship of the coverlet, is that what she's after?

But the king's infidelity was not limited to such favorites as Suzanne and Clementina, nor young widows like Avise. His gaze roamed further, and he acquired a taste for the wives and daughters of his barons. He resisted no one who took his fancy, seducing the daughter of a friend as readily as the wife of a visitor. He was the King of England, and that helped, but he was also charming and attentive, and rarely beyond arm's reach of a jeweled token. The women were flattered to have been chosen, and it was only later that they joined the forgotten clique, the group, the crowd.

But the barons were not charmed by the scandal that attached to their women. They snatched them away and withdrew to their fiefs, recoiling from the stench of perfume that billowed from the court.

And then, infected by guilt and rumor, King John grew jealous of his wife. If he was adulterous, then why not she? If he had his Suzannes and Clementinas, then surely she could be linked to a Robert or a René.

He decided she looked bored in his company, yet smiled with anyone else. Blind to all but his own seething jealousy, he convinced himself that Isabelle was spending too much time with young men. She was seeing too much of this earl's son, listening too avidly to that count's tales. She was standing too close, touching too readily. There was no question in John's mind but that Queen Isabelle was unfaithful, adulterous, profligate. Like husband, like wife . . .

His own clandestine activities helped nourish the rumors, and they in turn grew wilder. Sons of the nobility found themselves banished on some trivial pretext or, hearing their names mentioned, fled before the rumors reached the king.

He was already suspicious of his barons, fearing that the abortive invasions and high taxes would lead to unrest and insurrection. He kept an equally watchful eye on the clergy, confiscating the property of any who sided with Rome. And now he added his wife to the list of suspects, as though he did not have troubles enough. It was only left for him to bruise his horses and kick his dogs, and the pattern of mistrust would be complete.

Two years to the month after he had surrendered the citadel of Rouen, William Briouze came home. He had spent the time in a French prison, waiting for his wife and king to raise the money for his ransom. Six thousand marks was the figure Philip Augustus set on John's loyal baron, and he was surprised the chests took so long to arrive.

But he need not have been, for Briouze's wife, the immensely strong-willed Maud de St. Valèrie, had been forced to collect the coins herself. She had appealed to King John, received his promise of help, then waited for his contribution. Half a year later she was still waiting, and sent a fifth and sixth appeal from her castle at Skenfrith.

Then the happy day when the king's soldiers arrived with tangible evidence of John's affection for Briouze. Four hundred marks, and a letter in which he expressed the hope that his old friend would soon be free.

Without hesitation, the chatelaine rejected the gift. "I can spare no more time or paper, but you may tell the king this. His pittance disgusts me. However, for my husband's sake, I shall forget it was ever sent, and work that much harder to make up the loss. You, messires, will understand why I offer you neither food nor shelter. I cannot afford it, and anyway I will not see John's men gorge themselves whilst my Lord Briouze languishes in prison. Now take the money and give it back to the king. Tell him what I've said. Tell him he has confused friendship with parsimony. If you dare."

There were no further exchanges between the indignant John and the outraged Maud de St. Valèrie. The Briouze family were not impoverished, but the chatelaine found it necessary to sell off a large number of manorial lands and borrow heavily from her friends and relatives. The ransom was paid in installments, the last at the end of May 1208, and three weeks later Briouze entered the round keep at Skenfrith.

The household servants mistook him for an elderly visitor, one of Lady Maud's uncles perhaps, or a senior baron come to ask when her husband would be set free. They were dumbfounded to learn that this *was* William Briouze, for he was not yet sixty and looked older by half. His pockmarked skin seemed as if it would tear at a touch, and his once-belligerent expression had become wary. It was the face of a man who has been deserted too often, a man prey to the incubus of foul dreams. His hands shook even when they were not curled around a mug, and his voice had become querulous, as though he doubted that his opinions were any longer of value.

He shared his dreadful secret with his wife, repeating the story time and again, flaying himself with the truth. His description of the assembly hall at Rouen, of John's insensate fury, of Duke Arthur's last, inconsequential words—"Ensconce me down there with a chair and table and some of your husbanded candles, and I could tell you"—all of it was recounted in a gray, tremulous voice, and always the same, word for word. He'd had more than five years in which to rehearse it, and the horror remained undimmed.

Maud did what she could for him, this ravaged mockery of the ironhard William Briouze, and warned their friends to keep silent on the subject of Rouen. They did so, and were sufficiently appalled by the warlord's condition to waive the debts she had incurred on his behalf. This was a considerable help, for it allowed her to retain what was left of her hands. William's lands, of course, save that he was too ill to administer them.

The angular and embittered chatelaine said nothing about the murder, nor about John's subsequent flight from Rouen. Nor did she mention the pittance he had offered, but let the ingredients simmer, stirring them occasionally until she was satisfied that the merest taste would poison an ox.

Then, unbeknown to her husband, she sent a letter of abject apology to King John, pleading with him to visit his old friend, the ever loyal William Briouze. "Bring with you whomsoever you wish," she invited, "so that they may judge the true nature of fealty. William loves you, lord king, and, for myself, I realize I was wrong to reject your bounty. Come and stay with us, and you will see that even the most humble house reveres you."

She laid the flattery as thick as mortar, then went back to stirring the pot.

The king was delighted by the letter and responded in kind, forgiving the Lady Maud and assuring her that, as soon as it was convenient, he would visit her at Skenfrith.

But before he could leave the court, there were more pressing matters to be dealt with.

The first, and least important, was to resolve a stupid argument with two of his barons, Eustace de Vesci and Robert FitzWalter, both of whom believed he was having an affair with their women. FitzWalter had all but accused him of seducing his daughter, whilst de Vesci had taken it into his head that his wife had been disgraced. The thing was getting out of hand, John grumbled. One would almost think the barons *wanted* it to happen, and would feel insulted if their women failed to catch his eye. The wife of de Vesci? Well, there might be a grain of truth in it. But the FitzWalter girl? No. Absolutely not. He'd have remembered if— Oh, *that* daughter. FitzWalter had spawned so many, it was hard to tell.

The king shared a dinner table with de Vesci and approached the problem in his own inimitable fashion. Grinning mischievously, he told the baron, "I've heard talk that you're displeased with me, Eustace. Why should that be?"

"It depends," de Vesci said, "on what you've heard."

"Something to do with your wife. That she shared my bed on an occasion."

The baron moved in his chair, and for an instant John's grin faltered. But de Vesci was simply shifting his hips. "You must tell me, if you care to, King. *Did* she share your bed?"

"It's hard to tell," John puzzled. "In the darkness of the chamber, the heat of passion. You know how it is."

"I know who shares my bed, if that's what you mean."

"But difficult to say for sure. Perhaps it was the Lady—"

"Joanna."

"Yes, and perhaps not."

"I think not," de Vesci said evenly. "I think it was more likely to be a harlot. Someone you had only just met, and would not meet again. A common whore, that's who I think it was."

It took John a while to digest the insult. Then, blinking with anger, he said, "It's possible, for I only met your wife a few days ago."

When Eustace de Vesci stormed from the court he was accompanied by Robert FitzWalter and a dozen of their friends. Within months they had formed a core of opposition to the king, and raised the first visible banner of rebellion in England.

Until then, all John would admit was that he might have misjudged his audience. It did not pay to joke with men who had no sense of humor.

The second thing that kept him from Skenfrith was his dispute with Rome. The country had now lain under an interdict for more than a year, and both Pope and monarch had hardened their hearts. John still refused to admit the much-traveled Stephen Langton, and subjected the papal emissaries to insult and ridicule. They came and went, bearing a fresh ultimatum, another final warning, a last plea for sanity. And then, when their efforts were exhausted and the young Pope sufficiently enraged, the king was threatened with the most terrible sanction of all—excommunication from his Church and his God.

The threat was first issued in January 1209, but the bishops entrusted with the task lost their nerve and withdrew, and it was not until November that sentence was published, and even then at a safe distance, in the churches of France.

If Pope Innocent imagined that John would fear for his soul, he was disappointed, and the king fought back as though against an invader. He was now an outcast, denied all religious comfort and protection, a sworn enemy of Christians, a target for any man who believed in God. He was, by definition, an intimate of the devil, and all those who went against him would be blessed with the title of crusader.

England had been made to suffer—and was still suffering—under the interdict. And now its king was excommunicate. A good time John decided, to take his wife and a group of his uncommitted barons and show them the loyalty of his old friend, William Briouze. At least at Skenfrith he could keep an eye on the much-too-innocent Sparrowhawk.

For a man who had set as many traps as a poacher, King John might have sniffed more cautiously at Maud's invitation. But it was cleverly concealed by flattery, and the following April the chatelaine welcomed him to Skenfrith as though she, too, was eager to share his bed.

She asked to speak privately with him, and they walked around the base of the grassy mound before entering the keep. Hesitant at first, she seemed suddenly to find her courage and said, "I am deeply ashamed at having rejected your offer, lord king."

"What? Oh, that. It's gone and forgotten," he dismissed. "We both wish it could have been more, but it was not possible. Spare yourself any further torment, Lady Maud."

"I have," she murmured, "in a way. You see, lord king, I dared not tell my husband of my impetuousness, so I invented a happier tale. For his sake I said you had forwarded half the ransom, three thousand marks; not all at once, of course, but over a period of time. And that you had also written, 'Nothing less will do for

Briouze.' As soon as I had sent back the money I realized that you *would* have raised the sum—"

"Had it been in my power to do so, yes, assuredly."

"And that although you did not commit those words to paper—"

"They were in my heart. 'Nothing less will do for Briouze.' That's well put, Lady Maud, for it *is* how I feel. But what of the letter I did write?"

A nice squirm of contrition as Maud told him she had destroyed it. They continued around the base of the motte, and then John asked, "Do you wish me to echo your story, is that it?"

"For my husband's sake."

The king nodded thoughtfully, almost convinced that he was poorer by three thousand marks. "It's time I met him," he said. "Our responsibilities have kept us apart too long."

Briouze's condition caused some embarrassment, and John hurried over to clasp his trembling hands. "England is complete again, William, now that you're home. You must eat well, eat and rest, and then next year we'll lead a fleet across the Channel and deal the French a blow they'll long remember. By the way, where were you imprisoned?"

"Near Melun." He had not yet smiled at the king, though John was happy to do the work for him.

"Melun? I'll remember that. And once we've cut our way into their yard I shall claim back every penny of the ransom. They'll be selling their children as slaves by the time we've finished with them." He stared earnestly at the warlord. "Do you remember the words I used to your lady? 'Nothing less for Briouze; nothing less will do.' Something like that. Well, I'd rephrase it. Less than nothing will do for Melun!"

Behind him the pot had simmered and come to the boil. . . . Maud de St. Valèrie studied her guests. . . . The beautiful, dark-skinned Isabelle . . . The table of barons who had come to witness the king's popularity . . . The king himself, who had just claimed and quoted a lie. . . . Then, by moving her lips, the chatelaine of Skenfrith threw the scalding contents of her bitterness at John.

"Why should *you* wish to lay claim to the ransom, lord king? What has it to do with you?"

He turned in his chair, the smile meant for Briouze still in place. "Not all of it, no. Just my contribution, the three thousand—"

"There was no three thousand."

"But we— You told Briouze—"

"I told my husband nothing. It's true, I must tell him now, but the subject has never been mentioned until today." Gazing past him at the ruined warlord, she said, "I am not blameless in this, William. I may have kept you in prison a while longer than was necessary, and I have waited until this moment to admit it. But judge me on the truth. I'm sorry to say it, but it will be more hurtful to you than my own petty deceit.

"I sent the king six appeals for help, and only the last brought a reply. It also brought his contribution to your ransom—"

"Every penny I could afford! *More* than I could afford!"

"But it was not the sum he told you. It was not three thousand marks, William, but a miserable four hundred. And he never wrote 'Nothing less for Briouze.' At least," she added, taking his letter from her purse, "he did not include it in this."

As she unfolded the brittle parchment and tossed it within reach of the barons, John raged, "Out *there*, on the *grass!* You asked me to walk with you and—"

"And see how Skenfrith has fallen into disrepair. What else would you and I have to discuss, unless it's that incident at Rouen, when you used a stone jar as an instrument of murder?"

The barons leaned forward, drawn by an invisible halter rope. Queen Isabelle stared desperately at John, but he was fixed in his chair, his eyes on the merciless Maud de St. Valèrie. She in turn ignored him and gazed at Briouze. Smiling gently, she murmured, "Time it was out. You have carried this burden beyond all the limits, and you see how you're repaid."

Briouze said nothing, and no one but his wife could recognize any change in his expression. But for her the change was startling and complete. His pitted skin seemed less fragile, and the haunted look slipped away, like ice from a window. He clasped his hands together to stop them shaking, then nodded once. She had his permission to tell the story that the world waited to hear; a mystery story, a murder story.

The chatelaine recounted it with absolute fidelity, word for word as she had heard it from Briouze. John and Isabelle exchanged an agonized glance, but the queen's only interruption, a nervous snort of contempt for the *menteuse*, brought bleak stares from the guests. It all rang true. John's attempts to sweet-talk Arthur, and the young duke's arrogant rejoinders; the king's insistence on the English victories in Brittany and then, truest of all, his outburst of uncontrollable fury, the dreaded Angevin sickness.

Five years of recurrent nightmares had polished Briouze's memory until, as he had told it over and over to his wife, she had seen the pool of candlelight, the splinters of glass from the smashed goblet, the king's nephew with his wrists manacled and his thin lips moving as he mocked his captors. "What a silly trick, my lords. What an unworkable pretense. . . ."

And the visitors to Skenfrith could see it, knowing beyond doubt that they were witnessing the truth.

The King of England had bludgeoned Arthur of Brittany to death with a wine jar, then concealed the crime by passing the body through the window and dumping it in the river. No prayers for this member of the royal family. No burial in hallowed ground. And no gesture of remorse by the monarch-turned-murderer. Nothing so human from the wolf.

The king's party withdrew from the castle and rode south to Monmouth. From there John sent messengers to two of his loyal seneschals, Gerard d'Athies at Bristol and Engelard de Cigogné at Gloucester. Each was to assemble as large a force as possible and join him within the week. He had unearthed a nest of traitors who were hissing and crawling about the ramshackle castle of Skenfrith.

On the night the royal messenger left Monmouth, William Briouze sent his wife and family to an estate he owned in Ireland. He would join them as soon as possible, he said, but first there was someone he had to see, someone to whom he should have told the story long ago.

The Sparrowhawk remembered, too late, that she had not brought the buckle. Indeed, she could not say where it was, since her possessions were scattered all the way across England. It was the price of her husband's jealousy, for he seemed loath to let her out of his sight for anything but life's natural functions. So, hustled from London to Windsor, Oxford to Skenfrith, and now from Monmouth to the gale-lashed fortress of Pembroke, she had abandoned half her clothes chests and most of her jewelry.

The buckle was the one John had presented to Marshal, to hold in trust for his seventh child. The young queen had immediately stolen it back, vowing to deliver it herself and hurl it in the dust at Pembroke. That, she had promised, for my husband's gifts to another woman's brat!

But times had changed. The king had rained trinkets on Suzanne and Clementina, Avise and Joanna and God alone knew how many others. If Queen Isabelle was to reclaim them, she knew she would have to prise open every jewel box at court.

The ride to Pembroke left the travelers wet and miserable. Spring rains hung thin as mist in the valleys and swept from ambush around the curve of the bald gray hills. Ahead of John and Isabelle rode Gerard d'Athies and seventy ill-humored soldiers, while the ninety horsemen who comprised the rearguard were commanded by the equally uncomfortable Engelard de Cigogné. Between these two contingents were a further hundred and thirty royal troops. In all, excellent protection for the king and queen, and a formidable hunting party.

From what they had heard en route, their quarry was ten days or so ahead of them, and was probably now lurking in one of the towers at Pembroke.

King John had been there before, but he was once again awed by the sheer size of the place. The gatehouse contained not one but three portcullises, behind the first of which were massive double doors that could be bolted on both sides from holes in the roof. A few feet beyond was the second portcullis, and behind that another door. Then a board-covered ditch and a third metal lattice and a final, single door, plated with iron.

Among its other features, Marshal's home boasted a keep that rose more than a hundred feet above the inner bailey and, with walls that were nineteen feet thick at the base, was strong enough to support a dome of limestone blocks. It was said that Pembroke was one of the few castles where the roof did not leak. The dome was encircled by ramparts; again not one, but three.

It had its own mill, the wheels turned by the waters of the Pembroke River. It had its own boathouse in the form of a natural cavern, opening on the estuary. It had four separate assembly chambers, the Great Hall, the Northern Hall, the Norman Hall, the Oriel. And it had a dungeon, a circular pit sunk thirty feet belowground, into which prisoners could be lowered through a hole in the stone-slab floor. Marshal had never had occasion to use it, though he could think of several men who'd fit nicely down there.

The bedraggled column was admitted to the yard. The warlord greeted his visitors, then conducted the king and queen and their immediate entourage into the keep. The three-hundred-strong escort—the hunting party—were accommodated in the adjacent Northern and Norman halls, and offered ale and bread, to hold them until a meal could be prepared.

When she had shed her rain-blackened cloak, Isabelle beamed at Isabel. The chatelaine knelt to her namesake, and the queen said, "Are we too late in the day to meet your children, Lady de Clare? You've such a tribe of them, I can't keep pace. How many are there now? Seven, or is it eight?"

"Eight, my lady, though no more are stirring at present. And your own son, Henry? I trust he grows well and strong."

"And noisy," the Sparrowhawk tutted. "Another like him, and I swear I'd go deaf."

"I doubt it. I have five sons and can still hear when anyone speaks."

"When Earl Marshal courts you anew," the queen smiled.

"When anything sensible is said."

They laughed together, their suspicions confirmed. They did not like each other at all.

Marshal was akin to an Arab in more than the pigmentation of his skin. He believed in the Islamic rules of hospitality and treated his visitors to fresh-caught fish and a treasured stock of Bordeaux wine. Then, when the rulers of England and of Pembroke had exchanged enough insincerities to make their teeth ache, John asked the warlord to surrender William Briouze.

"We know he came to you. He deserted his castle at Skenfrith, and we have evidence that he sent his vindictive wife to find sanctuary in Ireland."

"She *and* her brood," Isabelle appended. "They have also taken on the coloring of traitors."

The king looked inquiringly at Marshal, then tilted his head to hear the warlord's response.

Marshal lifted his goblet and drained it. *And why not, by God? It's my wine.* Then he returned John's quizzical gaze.

"William Briouze," the king prompted. "We know he's here."

Again silence from his host, and the slow realization that he would not reply. John nodded at the loyalty of it, added wine to his glass, then reached across to fill Marshal's. "Listen to me, Pembroke. I understand your feelings. Briouze is your friend, as he was once mine. But, whatever he may have told you, he has shown himself to be an enemy of England, and when did you ever cosset the foe?

"Did he say anything about Duke Arthur? The Lady Maud did. A wild and vicious tale that has set new rumors spinning throughout the country. What did he tell you? That I had a hand in it?"

Since John had refilled his goblet, Marshal had let it stand. Now he glanced at his wife, who passed her own glass along the boards. It told John what he wanted to know, and he abandoned all pretense.

"Briouze left Skenfrith and came here, we know that much. Now, give him up before you lose my affection, Marshal. I have three hundred men in this place and, if I tell them to search it—"

"They will do so."

"—they will— Yes, they will do so. But I'd rather *you* told me. Is Briouze here, under your care?"

Marshal reached under the table to massage his knee. Then he grinned, hauled himself to his feet and nodded in the direction of the door. "We have not been as popular as this for years," he observed. "My friend and neighbor, Gerard de Barri, Lord of Manorbier. Gerard, stop shedding the wet. You're in the presence of our king and queen."

John also came to his feet and, because he had done so, his entire entourage rose from their chairs and benches. Gerard de Barri stamped his way into the chamber, bowed casually to the king, then strode around the table to embrace Isabel de Clare. "You'll save me, even if Marshal won't. A drink and a chance to warm my bones? You'd allow that, wouldn't you, young lady?"

Completely ignored, the queen snatched at John's sleeve. But his attention had already been taken, for in Gerard's wake came a dozen hefty knights, then a dozen more, then archers and cross-bowmen, then more of each, edging politely around the walls, yet threatening to send the oak floor crashing into the cellars. At least a hundred sidled into the room, completely surrounding the table. When the last had pushed his way clear of the door, the Lord of Manorbier said, "It's not my way to come uninvited, you know that, Marshal. But we've been out in the rain all day, and I could not have ridden another step, not even to my own fire-side. The others have joined—well, I suppose it must be King John's soldiery—anyway, they've joined them in the halls. It'll be a tight fit for a while, the royal contingent and my own few hundred ruffians, but it won't be for long. Now, sweet Isabel, for mercy's sake give me a drink."

"Be honored," she told him. "The king himself prepared this one."

Ah, yes, John thought, I see this little scheme. Briouze was here, is here, or is cringing at Manorbier. Their game's as clear as a joust. Marshal keeps his garrison out of sight, inveigles my three hundred into the halls and then, wonder of wonders, his friend cannot travel another step, but must arrive at the opportune moment with an overwhelming force. They've crowded us out, Marshal and his bull-faced neighbor. They knew we would come in pursuit of Briouze, and now they've squeezed us so tight we can hardly draw breath, let alone a sword. Oh, this is a well-managed insult. I'm bound to remember this.

The companionable Gerard recognized Engelard de Cigogné, winked at him, then grumbled on about the weather. The queen was looking from face to face, as was Gerard d'Athies, as was the outmaneuvered king. Other voices chimed, discussing local gossip, and the royal couple found themselves ignored. Where Maud de St. Valèrie had sought to hound them from Skenfrith, Marshal and Isabelle were content to let them be, inflicting a far deeper wound.

They would not say if Briouze had been there, nor if he was still in the district. And they would not even say if they had heard the popular story, which told of how King John had slain his nephew with a bottle.

But their attitude said it all. The Wolf and the Sparrowhawk were not wanted at Pembroke. The man who had guided John as prince and king was tired of the job. Lackland, Softsword, Shrewdhead—whatever they called him now—he could do as he pleased, but he would have to do it without the support of William Marshal, Earl of Pembroke and Striguil, the man who carried a limp and bore a scar, both of them earned whilst the King of England was floating away downstream.

Once again the royal party withdrew. The king snarled and cursed his way back to Monmouth, then suddenly brightened and held a midnight meeting with Gerard d'Athies and Engelard de Cigogné. He had thought of a way to smoke out William Briouze.

Leaving the barons to implement his scheme, John returned to the centers of government. D'Athies and de Cigogné sent him regular progress reports, but it was not until the turn of the year that they rejoined him at Windsor. They had traveled a thousand miles and spent a small fortune on bribes and information. They had not found Briouze, though the king was happy to reimburse them, for they had fulfilled their task and seized Maud de St. Valèrie and her eldest son.

The interrogation was short and brutal. The king offered Maud the chance to recant her lies about Duke Arthur and admit that the story was the product of her husband's diseased imagination. She refused.

He then demanded to know if Briouze had fled from Skenfrith to Pembroke.

"So you can brand Marshal a traitor? I don't know where my husband went when he left Skenfrith, though I wish I did, for I could then deny you the knowledge."

Her son was questioned under torture, but even his agonized screams revealed nothing. It seemed likely that Briouze had stayed away from his wife and family in the hopes of sparing them this.

John did nothing to suppress his loathing for the woman who had tricked him and told the world about Arthur, and he committed Maud and her son to prison. But it was imprisonment with a difference, for he left them to share a cell, a single wedge of bread and a mug of water.

They were pronounced dead eleven days later, the son's arms disfigured where his mother had gnawed them.

The king took more hostages, not only from within the English ranks, but from the malcontents beyond his borders. The fall of the Briouze family had brought a number of barons to heel, though others stiffened their resistance to a monarch who could kill his own nephew, outlaw his accomplice and inflict a lingering death on the chatelaine and her son. Some saw John as a man to be obeyed, but many regarded him as a monster, and drew pictures of a cage.

Queen Isabelle herself was little better than a hostage, for her jealous husband had assigned a dozen knights to guard her, claiming that his efforts would come to nothing if she herself was abducted.

"That's the least of your worries," she retorted bitterly. "But how do you know I won't be seduced by the guards? They look capable of it to me."

Abroad, Pope Innocent wrote to the man he had chosen as Archbishop of Canterbury, Stephen Langton, pleading with him to gain entry into England. "You have a brilliant mind," he encouraged, "and I am sure you will find a way to establish yourself in that godless country. However, if John will not be reconciled with us, I must declare him impenitent and take the necessary measures."

By which, Langton thought, he means an alliance with France and an invasion of England. No more than John deserves, though I do not intend my appointment to be celebrated in blood. There must be a way to make even that hard heart flutter.

Ironically, the answer was supplied by the man John had raised and ruined, the tragic William Briouze.

The death of his wife and son had torn apart the last shreds of resolve and he had fled to Normandy, then made his listless way to the Cistercian monastery at Pontigny, not far from his former prison at Melun. Pontigny had once housed the exiled Thomas Becket, and now served as a refuge for Stephen Langton, so the monks were not at all surprised when Briouze knocked at the gate. The place was getting quite a reputation as a sanctuary for those who had offended the Angevin kings.

Age and events had taken their toll of the warlord, and it did not need a practiced eye to see that he was dying. Langton behaved magnificently, cheering him when he could, comforting him when the nightmares reappeared. In return, the wizened Briouze told him about England and its monarch.

"He becomes more frantic by the hour. He trusts no one, spies on his friends, chains watchdogs to the queen. God willing, I shall not live to see it, but England will soon erupt. My wife . . . She met a hideous death, but she was not the only one. He hanged twenty-eight of the Welsh nobility in a single day. He's mad, or passing for mad, and he cannot last."

"How would you stop him?" Langton asked, nodding in sympathy as Briouze said, "With a knife in the belly."

"Do you think there is anything that would terrify him?"

"Everything does already; his actions bear witness to it."

"Suppose," Langton murmured, "suppose the threat of a French invasion became real. Could he stand up to it? Would England rally to him?"

"If I say no, you'll assume it's my personal bitterness."

"I'll make allowances," Langton said gently. "You tell me, and I'll judge for myself."

"Good. Then give your verdict, for I say no, he will not stand up to a real threat. He no longer has the support. And I'd go further. In my opinion, biased though it is against that wild animal, half the nobility would welcome an invasion. Mind you, I am not among them."

"Nevertheless, I shall do what I can to arrange it." He saw Briouze's expression and smiled. "Don't fret, William. Not a single French ship will reach England. Except the one that takes me across."

The Pope would not realize it for some time, but he had made a perfect choice in Stephen Langton. The archbishop was an Englishman by birth and, like William Marshal and too few others, he put the fortunes of England before all else. But he was not merely patriotic. He was also an inspired diplomat and happy to manipulate the heads of Church and State.

He replied to Pope Innocent, admitting that he was lost for an idea. He could think of no way to gain admission to the benighted island, nor sway its intransigent king. He would understand, therefore, if God's senior servant took the necessary measures.

With extreme reluctance, Pope Innocent contacted the King of France and commanded him to make preparations for an invasion of England. Philip responded obediently, though he insisted that it had never been in his scheme of things to carry the war across the Channel. He had already achieved his objective by the destruction of the Angevin empire, and he had no claim on England itself. He would only raise a fleet at the express command of Rome. However, since Rome so commanded . . .

In the spring of 1213, at the Council of Soissons, King Philip asked his vassals if they would support and assist him in a holy crusade against England. Their enthusiastic assent made his head spin.

Stephen Langton had already moved from Pontigny to the Norman port of Barfleur and, when he heard the news, he wrote immediately to King John. The scheme he proposed was a masterpiece of diplomacy, though the first reading drained the color from John's face.

Langton suggested that the King of England should surrender his realm in its entirety to the Pope. He should furthermore apologize for his misdeeds, make restitution to the clergy for the wrongs he had done them and the property he had confiscated, and then, with due ceremony, allow the monks of Canterbury to install the Pope's elect, the selfsame Stephen Langton, as head of the English Church.

If not, Rome and her allies would lend their considerable weight to the French crusade, and the godless island would find itself ringed by ships.

However, there was a choice. If King John agreed to mend his ways, the Pope would return England to him as a vassal state—for the nominal sum of a thousand marks—and accord it the full protection of the Church. In other words, John had only to submit and he would be transformed from an outcast into a beloved son. And would the French then dare attack, knowing they went against a child of Rome? The answer was no, but only if John's reply was yes.

At loggerheads with Scotland, Ireland, Wales, France and Rome, as well as his own mutinous kingdom, John read and reread the letter, then dashed off a reply. The Pope's elect was welcome in England, and God grant him a smooth crossing. The contrite king would be on the beach to meet him, and would make obeisance there and then to their father in Rome. He would reinstate every last clergyman and pay back every lost penny. He repented of his sins and craved the archbishop's forgiveness. He had wandered far from the path, but he was not yet beyond redemption.

And that, he thought, should satisfy even a fairground juggler like Langton.

On May 15 John surrendered his realm to the Pope and received it back a few moments later from Stephen Langton. The king kissed the episcopal ring and escorted the archbishop up from the beach. They were all smiles, and Langton was enchanted by Queen Isabelle.

On July 20 he lifted from John the sentence of excommunication and set in motion the raising of the interdict on England.

Sometime in August, John was visited by a distant relative, Otto of Brunswick and claimant to the throne of Germany. The two men aired their troubles, talking each other down whenever they felt the attention slipping away. Otto bemoaned the civil war that had divided Germany for fifteen years, whilst John took him step by step through England's twelve-year war with France.

"You have my sympathy," they said. "I understand. Take my own situation, beset on every side by enemies—"

"I know better than you think," they said, "and I'm reminded of the time when the devil himself would have fled. The only thing that kept me in power—"

"As it did me," they said. "The knowledge that I had God and right on my side and was being, well, tested as it were—"

They kept it up throughout Otto's visit, then signed a declaration of alliance. Otto would help John mount an invasion to recover the lost territories, in return for which the Angevin would aid the Swabian against all rivals and pretenders. They would take the field next year, Otto attacking France from the north, John sweeping up through Poitou and Touraine, and thence to Paris. They would catch the French fish between their mailed gloves and squeeze him until his good eye started from his head!

But they were so busy scheming that John overlooked another meeting, this one between Stephen Langton and a group of dissident barons. It took place in a side chapel of St. Paul's Cathedral, where the archbishop put forward the idea that King John should be asked to reaffirm the ancient laws of England. The idea met with general approval, though no one volunteered to demand his seal. It would be enough if he agreed to honor the laws of his predecessors and his own coronation vows. So long as John restrained himself and did not further antagonize the nobility, there'd be no need for wax and ink and parchment.

9

FIELD AND MEADOW
May 1214–June 1215

It had started wonderfully well.

True to his promise, Otto of Brunswick had raised a formidable army in the north, embracing anyone with a grievance against France. The counts of Holland, Flanders, Boulogne and Namur had joined him. His father-in-law, Henry of Brabant, had been recruited, along with the dukes of Limburg and Lorraine. The lesser nobility were well represented, and the northern force—the left-hand glove—comprised six thousand horsemen and some eighteen thousand infantry. Strengthened by an English contingent under the command of the Earl of Salisbury, the army assembled in Flanders, waiting for King John and the right-hand glove to sweep up from the south.

And down there, in Poitou, it had also started well.

The success of Otto's recruiting drive had contributed toward John's own attempts to raise an army. Barons who had hitherto regarded an English expedition as doomed to failure were impressed to learn that Holland, Flanders and Boulogne had already rallied to the cause. As a result, King John was able to lead a significant force across the Channel and into the port of La Rochelle.

Needless to say, he took the Sparrowhawk with him. And, on the pretext that they were in foreign territory, he doubled her bodyguard. Whoever approached her was warned off, or his conversation reported to the king. The most innocent exchange was studied for hidden meaning, and the guards themselves were replaced at a moment's notice. Isabelle suggested to her husband that he shackle her wrist to his—"Or would that be too much of an encumbrance in battle?" He ignored her comments, but if one knew the king's whereabouts, one would know the queen's.

The English army made several incursions into Poitou, recapturing a number of castles and securing the fealty of the local barons. The invaders passed through Angoulême, Isabelle's birthplace, then pressed on into the county of La Marche, home of John's most dedicated enemies, the ever militant Lusignan brothers.

Now completely gray on the head, yet still called le Brun, Hugh of Lusignan and the ferocious Ralf of Exoudun hungered for battle. They had allowed King John to take them by surprise at Mirebeau, but they were on home ground today. One glimpse of the high-heeled monarch and they'd let fly with the best-fletched arrows they possessed. One glimpse, that's all they asked, and they could add regicide to their list of achievements.

But once again they allowed their emotions to hold sway. Hearing that the English force was in the vicinity of Moncontour—in whose nearby valley the brothers had been ambushed, and the child Isabelle snatched from them—they abandoned caution, rode straight at their enemy and were immediately surrounded.

King John reveled in their defeat. The Sparrowhawk was brought forward to gaze at the broken-nosed Ralf, and at the Lord of Lusignan, the man she might have married.

She told Hugh, "I scarcely recognize you. You're like a varnished board that's been left out in the weather. You've lost all your color."

"So I have," he replied, "whereas you, my lady, have stayed in the bedchamber and kept your looks. It seems odd to address you as Queen of England, though you've been so long enough."

Annoyed by his remarks, Isabelle queried, "Why odd? As you say, I've been the queen long enough. Thirteen years, if you reckon it. And, contrary to what you may think, I do not spend all my time in the bedchamber. I'm better traveled than you."

"I'm sure you are," he yawned. "I did not say it was the same bedchamber."

When Hugh and his brother had been taken away, Isabelle rounded on John. "So the vile rumors spread, eh, husband? Even out here they believe I'm a—what, a salacious flea that hops from bed to bed? Well, I'd have to be a flea, wouldn't I, to get past the guards? Now why do you look at me like that?"

"Because I never heard a rumor that was not founded in truth, that's why."

"Oh, yes!" she exclaimed. "I know of many that have no root. After Mirebeau, for example? When the French believed you were a descendant of the witch Melusine? When they stared at the sky, expecting to see you flap your way to Paris? That was a rumor, though without much substance, as I remember." She turned away in disgust, and the bodyguard closed around her.

The capture of Hugh and Ralf might have started a landslide, sweeping away all opposition in the south. The situation was akin to John's victory at Mirebeau and, waiting patiently in Flanders, Otto of Brunswick flexed his strong left glove, ready to clap it against the right.

But before the mailed hands could meet, King John learned that a French army was poised on the border of Poitou, and that it too was awaiting the clap of combat. He wrote home to England: "God has given us the opportunity to press our attack against our chief enemies, the masters of France. Now we shall venture beyond the palisades!"

And then, from all quarters of the English army came evasions and apologies. The local barons, who had recently sworn fealty to the king, were content to advance, castle by castle, securing England's rights. But they were less inclined to meet the French on the open field and, should such an event occur, they wished to be excused.

Things had changed dramatically in the past few months, and might very well change again. As the Poitevins saw it, there was no point in alienating either side. If the French army withdrew, the local barons could once again rally to the English flag. But if battle was joined and the expeditionary force defeated, it would be as well to greet the French with wide, innocent eyes.

Denied the support of the Poitevins, John's courage faltered and failed. He took his army back to La Rochelle, and the right hand beckoned to the left. It was Otto's turn to make a grab at the slippery fish.

Leaving his southern contingent to contain John in Poitou, Philip Augustus led his main force north from Paris in search of the Imperial army.

By a series of mismaneuvers, the adversaries passed within a few miles of each other, the French crossing the border into Flanders, the Imperialists advancing southward into France. The afternoon and evening of July 26 saw the two armies making frantic efforts to avoid an attack from the rear. They wheeled about, drew level once again and squared off on an undulating plateau near the border village of Bouvines. Scouts returned with exaggerated estimates of the enemy's strength, though daylight would show that the forces were evenly matched. The French were numerically superior in cavalry—if only by a thousand or so —but fielded less than Otto's eighteen thousand foot soldiers. It was still a massive display of strength by both sides, and the ground trembled beneath the weight of fifteen thousand destriers and fifty thousand men. Torches burned throughout the night as the armies prepared for that rarity, a set-piece battle.

They knew little of tactics and cared less. The archers and crossbowmen would occupy the front ranks, loose their shafts, then bunch together, leaving gaps through which the cavalry could spur out onto the field. If the infantry did not part quickly enough, they would be ridden down by their own horsemen, impatient to charge. So it paid to listen for the trumpets and dodge the pounding hooves.

The knights themselves placed their own interpretation on trumpet blasts and the roars of their commanders. More often than not, they set their sights on a particular banner, or took the opportunity to resolve some long-standing feud. They would charge forward in line, then break away, or veer in front of their companions, howling a war cry and spurring at their favorite foe. Had Richard Lionheart been alive, or the great German emperor, Frederick Barbarossa, the knights would have been content to gallop out and drive an iron wedge deep into the enemy lines. But there was no Coeur de Lion, no Redbeard, not even a William Marshal, and Otto's disparate allies singled out their own personal targets.

The French were better disciplined, for they were united under

a common banner, the golden fleur-de-lis, though even they welcomed the chance to settle an old score. Where better than in the
turmoil of battle to repay an insult that had rankled for five or
ten years? How better to commit murder than as an act of war?

Next morning, July 27, the battle lines were drawn up across
the plateau. The armies stood face to face, each assembled in
three divisions, wings and center, with the infantry in front, the
cavalry pawing the dry ground fifty yards behind. Six contingents
ranged against six, the sky paling and the archers letting fly as
they measured their range.

The village of Bouvines lay three miles from the border, three
miles inside France. So it was Otto who had invaded, and Philip
who sought to drive him out. The French, as the injured party,
opened hostilities, cheering as their first concerted flight hissed
across the open ground and took its toll of the enemy.

The Imperialist left was led by Count Ferrand of Flanders, the
right by Renaud of Boulogne and the Earl of Salisbury, the center
by Otto of Brunswick and the mass of the allied nobility. The
three Imperial divisions answered arrow with arrow, then echoed
the cheers.

The French left was commanded by the counts of Ponthieu,
Auxerre and King Philip's brother, Robert of Dreux, the right by
the Duke of Burgundy and the warrior bishop, Geurin of Senlis,
the center by the king and seventy Norman knights. The French
archers replied to the Imperial response, and then the arrows
flickered back and forth, thinning the lines.

Bishop Geurin was the first to lose patience, and he led a detachment of French knights directly against his adversary, Ferrand of Flanders. With a howl of anger, the counts of Dreux and
Auxerre followed suit, enraged that their bishop should have
dared to start the charge.

The Imperial left responded, its example followed by the
right. Horsemen thundered from both wings of the armies, Senlis
at Flanders, Boulogne and Salisbury against Dreux and Auxerre.
The French infantry advanced in the center, and the Imperial
bowmen shortened their range. But even before the cavalry had
crossed the open ground, the short-lived discipline collapsed. The
knights had chosen their individual targets, and now they
slammed down their visors and spurred away from the groups.

It was an age in which kings and emperors were required to fight. Not enough that they governed from a throne and conducted their wars from a pavilion; if they were leaders at all they were expected to prove it in both court and conflict, and their behavior on the field did much to inspire or dishearten their troops.

Many times in the past, the death or capture of a monarch had been enough to halt an army in mid-stride. The cry "The king is taken!" could turn certain victory into sudden defeat, the soldiers discarding their weapons and falling listlessly to the grass. The loss of a royal banner, usually flying from an ironbound mast and defended by an elite corps of knights, left the army without a rallying point. They fought best for what they could see, their commander in chief in his battle crown, their flag at its masthead.

Awkward then for the Imperialists when Otto of Brunswick was grabbed around the neck and wrestled from the saddle. He fell heavily, his visor jammed shut, and lay kicking like an insect, pinned down by the weight of his armor. Fortunately, his bodyguard had been selected for their military prowess and they hacked a path to his side, wrenched open his eagle's-beak visor and set him back on his horse.

Then it was Philip's turn to put his life at risk. Separated for the moment from his guards—the same giants who had hemmed him with shields at Château Gaillard—he was riding across the field when one of Otto's knights swung at him with a halberd. This long-handled weapon, part spear, part hook, part ax, was much favored by the men of Saxony and, although the knight failed to slice Philip across the chest, he managed to unseat him.

The French king fell with no more grace than Otto. His visor remained free, but he was winded by the impact and momentarily blinded by dust. He lay on his side, waiting to be cut by the ax blade or run through by the spear tip. *The plateau's a mile or two from the border. . . . At least I shall be killed in my own country. . . . Forgive me, Almighty Father, for I have sinned. . . . Receive now the spirit of your servant.*

He twisted violently as something crashed onto his shoulder. A second weight fell across his legs, while a third clanged against his helmet. Still blinded by the dust, he abandoned his confession and writhed under the weights, fumbling in an effort to identify the burden. Was he to be crushed to death? Is that what Otto had ordained as a fitting punishment for his enemy? Crushed until the bones snapped and the body became a shapeless sack?

His fingers curled around a studded rim and he gave a half-cry of relief. He had been buried beneath a pile of shields. His bodyguards had found him and covered him with their own protective blanket. They would let him get up when the time was right.

The plateau of Bouvines was now littered with bodies, scattered weapons, thrashing horses and the ghastly bric-a-brac of shoes and gloves.

Otto had recovered from his fall, only to have his destrier collapse beneath him, an arrow through its eye. He went down a second time in a flurry of straps and metal, broke his wrist as he landed and once again lay at the mercy of the French.

But his guards were still there, and they dragged him free, dumped him without ceremony across a saddle and hurried him from the field. The pain of his injured wrist left him too faint to hear anything they might have said, though they would be the last to admit the truth—that the Imperial lines had been turned. King Philip was up and about, bruised but otherwise unharmed, and his reappearance had given fresh heart to the army. The German halberd had missed its mark, and men had seen the shadow of God's hand as He had deflected the blade.

All day long, a day without end, the battle had swung and swayed. The Imperial archers had loosed as many shafts as the French. Their knights had ridden as far and probed as deep. Their commanders had fought as bravely and howled as loud. Yet the results showed otherwise.

The German left had been all but annihilated, the eagle banner pulled down, the Earl of Salisbury bludgeoned senseless by none other than the pious Bishop of Senlis. Renaud of Boulogne had been captured, as had Ferrand of Flanders and one hundred and thirty of the invading nobility.

Against this, the French casualties were negligible, and not a single man of rank had been killed or captured. It seemed that the French arrows had struck their targets, whilst those of Germany, England, Holland and Boulogne had all gone astray. Two well-matched forces employing the same tactics, or rather immersed in the same confusion, yet denied the same success. No wonder the French crowded around their king and bowed their heads as the militant bishops gave thanks for the victory. No wonder the Imperial army crept away, each contingent to its own country, the alliance shattered beyond repair.

It was known thereafter as the Battle of Bouvines, the decisive triumph of France over her combined enemies. Bouvines had supplanted Mirebeau. Bouvines had echoed Gaillard. Bouvines had set the seal on French domination, wherever France cared to appear.

John winced at the news, vowed swift and terrible revenge, and stayed as long as he dared at La Rochelle. Then, when he heard that Philip had started south, he took his wife and court and army back to England. And back, as he suspected, to the greatest conflict of all.

The barons reeled from the shock. They spent the winter sifting the various reports and, dissident or royalist, reached very much the same conclusion. King John had failed to take advantage of his early successes in Poitou, failed to meet Philip's southern contingent and failed to assist Otto in the north. It could have been woven into a tapestry or set as a mosaic pattern in the floor; a lesson for the future. The King as Invader—The King Irresolute—The King in Retreat. John himself should be made to stand before the tapestry or kneel on the floor for hours at a time, contemplating the images of disaster. It was a nice thought, though no one supposed he would learn from the arrangement of stones and stitches. A harsher lesson was called for.

By the time he was settled in his winter quarters in London, he knew who to blame for his defeat. The Poitevin nobility, of course, for having refused to engage in a pitched battle with the French. But also those English barons who had stayed at home. Had they supported the cause and crossed the Channel, the Poitevins might well have fought on, encouraged by the size of the invading force. Who could say that the French would not then have retreated, or called to Philip for help? The more John thought about it, the more certain he became. If England had rallied at the outset, Poitou would have held firm and the enemy would have been vanquished, torn to pieces by John's army in the south and routed by the Imperialists in the north.

It was all the fault of the dissidents in England, and they would pay for their cowardice.

He meant that literally, for the expedition had left him almost bankrupt. The barons would pay three marks for every knight they had failed to equip and send abroad, plus an individual fine in lieu of their own presence on the field. However, many of them still owed back taxes, or refused to ransom the wives and children he had taken as hostages. The thing had begun to spiral, with John adopting more extreme measures to combat the growing intransigence of his barons. His demands were greater than any made by Henry and Richard, his methods of exaction more brutal, more bitterly resented. He had lost England's empire overseas, run foul of the Pope and so committed the people to the darkness of the interdict. He had flouted the laws of his predecessors and his own coronation oath, and alienated the nobility to such an extent that talk of war now meant war against the king.

And on that fragile dish he heaped his demands for further taxes and another punitive fine. The dish broke.

When he saw them he thought they had come to arrest him—or worse. They had entered the chamber without warning, eighteen of his most aggrieved barons led by Robert FitzWalter and Eustace de Vesci, and all in full armor. His first instinct was to run, but the group moved aside and he saw the Archbishop of Canterbury cross the floor.

King John had spent the first few weeks of winter in the Tower of London, then moved upstream to a smaller riverside fortress known as the Temple, situated just beyond the city's west wall. It was here that Stephen Langton and the dissidents found him, seated at a desk and in conference with officials from the treasury. The desk and flanking tables were covered with documents, proof of what a man owned and therefore owed in tax.

The king came to his feet, decided to make light of the intrusion and asked Langton if he was any good at figures. "I'll admit I'm not. Come and sit beside me and help me work out—"

"You know these men," Langton interrupted, "so you know they are not your friends."

"Yes, I know them, primarily as debtors to the Crown, but that does not explain how they got in here without—"

"I dismissed your guards, that's how, lord king. As I hope you will now dismiss your collectors."

"And why should I? Is some act to be performed here that you cannot let them see? Why are your companions wearing hauberk and helmet? The war's on the other side of the Channel, if they care to pursue it."

"Until recently it was," Langton agreed, "but it looks like spreading. Dismiss the officials, lord king."

John's hand went to his head. He struggled to prevent it, but the scene reminded him of an earlier confrontation between king and Canterbury. His father, Henry II, wishing for the death of that incorruptible archbishop, Thomas Becket. . . . A few muttered words, and Henry's knights had ridden to the Cathedral, bullied their way past the priests and murdered Becket at the foot of the altar.

And now Becket's successor had brought armed henchmen to the king.

"Dismiss them," Langton offered, "and I'll stand between you and the nobility. I've read my history, but there'll be no bloodshed today. We are here to address you, that's all. The armor was merely to discourage resistance. You see, my lord, no one trusts you any more."

John took his hand from his scalp, told the officials to wait outside, then asked the intruders to say their piece. "I can't imagine what form this resistance would take, but if you feel more secure in metal—"

"I dare not threaten you," Langton said, doing exactly that, "but you'd be advised to swallow your taunts. I promised to stand between you and the barons. I did not promise to fight off eighteen of them."

A weary sigh from the king, a theatrical shrug of patience and then, "Very well. I shall make no more comments. I shall sit here, at the desk, and hear what anyone has to say."

FitzWalter was so determined to speak that his lips were already moving, but he allowed Langton to forestall him, and it was the archbishop who delivered the address.

"May I speak without interruption, lord king?"

"However you like." John waved. "I'm an audience."

Langton nodded slowly, aware that the king would never rid

himself of his ripostes. Nothing so simple as "Yes, I am listening." Always the more sarcastic "However you like, I'm an audience."

"Things have gone too far," Langton said. "Or, to make a point of it, you have gone too far. Those barons who supported you have been left near-destitute, whilst those who deny your right to impose tax after tax have had their wives or children snatched from them, or have themselves been held in contempt. In this, amongst other things, you've gone too far."

"Pray continue," John purred. "I'm hearing the squeal of rich men made less rich."

"The Church also has a strong case against you," Langton said. "You have yet to return many of the confiscated properties, and there are a number of outstanding artifacts that were last seen in the hands of your collectors. You tax the Church, no doubt of that, but you also tax its friendship."

Fiddling with the papers on his desk, John asked, "Is there more to come?" He saw Robert FitzWalter take a step forward, and let the parchment lay. "Yes, of course there's more. You're here to air a general complaint, aren't you, Stephen? You'll drag in all the defeats abroad, remind me of my weaknesses, describe the chasm that now stretches between the king and nobility, then finally issue some terrible warning which will, by chance, absolve the Church from any further payments and leave malcontents like FitzWalter and de Vesci as petty monarchs on their not-too-petty fiefs. Or do I misunderstand you?"

"You misunderstand," Langton said quietly. "We are here to ask you to cease and desist in your actions; to return all the hostages you have taken, together with such property, money, jewels and possessions as can be individually valued at more than one silver mark. Furthermore, we ask you to make the fullest restitution to those barons from whom you have abducted wives and children, to take the vows of a crusader, reaffirm your love of the Church and the laws of England's greatest king, Edward the Confessor. Ah, yes, and to bestow your mother's dowry on your brother's hapless widow, Queen Berengaria. The Lady Eleanor would have liked that, and so would Richard. It'll mean you have to get most of it back from Queen Isabelle, though I'm sure you'll find a way."

John gazed at him, then at FitzWalter and de Vesci. He fiddled with the papers again, laying one over the other. The dissidents watched him, but none of them wished to break the spell of Langton's address.

Eventually the king said, "Well, now, that's quite a list of wrongdoings. Quite a show of distaste. And, if I don't accept your terms, I suppose you'll retire to your castles and monasteries and defy me until the end of time."

"On the contrary," Langton said. "We shall emerge from those selfsame buildings, declare war on you and remove you from the throne. It is not what we want, but you leave us little choice. You will either accept our terms, and that would be the wisest course, or you will have the crown lifted from your undeserving skull. The end of time? God knows, Softsword, your end will come quicker than that!"

He coughed, embarrassed by his outburst. Unseemly behavior for the Archbishop of Canterbury, though much enjoyed by the barons. As for John, he stared from behind his desk, not yet able to believe what he had long suspected—that the wolf pack would one day turn on its leader, using the tricks he had taught them.

He asked for time to consider their demands. FitzWalter and de Vesci wanted an answer there and then, but, grudgingly, they allowed Langton to overrule them. It was agreed that John would meet the barons at Northampton on April 26, the first Sunday after Easter. At which time, he promised, he would deal conscientiously with their complaints. And, in an unspoken afterthought, with them.

The Sparrowhawk listened, memorized what she heard and grew daily more fearful of the future. Of England's future, and John's, but more especially her own.

The king still insisted she travel everywhere with a bodyguard, though the guards themselves had become tired of their assignment. So far as they knew—and it would be too bad for them if they did *not* know—Queen Isabelle had remained faithful to her husband. They still presented their reports, though these were now a mere formality, a weekly assurance that his wife was his and his alone.

Risking a bloody nose, other members of the garrison described the queen's guards as "the chastity belt." It was an inaccurate term, but one that struck home. The guards were all battle-hardened warriors, and heartily sick of traipsing after their innocent young charge. They felt ridiculous, accompanying her on walks, shouldering their way around London's open markets, stifling a yawn as she and her handmaids discussed the comparative merits of a pair of shoes or a bolt of cloth. Christ's eyes, they moaned, if they ever left the army they could set up as merchants and make good use of what they had learned.

Their lack of interest in the job allowed Isabelle greater freedom of movement, and as she heard John formulate his plans and dictate his letters, she made life as dull as possible for her guards.

She visited the markets two, and then three times a day, dithering over a simple purchase, returning in confusion to the Temple, then insisting that her escort take her back for another look at the goods. A few weeks of that and they were paralyzed with boredom. They pleaded with her to be more decisive, but this only meant that she shopped impulsively, regretted it later and blamed them for the mistake.

"One would think you were in league with the stall-holders, the way you urge me to part with my money. There's nothing for it, messires; I don't like what I've bought, so I'm going to exchange it, or reclaim my coins. You'll hear some pretty language if I try to get my money back from those marketeers."

On March 4, a day Queen Isabelle would remember, the guards made no move to accompany her on her declared search for a pale green kirtle with pendulous cuffs. They knew where she was going, and why; they knew she would either buy the gown and regret it, or make this the first of a dozen exploratory trips. A pale green kirtle? With pendulous cuffs? Sweet Christ, they could take no more of it.

And so, for the first time, in the guise of a silly, feminine mission, the Sparrowhawk left the Temple castle without an escort. The market lay to the east, within the city walls. Isabelle turned west and crossed half a mile of open, marshy ground, following the curve of the Thames. No one recognized her until she reached the courtyard of Westminster Palace and asked to speak with the primate of all England, Stephen Langton.

He brought her a warm blanket and a glass of wine, then sat quiet as she betrayed her husband. She told the archbishop that John had no intention of meeting the barons at Northampton, but had written to the Pope, appealing for help, and to Flanders, Germany and twenty other places, urging their leaders to send mercenaries to bolster the English throne.

"I think you underestimate him, Langton. He storms and threatens in the privacy of our chamber, and I know he will not agree to your terms. Long before Easter, or whenever you're supposed to meet him again, he'll have an army at his back. He feels trapped, and he'll turn on you, mark my words. This is not Normandy, with its postern gate of Barfleur. Nor is it Poitou, with its outlet at La Rochelle. This is England, and where can he go from here?

"He will fight you, Langton. I don't say he'll win, but he will turn the ground slippery underfoot, razing towns and castles, burning crops—if it's the right time of year—and generally pulling down the stones. Invite him to a meeting, and he won't turn up. But wage war against him here, in his own country, and he'll see England destroyed before he submits. I thought you should know what's happening, that's all."

Langton nodded, then leaned forward in his chair. "You took a risk walking across the marsh. It's a favorite haunt for brigands." He glanced at a servant and curled his hand around an invisible glass. "I believe I'll join you, my lady. This is really the first time we've spoken together, tête-à-tête." The glass arrived and he stared at the dark liquid, then raised his eyes to the queen. "So your concern runs deep enough to bring you out here. I'm impressed."

"I thought you should know," she repeated.

"Indeed I should, though that's not exactly what I meant. I am impressed, certainly, but more than anything by your desire for self-preservation. You're terrified, aren't you, Lady Isabelle? You can see the country running with blood—how did you put it, slippery underfoot?—and the throne toppling, and a ship waiting to transport you back to Angoulême. That's what concerns you, along with the fear that the ship will carry neither jewels nor coin.

That's why you've ventured upriver to lay bare your husband's secrets, because you do not want to fall so far to the ground, nor ride so high in the water. You have come here to save yourself, my lady, even if the King of England can't be saved."

Stubborn to the last, she said, "I thought you should know what was happening, no more than that."

Langton turned his glass, glanced across the rim and murmured, "Rather more, I'd say. Some private scheme of your own, whereby you might retain your crown? What is it, Lady Isabelle? What would you have me do?"

She had practiced the phrase on the marsh, but the words still distorted her lips. "I want you to—I want the Earl of Pembroke sent for. Offer him whatever's necessary, but get him here. I want William Marshal at your side, to bring some sense to this holocaust. There's no one else I can think of."

"Don't shy from the truth," Langton told her. "He's the obvious choice, and we both know it. I am glad you told me of the king's preparations and so forth, though most of his actions were already known to us."

"And the Earl of Pembroke?"

"Oh, didn't I say?" Langton apologized. "I sent word to him a month ago. He's already on his way, he and his neighbor, the Lord of Manorbier. If they can't implant some sense in the situation, we shall all be running for the boats."

The arrival of William Marshal and Gerard de Barri came too late to prevent the first violent act of insurrection against the Crown. It took place at Northampton, where, as the day of the agreed meeting drew to a close, the dissident barons realized the king would not appear.

It was rumored that John had approached to within twenty miles of the rendezvous, but refused to advance any farther until the rebel leaders disbanded their force. A sensible request, if it was true, since Robert FitzWalter and Eustace de Vesci were backed by forty militant barons and almost two thousand knights.

But FitzWalter had lost patience. A troublemaker at the best of times, and still convinced that his daughter had been ravished by the king, he was in no mood for conditions or compromise. John had vowed to attend the meeting on April 26 at Northampton, and he had broken his word. Nevertheless, the meeting *would* take place, if not today, then tomorrow; if not in the city or under its walls, then twenty miles down the road.

Aware that John employed a legion of spies, FitzWalter gave them something to report and detailed men to burn several of the more prosperous-looking houses. If the king was on high enough ground and cared to glance northward during the night, he might see the sky glowing red above the city.

This pointless and vindictive act was followed by another, for the dissidents trotted south to John's rumored encampment at Brackley, learned that he was not there, nor had ever been there, and vented their spleen on the innocent townsfolk. They stopped short of outright murder, though no one could be sure that all the occupants had escaped from the burning buildings.

The violence spread. The few moderate voices were drowned out, and it seemed that England, having done so poorly abroad, was now determined to punish itself at home. The royalists and mercenaries were committed against the growing force of rebellion, yet they were all flagellants, prepared to draw blood from each other and lay their thongs across the rib cage of the country.

Langton, Marshal and the big-girthed Gerard de Barri rode north to intercept the dissidents. They brought with them a list of proposals—a rough draft of what would come later—but neither FitzWalter nor de Vesci would discuss it. They had struck a blow at Northampton and another at Brackley, and they were now on their way to London. Numerous towns and fiefs had gone over to them. Their blood was up. They were in full cry after the wolf. They had no need of well-balanced documents, or talk of restraint. Softsword had taxed them up to the hilt, lost an empire and failed to keep his rendezvous. Now he would get his just deserts, and they would come at the end of a sword, not the tip of a quill.

At the age of sixty-nine, scarred and limping, yet once again in harness, William Marshal could still recognize an opportunist when he saw one. He discounted Eustace de Vesci, as he had always discounted the younger Lusignan brother, Ralf of Exoudun. They both did what they were told, Ralf by the more positive Hugh le Brun, de Vesci by the more ambitious Robert FitzWalter. It was FitzWalter who would set England ablaze, if he was not first damped down.

"Tell me how it will go," Marshal asked. "An invasion of London, and then what?"

"And then, if you wait you'll see," FitzWalter retorted. "We'll seize the king, and there'll be a trial, and then he'll be put away for the rest of his life."

"And how will Rome take it, when she learns that you've imprisoned her new-found vassal?"

"Do you know," FitzWalter measured, "I do not care—*that*—what Rome may think or do."

"Nor how King Philip receives the news?"

"Nor how the Frenchman receives it, no."

"Nor that England will be left without a monarch? Or do you intend to pay homage to Queen Isabelle?"

FitzWalter turned away, his arms raised to signify that he was at a loss. Then he swung back, grim and belligerent. "What is your purpose, Earl Marshal? Why this swarm of questions? You are not directly on John's side, nor on mine. You've got a leg either side of the wall, so why should I confide in you? Excuse my forthrightness if I say you're, well, you're worked out."

"I was worked out ten years ago," Marshal corrected. "But if I answer your questions, you can then answer mine. What's my purpose? To avoid civil war and to bring the contentious parties face to face, *without* the benefit of arms. And why should you confide in me? Because, you bloody upstart, I make a better confidant than an enemy! You've burned out a few innocent civilians and think yourself irresistible. But submit to a proper test. Ask around and see who would back Robert FitzWalter against William Marshal. Excuse my forthrightness when I say you'd be left shivering in the cold."

The rebel leader did ask around, and the evasive answers told him Marshal was right. The dissidents would willingly fight the king, but they would not go directly against Stephen Langton, William Marshal, nor any of the earl's friends and neighbors. The object, after all, was to trap the wolf, not fight the primate of England or the master of Pembroke.

Nevertheless, FitzWalter continued his march on London. He also adopted the pious title of Steward of the Host of God and Holy Church, thus dignifying his attempts to pull down the king.

On May 17, 1215, the rebel army—the Host of God and Holy

Church—seized the capital, save for its impregnable fortress, the Tower of London. Many of England's eastern and northern counties had joined the revolt, though the west and southwest remained predominantly loyal to the Crown.

King John and Queen Isabelle had been forewarned of the rebel advance and fled from London to their castle at Windsor. They were joined there by the pair who had captured Maud de St. Valèrie, Gerard d'Athies and Engelard de Cigogné, and by Marshal's special enemy, Constable Saldon. They waited in desperation for a letter of support from the Pope, or for news of a mercenary landing. The former would unsettle Langton, whilst the latter might draw FitzWalter and his army down to the coast. But until that happened, the royal family were advised to stay put. Windsor was as impregnable a stronghold as the Tower of London and, by the time the rebels moved against it, help would have arrived from overseas, God willing.

But Isabelle's betrayal had encouraged the archbishop to send letters of his own. He had assured his old friend, Pope Innocent, that the situation was under control and that John—child of Rome—would not be harmed. Then, adopting a different tone, he had warned off the king's allies in Flanders, Germany and Boulogne. "This is an internal affair," he told them. "You have your own problems with Philip of France. It's better that you should guard your own borders than try to cross ours."

John did not know it, but his allies had already arrived at that very conclusion.

In early June, Robert FitzWalter moved his headquarters to Staines, a few miles downriver from Windsor. He was not equipped to besiege the castle, but if he could not break in, at least John could not wriggle out.

Meanwhile, Archbishop Langton, Earl Marshal and others continued to work on their provisional draft, expanding it from its original twelve clauses into one that contained more than sixty. It went by a variety of titles; the Charter of Liberties; the Articles of the Barons; the Great Charter, or in Latin, Magna Carta.

They discussed how best to strike the blow. The leaders, moderate or militant, were all willing to visit the king—if he'd admit them—though they agreed that he should, by rights, come to them. At one stage in the proceedings FitzWalter's chief supporter, Eustace de Vesci, strode forward as though to snatch the document, only to find himself pricked by a porcupine of swords. His knights started to his rescue, then halted as the Lord of Manorbier shoved his armored belly in their path. "This isn't a game, messires. And, if it was, your leader is not good enough to play. Back you go. That's the way. You leave these things to Langton and Marshal."

In the event, it was decided that no one would deliver the scroll. Instead, King John would be invited to meet the barons on neutral ground, preferably one of the flat, swampy meadows between Windsor and Staines.

Ever respectful of property, Marshal searched the riverbank, found what he wanted, then made inquiries as to the owner of the land. The meadow belonged to a farmer who described it as the running middle, simply because one side was flanked by the Thames, the other by a gully. It was by no means in the center of the river, but Marshal was content to abide by the farmer's wishes and paid generously for an indeterminate lease on the stretch of ground called Runnymede.

When the pavilions had been erected, the fence posts hammered in, the surrounding trees cut down to prevent an unseen attack, and a special guard from Pembroke and Manorbier positioned where they could keep a watchful eye on both royalists and rebels, Stephen Langton sent emissaries to Windsor. They took with them a copy of the charter and requested the king's presence in the meadow.

He remained in the castle as long as possible, at first refusing even to look at the charter, then rejecting half its clauses, then maintaining that he would put his seal to nothing under duress, and finally pleading illness.

He did not admit that, on June 8, he had summoned Gerard d'Athies, waited an hour for him, then instituted a search of the castle. The search had failed to reveal either d'Athies or Engelard de Cigogné.

"What a shame," Isabelle commented bitterly. "If we'd known their route, we could have followed them."

By June 15 King John had run out of excuses and friends. Less than ten knights remained at Windsor. The royalists in the west had made no move against the rebels. The Pope had dispatched no army to liberate his vassal. The eagle of Germany remained in its homeland.

That same morning John sent word to the barons. If his safety was guaranteed, he would affix his seal to their charter. Stephen Langton went to collect him from the castle, leaving Marshal to check the ground.

The document had been prepared in haste and would be later revised and improved. It attempted to clarify feudal law—much of it unwritten until now—to air the grievances of the barons and limit abuses by the king. It was directed against foreigners, weighted heavily in favor of the English nobility, and of little immediate value to the common people. Self-interest was apparent, as was the idealistic belief that, long ago, before the Angevin kings had left their ruthless imprint on the country, life had been fair and just.

The meaning of the charter was, in places, impenetrable, in others clear and succinct. It was both comprehensive and parochial, generous and vindictive, but, most important of all, as timely as the sun at dawn, the moon before dusk.

Langton's hand could be seen in the first clause, in which John confirmed that the English Church should be free, its rights undiminished, its liberties unimpaired. The Church would henceforth elect its own officials, without interference from the king. There would be no more royal favorites pushed into place, and hopefully no more interdicts.

One clause stated that no widow or heiress should be compelled to remarry against her will, an unpleasant practice that had allowed the king to reward his friends with lands and titles, no matter how gross the men appeared to the chatelaines.

Another clause barred royal officials from seizing land as payment of a debt, so long as the debtor could offer jewelry, horses, any movable possessions that would save his home or fief.

Another forbade the levy of taxes without the general consent of the barons. No more impositions at the whim of a bankrupt king.

Another, which concerned merchants, craftsmen and farmers, declared that, whatever the man owed in fines or taxes, he should be allowed to keep the tools of his trade. What advantage was there in confiscating his stock or plow? Much better to let him work and repay the money, little by little.

Another, this time for the benefit of the nobility, stated that earls and barons should be fined by their equals, not by the king and his cronies from the Exchequer.

Another, showing a nice regard for detail, denied any royal official the right to take a horse or cart without the owner's consent.

Another placed the same restriction on timber.

Two more, and these the longest-lasting of all the clauses in Magna Carta, maintained that no free man should be seized or imprisoned, stripped of his rights, outlawed or exiled, destroyed or condemned, save by the judgment of his peers and the law of the land. Furthermore, no one should be forced to pay for justice nor denied it.

From these assurances alone the people of England would one day derive the greatest comfort and security. It would take time for the words to spread and be understood, and even then there would be abuses, always abuses. However, these essential rights had been committed to paper; no man should be condemned without a fair trial, and justice should not drag its steps.

Another clause, a direct stab at the king. All hostages were to be returned.

Another, a personal thrust from William Marshal against those men who had tormented his friend Briouze, and brought about the hideous death of Maud and her son. The demand that Gerard d'Athies and Engelard de Cigogné be removed from office, and that they never again hold a position of trust in England.

Another, a sweeping blow at foreigners—at the likes of d'Athies and de Cigogné—requiring that all justices, constables, sheriffs and their ilk were to be appointed from among those who knew the country and cared for it. In other words, Englishmen.

In keeping with that, another clause sought the removal of all foreign knights, bowmen, attendants and mercenaries, together with their horses, weapons, relatives and pets. England had enough problems, without an influx of troublemakers from abroad.

There were other clauses, all contained on a single sheet of parchment, twenty inches wide by thirteen high. The close-written lines were enough to blur the sight, though King John managed to press his seal into the warm wax before dragging his sleeve across his eyes. It was the strain of reading, he insisted, not acknowledgment of what he had read.

Making sure that FitzWalter and de Vesci kept their distance, Langton and Marshal escorted the king to the edge of the meadow. They did not ask where he was going, and he did not tell them. He was still King of England and, even though his powers had been made public, there were some things he intended to keep to himself. A man's destination was his own business. As were his feelings. And his fears.

10

⁓•⁂

THE DROWNING OF THE TUSKY BOAR
June 1215–October 1216

In the event, the king chose the Tower of London in which to fall sick. No one knew how he had reached the fortress unrecognized, only that he had left Queen Isabelle at Windsor and dismissed his pathetic retinue ten miles from the capital. From there he had gone on alone, perhaps by river, perhaps circling London to approach the Tower from the east. Whatever his route, he avoided capture and entered the castle during the last days of June.

His was no commonplace illness, no mere chill or fever. It was the Angevin sickness, and it struck terror in the garrison.

They would emerge later and recount what had happened when a demon had taken possession of a king.

He turned his teeth against stone pillars faced with plaster, biting at them as though to bring down the roof. He thrashed the floor, snapping his fingernails, tearing the skin, then sprang to his feet and ran shrieking at the walls.

He had seen many men chew their shields, or hack mindlessly at the furnishings of a private chamber. His father, Henry II, possessed by the same demon, used to spur his horse until it dropped, then stumble onward, wrenching branches from the trees, or hurling rocks that no two normal men could lift. Richard Lionheart had been similarly afflicted, though he had preferred to wreak havoc with a massive, double-headed ax. The family had been goaded, each in their own way, and this now was John's.

He prowled the corridors, leaping at shadows, snarling at

sounds. He used whatever he could find as a weapon, running forward with a curtain, then draping it over nothing at all and fling-
ing himself upon his imagined foe. From time to time he dropped
with exhaustion, though even in this he was unreliable, and the
guards had learned to leave him where he fell. They put out
food and drink, then as often as not found the dishes shattered,
the bread and meat dry on the floor.

They did not know where or when he would next appear. They
heard him shriek, heard the clash of metal against stone, heard
the rap of his heels on the oak boards. A few of the more boast-
ful guards claimed to have seen him, but their companions were
unwilling to accept that the king's arms had become black, rustling wings, or that he could turn from man to toad to bat at the
blink of an eye. He might be a descendant of the witch Melusine,
but whether he was or not, they thought it best to keep out of his
way.

He haunted the Tower of London for almost a week, his mind
distorted by suspicion. The conspiracy had been so gigantic, so
universal, that he was never at a loss for a name. It was all the
fault of Audemar Taillefer and the two hulking porters who had
carried his litter, what were their names, no matter, it was their
fault for denying him their support against the Lusignan brothers,
that murderous pair who had pursued his mother, sweet Eleanor,
theirs and Marshal's and Briouze's, don't forget Briouze and that
tragedy of Gaillard, Roger Lacy, they and the fishermen from
Rouen who had failed to tell him that the tide had turned, don't
forget them. . . .

It was the fault of that angular bitch, Maud de St. Valèrie or,
if not hers, of that fat-bellied Gerard de Barri, yes, he and his
namesake Gerard d'Athies, the traitor of Windsor like Engelard
de Cigogné, deserters both and akin to Otto and the weakwater
henchmen who had fled with him from the field of Bouvines.

The extent of the conspiracy was breathtaking, for it included
not only FitzWalter and de Vesci, God spurn their souls, but
Langton and the Church and, most grievous of all, the predatory
Sparrowhawk.

They were in league, as they would have to be if they were to
find the courage to go against King John of England. . . .

And then the shrieks and mutterings ceased. The passageways

no longer echoed his footfall. The food was left undisturbed. He had departed as surreptitiously as he'd arrived, and even the more incredulous guards found themselves thinking about bats and toads.

The charter had solved nothing. Fifteen years of mistrust could not be eradicated with a sheet of parchment and a wax seal. The rebels remained under arms, their leaders convinced that John would soon renege. He had agreed to their demands, but done precious little to implement them, and FitzWalter was determined to keep his army in battle array until at least half the conditions had been met.

His suspicions were well founded. As soon as the king had recovered from the Angevin affliction and returned to Windsor, he sent a fresh appeal to the Pope. He told Innocent that he had been forced to sign the charter under duress, and that the self-seeking FitzWalter had his eye on the throne. "I am an obedient child of Rome," he pleaded, "and I look to you for deliverance. We are all your children, here in England, and you must save us from the ambitions of greedy men."

Then, conveniently forgetting that he had included Otto and the Imperial allies in the grand conspiracy, he wrote to Germany, Flanders and Boulogne, begging them to send a mercenary army to his aid. "We were ever friends, you and I, and I look to you for deliverance. We are all your friends, here in England, save for a few ambitious men."

The Pope's reply was disappointing, for he offered a general panacea, urging all the factions to behave with moderation and keep their swords in their scabbards. Calm yourselves, was his message; see the other man's point of view.

Otto's response was more encouraging, though John was less enchanted to hear that Philip Augustus was astir. The reason was not clear, but the French commanders were congregating in Paris and the fish was said to be smiling uncommonly wide. Take care, was Otto's warning; Philip never yet smiled to another man's advantage.

So whilst John and FitzWalter beckoned with their banners, the Pope counseled patience, Otto dispatched mercenaries and the French court spoke in a whisper. Langton, Marshal and the other moderates sniffed the wind, not liking what they smelled. The charter they had worked so long and hard to perfect was in danger of being torn to pieces. There were too many men in armor, too few in the council chambers.

It started slowly, gained momentum and then, like a runaway barrel, split and spilled its contents. War broke out in a dozen places and, once again, horsemen thundered through the dry autumn valleys, plowed through the mud of winter, advanced a mile a day in the snow. The royalists surrounded London and overran several of the eastern counties. They took the great castle of Rochester and a dozen lesser fortresses, and it finally occurred to the rebels that, far from being defeated, King John was turning like the wolf. The mercenaries from Germany and Flanders had helped bolster his cause, and Magna Carta was nothing more than a distant memory, a confession to be extracted and signed, then dismissed as so much paper, so much ink.

This was civil war; henceforth all conditions would be met on the spot, or rejected at a rope's end. The only words to be made permanent were those that someone might care to chip on a tombstone.

Panicked by John's resurgence, the rebel leaders acted irrationally. So deep was their mistrust of the king, so desperate their need to supplant him, that FitzWalter and de Vesci turned their eyes toward the Channel, looked across it, across Brittany, across Normandy, across the vanished border. Hard to believe that men who had fought to preserve the Angevin empire against its greatest enemy would allow their gaze to settle on the distant city of Paris. But where else could it rest if they were to offer the throne of England to the King of France?

"Yes," Philip nodded, "so we've heard. They really are a benighted race on that island. I'm sure that whenever two of them agree to play chess—if they ever *do* agree—they first hack at each other to decide who starts. It seems to me that England is the one country that can be spared all foreign enemies. God knows, she makes enough of them at home!"

He spent several weeks studying the requests and invitations from the rebels. Like John, Philip Augustus was a child of Rome, and he was hesitant to incur the wrath of Pope Innocent. On the other hand, France would not be invading the island so much as liberating it from the oppressive—and some said lunatic—John Softsword.

However, Philip himself would not go. He was over fifty now, completely blind in one eye, partially so in the other, bald and overweight and no longer interested in venturing abroad. He would send his son, Louis, then listen to the young man's stories about the race that fought each other for the choice of pawns. He'd let Louis find out if the English throne was still on offer.

On May 21 the French prince landed at Stonar on the Kent coast, choosing that beach because it was flat and pebbled and ideal for his machines. He was a serious young man, not yet thirty, but already the model of his father. Neither acted rashly nor courted the crowd. King Philip was known as a chilly fish, intelligent and farsighted. Louis as a man who could be surprised by nothing, since he took surprise itself by surprise. He devoted so much of his thinking to the future that his friends asked him what life was like five years on.

And now he stepped onto the beach at Stonar, already aware that the hard-packed pebbles would take the weight of his twelve hundred mounted knights and forty-six assorted catapults, *perriers*, rams and mangonels, more siege machines than either the royalists or rebels could muster.

English scouts spurred inland and reported to their leader. King John was at Canterbury, arguing with Langton and Marshal. There was not much the three men agreed on, though they all accused the scouts of exaggeration. Twelve hundred knights, maybe, but not forty-six machines. There were not as many as that in all England, not of the size the scouts had described.

Marshal said, "If this *is* a French invasion, it's at the behest of FitzWalter. King Philip would not have sanctioned it unless he had an answer ready for the Pope. So those twelve hundred knights and their however-many machines are bound to join the rebels as soon as possible. If that happens, then you, my lord king, will be once again in a corner."

"That's not such an elusive thought," John snapped. "It had already occurred to me. But dare I ask what you would do in my position? I know you're against this war in all its forms, Earl Marshal—"

"Against the civil war, yes. But I'm equally opposed to foreign invasion. I don't know who leads them, Philip or his son, but they are not here for a change of air. If they help FitzWalter, they'll want something in return. Very likely your crown."

"And so?"

"So you'd do well to intercept them and snatch their machines. They are a sure sign of confidence, the property of an army on the advance. They're the first things to be abandoned when men flee, but they'll make a pretty picture, rolling up from the coast. My advice is that you find them, and take them over."

"Will you ride with me? And you, Langton?"

No, they said, no more than they'd ride with FitzWalter. The king had asked what they would do in his position, but they were not in his position. If they were to travel anywhere together, it would be to the nearest conference table.

Left to fend for himself, King John led his troops in search of the machines. But he failed to locate them, lost his nerve and retreated to Winchester.

Ten days after the landing, Prince Louis reached the outskirts of London, to be welcomed by FitzWalter and de Vesci. In awe of the rams and catapults, they asked if he would harness them again and accompany the Host of God and Holy Church in pursuit of the wolf.

On June 5 King John alerted his wife and escort and they fled from Winchester, this time hurrying to the one sure sanctuary of Corfe. Learning from FitzWalter perhaps, he had left the cathedral city in flames.

A few weeks at Corfe, and the royal couple had fallen prey to a new obsession. The fortunes of war were swinging too wildly for either side to claim outright victory, or be forced to acknowledge defeat. However, John and the Sparrowhawk were faced with one inescapable fact; they were running short of money. If they could not pay the mercenaries, the men would quit the field or, worse, offer their services to FitzWalter. Without mercenary support, the royalist barons would be disinclined to fight on, and some of them might also turn their cloaks. The balance would tip more steeply in favor of the rebels, until even the king's body-guard began slapping their empty wallets.

But this was hardly an opportune time to impose taxes on the people of England.

There *was* money, of course, though in a different form. John had already recovered a large proportion of it at Winchester, and he now wrote to more than twenty monasteries, warning them that he was coming to reclaim what was his. Queen Isabelle shared his obsession, for she was determined to collect her own scattered valuables.

At the end of July they set out on their treasure hunt.

Meanwhile, Stephen Langton had returned from an unsuccessful peace mission to tell Marshal that the rebels and their allies were falling out.

"I don't know what FitzWalter imagined when he welcomed Louis and his twelve hundred chevaliers, but I'd say he's finding the price too high. The French claim that the English are a manuscript of meanness, and cite the lack of decent wine as an example, whilst FitzWalter's cronies accuse the invaders of unearned arrogance and insist that they only crossed the Channel in search of a foreign title. Anyhow, they still refuse to meet King John."

"Who still refuses to meet *them*," Marshal added. "And so it will go until England's burned flat, or one of the adversaries takes an arrow in the chest."

"Well," Langton said ambiguously, "we must continue to pray."

The months that followed were stained by acts of appalling savagery. Armies met to skirmish, or smashed their way through unwalled towns and villages. Mass hangings were as regular as markets and, if the victims were royalists, then rebel sympathizers would be found to decorate another stand of trees. The king's troops were the most savage of all, and it was said that whatever they did not destroy in their advance, they would ruin on their return. The soldiers from both sides charged their normal fee for victory, raping the women, no matter if they were nuns, and looting the houses, no matter if they belonged to God.

Perhaps because he wished to impress his cutthroat army, or because he no longer feared for his soul, King John participated in the hangings and insisted on being the first to set a torch to the altar. His followers applauded, though they wished he'd shown such determination fifteen years earlier.

He was accompanied throughout by Queen Isabelle, who saw no reason to condemn his zeal. She preferred not to witness the atrocities, but was content to watch a monastery burn. The Church had always obstructed her husband. He was simply removing a few of the obstructions.

From time to time the royal couple detoured to continue their treasure hunt. The army was now followed by an ever lengthening column of carts and sumpter horses, jealously guarded by two hundred of the king's friends and favorites. They had a good idea of what the carts and saddlebags contained, but on pain of death they kept their fingers from the straps.

A messenger brought the happy news that Eustace de Vesci had been killed near London. The king's epitaph for the rebel was "Amid poor surroundings, I hope."

In the last days of September, the royal army drove a group of rebel barons from the fenland city of Lincoln. Its gallant defender was a woman, Nicola de la Haye, and Queen Isabelle smiled fixedly as John embraced the chatelaine and escorted her into the privacy of her chambers. The queen's bodyguards winced at the expression that scourged the smile from her lips. They all knew the king would not reappear before morning.

From Lincoln the army moved southeast to Boston, on the edge of the broad estuary known as the Wash. Judging the tide to perfection, the cavalcade of horses, infantry and baggage carts crossed the sandbars and reached the village of Lynn on the southern bank. There, the king led a detachment of his guards to the nearby monastery and reclaimed two more ironbound boxes. He decided to break his journey, and the monks entertained their visitors as best they could. Unfortunately, the local well was being cleaned, and the priests were making do with impure river water. The years they had spent on the fens had inured them to the commonplace diseases, but the king was out of bed most of the night, his bowels loosened by dysentery.

The next stop was Wisbech, farther from the coast, though still on the edge of the estuary. John suffered the ride in silence, and Isabelle affected not to notice his frequent visits to the ditch.

At Wisbech, the king again searched out the monastery, where its abbot fidgeted with the sleeves of his habit as he explained that the boxes entrusted to him had been transferred to the abbey at Swineshead.

"FitzWalter's men were in the district a month ago, though by God's grace they passed us by. However, we heeded the warning and sent—"

"Where is this place, Swineshead?"

"Over there, my lord, on the north side of the estuary. One can see the tower of the abbey from our own turret. If you'd care to climb up with me—"

"I would not." It was too late now to start for Swineshead. The cavalry would get there before dark, but the baggage train made less than three miles an hour, and John was loath to leave it undefended. Besides, he was still afflicted by dysentery, and too exhausted to ride farther. He would continue the treasure hunt in the morning.

The army had reached Wisbech on October 11, 1216. The King of England—the heritage of England—was one day from disaster.

The army would descend from Wisbech to the corrugated sands of the estuary, cross the sunken plateau and descend again to ford a narrow river called the Wellstream. The cavalry would go first, followed by the infantry, then the baggage train and its escort and finally a rearguard of knights and archers. It would be an easy enough passage, two steps down to the river, then two up to gain the northern bank. Local guides had been procured and, to avoid any repetition of the fiasco below Château Gaillard, the tide had been checked and checked again. The sea would have retreated from the estuary by midmorning, and the Wellstream could then be forded without risk. Swineshead Abbey was ten miles from Wisbech, though the estuary itself was less than half that width. The October sun promised to burn off the mist, and there was no reason why the army should not enjoy a midday meal at Swineshead.

There were quicksands here and there, but the guides went ahead with long bamboo poles, shouting if they judged the ground infirm. John and Isabelle rode near the head of the column, though from time to time the king trotted back to make sure the wagons were making good progress. A slight breeze blew the mist to rags, and the carters found it easier to keep in line.

The Wash was not entirely flat, but as the tide ebbed it drew all but a few inches of water from the depressions. The mist continued to thin, until the villagers of Wisbech could see the mile-long column snaked out across the sand. In the monastery tower, one of the monks glanced inland, then pointed at a distant line of rain clouds. "At least the army's been spared a drenching," he remarked. "With luck they'll cross in bright sunlight."

Following the guides, Queen Isabelle was fascinated that they could probe two seemingly identical patches of sand, yet warn that one of them was unsafe. She wondered if the quagmires could really swallow a horse and rider and, if so, how many incautious travelers were embedded, deep in the estuary. The grisly image made her shudder and she stayed in line.

The cavalry reached the Wellstream, urged their horses into the water, then yelled that they were dry above the boots. A flurry of spray, and the leading riders spurred up the far bank and onto the next rippled plateau.

In the west, the storm darkened the sky, whilst the estuary remained warmed by the sun. Before long the first wagons would reach the Wellstream.

Then one of the carts shed a wheel and there was a slight delay as guides were sent for, to probe a new path around the stricken conveyance. Soldiers struggled to lever the axle clear of the sand and hammer the wheel back in place. John crossed the Wellstream for the fourth time, riding back to supervise repairs. He had slept badly the previous night, and looked forward to reaching Swineshead. The monks there made excellent cider, he'd heard, and he ran his tongue around his mouth in anticipation.

Another wagon was driven carelessly wide of the path, the horses floundering in quicksands. Nothing could be done for them, so they were cut loose and the contents of the cart shared out among the next three in line.

The king returned to the river, forded it again, then reined in, scowling. The water had dragged more than usual, and he was wet to the knee. He squinted upstream, saw the banks of sand, the distant outcrops of reeds, the faint shape of bushes and then, with the merest flicker of his eyes, the storm clouds in the west.

It was raining there, and the rain was filling the river. . . .

He yelled at those on the southern bank, telling the escort to speed the baggage train, then beckoning wildly at the leading carters. "Come across! The water's rising! Get those carts across!"

One of his knights rode alongside, a guide clinging to the cantle of his saddle. "He has something to tell you, lord king." A vicious jab at his passenger and, "Go on, man, say it out!"

Still armed with his bamboo pole, the guide slithered to the sand, bowed at John and muttered, "With your permission, my lord king. I've lived in this region for, well, since I was a boy, and I know how the waters run. Things change with the time of year, even the land changes, and the estuary was a good bit deeper the first time I ever crossed it."

His concentration divided between the storm clouds, the height of the river and the progress of the carts, John glared at the man and snarled, "Not your history. Not now. What is it?"

The guide blinked and went mute with fear. The first cart was crashing through the water—and drifting a little in the current.

"What *is* it?"

"If you would be advised, my lord king."

"I'll be *told!*" John howled. "*What is it?*"

"It'd be safer to ford farther up. When the sea comes in it meets the stream and—" He twirled his hands, one right, one left, to show what happened when the waters converged. "As you see, the river's narrow along here, and now that it's filling up it'll begin to race. It'd be safer to cross up there, my lord, just this side of the reeds."

John stabbed a finger at the knight. "You! Take him along the bank. He'll show you where he means. Christ's eyes, messire, haul him up! Get him up with you!" He turned to shout at the carters, directing them to follow.

The first wagon had gained the northern plateau, and John recognized it as the one that had shed a wheel. He watched it lumber past, looked away, then cursed and went after it. Gesticulating at the man to slow his team, he drew level and said, "How did you regain the lead?"

The drover was puzzled by the question. "Now that we're un-laden, we just—"

"Unladen! But why?"

"To make the cart light enough to lift, my lord. It was the only way we could get the wheel back on. But the chests are quite safe. They're in the other wagons."

Quite safe, John thought, though still on the wrong side of the river.

The cavalry and infantry had all crossed the Wellstream and were spread out along the safe path that twisted between the stretches of quicksand. Isabelle had already reached firm ground, where she dismounted to wait for John and the baggage train. Almost three miles separated the northern edge of the estuary from the rain-filled river, so she could not see what was causing the delay.

Below her, on the sand, a number of local guides were talking heatedly with the advance troop of knights, whilst the infantry toiled up from the plateau and flopped down on the bank. She watched several of the knights wheel their mounts and gallop back toward the Wellstream, some riding alone, others with a passenger.

It was odd weather, the sky clear overhead, yet black at the shoulder.

The contents of the narrow gulley flooded seaward. Flanked on the south by two miles of sand, on the north by almost three, the Wellstream could not be circumnavigated, not if one wished to travel from Wisbech to Swineshead.

The first half of the morning had gone and now, as the day advanced, the tide ran in to fill the Wash. It met with no impediment, bubbling across the sand, the waves overlapping, swirling forward at the pace of a striding man. Ahead lay the line of carts and frantic drovers, but they were no real obstacle, for they could be lifted from the ground, tipped off-balance and sunk. However solidly built, they could not stop the sea from coming in at its appointed time.

When it happened, it proved irresistible. The wagons and their escort, now joined by the rearguard, were still maneuvering on the southern plateau. The sea swept against them, filling the depression and obliterating all marks of safe passage. From the opposite bank, King John saw two of the carts tip forward into the river, whilst others were mired in the quicksands. He screamed at the drovers to go back, then clutched at his saddle as the incoming tide caused his horse to stumble. The knights who had stayed with him or ridden back across the northern plateau reached out to steady him, but he flailed about, still screaming commands. "Take them back! The water will carry you. . . . the water . . . It'll float you back. . . ."

But the evidence showed otherwise, and it was not only those on the southern plateau who were trapped. The marks of passage had now dissolved in the water on both sides of the Wellstream, and the quicksands were once again concealed.

The knights took a more determined grip on their king. One sensible man reasoned that the riverbank must be firm, else it would have already subsided, and the riders led John alongside the gulley and away from the curling tide. His agony was pitiable, though he had never had greater cause to weep than now.

His carters and their horses, the escort and their horses, the rearguard and their horses were all left to drown. So, too, were the contents of the boxes, chests, coffers, bags and bundles that the king and queen had accumulated during their treasure hunt. And in these were contained the crowns and regalia of England, the cups and chalices of white gold, yellow gold, silver and bronze, the swords and scepter, the flagons, rings, belts and buckles, the pendants and brooches, the crosses and candelabra, the caps and spurs of office, the seals and documents, the jewels amassed by the monarchy over the years, the buckle stolen by Isabelle from Marshal's room, the silver clasp given to the king by the diplomatic Hubert Walter, the clasp that depicted a tusky boar, John's reward for valor.

It was all lost, this sparkling heritage of England. Or perhaps it was not entirely lost, since England herself had taken it into custody.

The sea washed the bank below Wisbech. It spread across the southern plateau, forced its way against the Wellstream and filled the gully, until there was no longer any trace of the river. On the northern flats, the sea advanced unopposed, running under the lea of the bank and watched in silence by the guides and cavalry, the infantry and the drover of the single, unladen cart. And by the Sparrowhawk, who saw the glint of sunlight on the water as the turning of a diadem.

She did not look for her husband. Drowned or saved, it made no difference, for he was dead in her eyes. He had lost her everything she possessed, so it was only fair that they should lose each other.

One of the guides had left his bamboo pole in the sand. It had been tilted a little by the incoming tide, but it served as a measure and they watched the water rise and cover it.

Men were praying now or grouping together with their friends to discuss the future. They had seen the distant horsemen ride inland, presumably along the riverbank, but they could not tell if King John had been amongst them. They hoped so, for England's sake and his, and especially theirs. This was not a good time for the monarch to die. He had yet to name his successor, else the country would be further divided between those who would pledge their allegiance to his son Henry, a nine-year-old child, or to Prince Louis, a foreigner, or to Queen Isabelle, a woman. So God grant that John had been spared the quicksands and the sea.

It took the riders two hours to complete the horseshoe route, leading the king inland, then turning away from the upper reaches of the Wellstream and trotting back along the northern edge of the estuary. John's illness had been aggravated by the sleepless nights, the lack of food and the wild exertions of the crossing. He was sweating profusely and retching in the saddle. His escort mistakenly believed that Isabelle would be inconsolable, and hurried to reunite the king and queen. Also, for more selfish reasons, they were eager to be rid of him. His condition was grave, and now that they'd brought him from the estuary, they wished to be known as his saviors not his pallbearers.

Members of the advance troop spurred to meet them. Queen Isabelle was informed, but she remained where she was, her gaze fixed on the jeweled water. John was led to her and, in her own time, she looked up at him. His face was beaded with sweat, his mouth slack, his hands limp at his sides. The knights wanted to leave them alone, but two men were required to hold the king in the saddle. They averted their eyes and feigned deafness, though

Isabelle did not care who witnessed the reunion. Such as it would be.

"How many of the carts returned to the village?"

He shook his head, spraying sweat.

"I see. Then we are destitute, you and I. And I because of your mismanagement, because you once again failed to do things right. Where will you go now? To Swineshead? I need to know, if I'm to put as great a distance as possible between us. Oh, don't gape, my lord. You must be aware that I shall no longer keep step with you. You're in poor condition to enjoy a mistress, but if you can find one, I'll applaud. As for me, I shall make my own way, and not necessarily within this kingdom. I'd feel too conspicuous, wearing a cheap wooden crown, whilst I waited for someone to fashion one from iron. That's all I could afford, now that you've drowned the rest."

"Take me to the abbey," he croaked. "My blood's poisoned. There are things I must set down, things you should know in case I—"

"Succumb to your illness? But you won't, my lord. There are still two treasure chests at Swineshead. You'll recover just by trying on the rings and bracelets. You are dead to me, and have been since midmorning, but England will hear your heel tap for a long while yet." Addressing the knights, she said, "Lead him along, messires. Get him to his boxes. That'll cheer him." She turned toward the estuary again, even now hoping to see a sealed chest bobbing in the tide.

The remnants of the army reached Swineshead, where the king immersed himself in an herbal bath. The monks warmed a bed for him, but he left the stones to grow cold and insisted on a meal of peaches and their excellent cider.

They told him that the crop had been very poor that year, but he slapped the table and accused them of false modesty. Then, correcting himself, he said, "Who knows? You may be right. But you must let me judge the pressing for myself. And another thing, I'll beg a sack of those herbs. They've drawn the fever right out of me."

"Which the night air will quickly put back, lord king. If you wish to eat and drink, at least do so in the warm. We can find whatever you want, and bring it to your bed."

"God's eyes," he complained, "it's you who'll put the fever back if you leave me with an empty belly. I'm only asking for fruit and drink."

Fruit in the shape of a dozen peaches, and enough cider for a family. His speech became slurred, his movements imprecise, his mood relaxed and forgiving. Queen Isabelle would join him in a day or two, he asserted, or wait with her children in the south. She had a sharp tongue when she wanted, did the Sparrowhawk, though she had clearly been distraught with worry. And the loss of the treasure, a terrible mishap, though perhaps at the next low tide the bulk of it could be reclaimed.

He mumbled at his companions to organize a search, protesting drunkenly when they reminded him that the tide would be at its ebb soon after midnight. "What of it? There are torches and tapers, aren't there, even on the fens? Go on, go on, get a search started."

When he had finally sunk into a torpor, his knight carried him to bed, then returned to the refectory and barked at the monks. "Must you look so disapproving, brothers? You make the stuff and sell for a profit, so why should the king not drink it?"

"It's not that he drank it," they retorted, "it's that he never stopped. Likewise with the peaches. He ate them as though they were berries, when he'd have been better off chewing dry bread."

"He ate what he wanted to eat. Anyway, you underestimate his strength."

The monks said yes, possibly.

In the morning he was too weak to whisper. The fermented apples and unripe peaches had turned to vinegar in his blood. He was doubled over with spasms and could neither dress himself nor walk unaided. The knights panicked, refused all advice from the monks and led the king on a hectic ride from the abbey, first to Sleaford, then west to Newark. By the time they had reached the castle there, they were aware that, although John's mind had begun to wander, his body would take him no farther.

They sent messengers to warn Queen Isabelle, Stephen Langton, William Marshal, anyone who might catch at the trailing reins. The storm that had made the Wellstream impassable now moved north, as if to stalk the king. The castellan of Newark was absent, and the knights laid John in the great oak bed, then clustered around, striving to hear him above the rattle of the shutters and the moan of the wind. It was an eerie scene, and not improved by the king's sudden attempts to claw at his skull or grind his teeth to the roots.

In a moment of lucidity, he spoke of Marshal as England's unswerving champion, and told the knights to entrust Prince Henry to his care. "My son will rule this country, under God, but he needs the Arab to advise him." Then, with a shudder of self-pity, he added, "You see what I have come to, through my defiance of that gaunt old man."

A few hours later, he managed to dictate a will, naming thirteen men as his executors. The Abbot of Croxton arrived in time to hear his confession and administer the sacraments. The wind blew between the shutters and extinguished a candle flame. By the time the wick had been touched to another and relit, the king was dead. It was October 18, 1216. In no other way was it important in the calendar, and it was not long remembered in the land.

But King John would be remembered and, with few exceptions, reviled. He had failed to stand comparison with his brother, the physical giant Richard Coeur de Lion, and he had lost England her empire. But more damaging to his memory, he had mocked and persecuted the Church, and it was the Church that produced the great chroniclers and annalists of the age. King John could act as he saw fit whilst he was alive. But he could not govern what the monks had to say about him afterward. As no one can.

Aftermath

Queen Isabelle's talk of wood and iron was too pessimistic. In the treasure chests that were still safeguarded at Swineshead, she found a gold coronet, small enough to fit the head of a woman, or a child.

The moderates and royalists contributed toward an outfit for the dead king, and another for the nine-year-old Prince Henry. John's body was gutted and cleaned, then taken to Worcester, where it was dressed in a cloth-of-gold tunic, the fingers gloved and curled around an inferior scepter and a plain, burnished sword. Ironically, he was deprived of his high-heeled boots, and his feet shod in a pair of everyday sandals. As a pious touch, and possibly for concealment in the afterlife, his head was enclosed in a monk's cowl.

As soon as his body had been interred, his son was collected from Devizes and taken under guard to Gloucester. The rebel leader FitzWalter was still about, and with him Prince Louis, so there was no time to waste. If the child Henry was not crowned as soon as possible, Louis might well proclaim himself king.

At Gloucester, the young prince responded in a shrill, clear voice as he was first knighted by William Marshal, then crowned King of England. In a third, brief ceremony, the seventy-year-old Earl of Pembroke was appointed Regent of the Kingdom and given command of the army that would, it was hoped, drive Louis back across the Channel—minus his machines.

The death of John brought a number of barons to the court of King Henry III. Some of them spoke down to him, while others told him bluntly that their quarrel had been with his father, a stain on the land, but that they now wished to exchange a kiss of peace and pledge their allegiance.

Ever at the boy's shoulder, Marshal assessed his behavior and allowed himself a grunt of approval. He was sure he had been neither so calm nor so courteous at the age of nine. Nor, he knew, had John, and it led him to wonder if, after all, the dead king had been right to suspect the Sparrowhawk. John had sired enough bastards of his own, and Queen Isabelle was still one of the most attractive women around. It was a scurrilous thought, and Marshal would keep it to himself. Even so, he could not deny that young Henry's demeanor owed nothing to the wolf.

The rebels had suffered a setback, but they were not yet ready to quit. In December, ignoring the weather, Prince Louis captured Hertford Castle and routed a force of royalists. The English barons were turning their cloaks more often than a bedsheet, and Marshal sought out his friend and neighbor, Gerard de Barri. Together, they raised a force of seventy knights and almost two thousand men, selecting them for their love of England, military prowess and dislike of traitors. It was an elite contingent and, stealing from FitzWalter, Marshal christened it the Host of Right and the Crown. Assisted by the big-bellied Gerard, he drilled the troops throughout the winter. Then, in spring, he left the king with men he could trust and went in search of the rebels.

On May 20 at Lincoln, the Host of Right and the Crown met the Host of God and Holy Church. Prince Louis was elsewhere, but FitzWalter rode at the head of his army, and Marshal at the head of his chosen force.

The fight for Lincoln lasted most of the day. The brutal and energetic FitzWalter was everywhere, howling his orders, surviving the death of his horse, snatching a double-headed ax as though he dreamed himself the Lionheart.

Against him went the corpulent Gerard de Barri and the hobbling William Marshal. But it was Marshal who, at seventy, gave the lessons. He too had lost his horse, and went forward on foot, well supported by the Host of Right and the Crown. In that single action he isolated Robert FitzWalter, disarmed him as he had once disarmed the belligerent Ralf of Exoudun, then limped on alone to engage in single combat with a French champion, the Count of Perche.

The Frenchman cut Marshal on his bad leg, but the very deadness of the tendons allowed the earl to stay upright long enough to kill his adversary with a direct thrust at the neck.

The rebels discarded their weapons and, supported by Gerard de Barri, the Regent of England dragged himself across the grass to speak with FitzWalter.

"A nice jab," the rebel commended. "God must have been looking elsewhere at the time."

Breathing heavily, Marshal said, "I think not. I think it was meant to be seen. I think it was proof of what I told you, you bloody upstart. If you go against me, do not do so with any expectation of success." Tired and sick of the bloodletting, he glanced at Gerard. "Take this man into a safe prison. And tell his French friend to go home."

Prince Louis was not the only one to depart the kingdom. Queen Isabelle left, aware that there was no place for a dowager queen in the masculine court of England. She returned to Angoulême, struggled to reassert her authority against France and the neighboring warlords, and eventually smothered her contempt for the man who had lost her, Hugh of Lusignan. More than that, she married him.

He was no longer the active suzerain, but she was better off in his bed than his dungeon, and they worked together to resist the intrusions of the Crown.

The Sparrowhawk would make a name for herself, not only as the onetime Queen of England, but as the woman who'd sent her servants to poison the King of France. Happily for that monarch—the grandson of Philip Augustus—the would-be assassins were discovered and hanged from the gate. The Sparrowhawk attempted suicide, failed even in that, and was described by the writer, Matthew Paris in his *Chronica Majora* as "rather a Jezebel than an Isabelle."

The prisoner FitzWalter took the advice Marshal had given him and became the crusader FitzWalter.

"You can avoid the boils of imprisonment, upstart, and possibly save your soul. You love to fight, so put some purpose behind it and fight the devils of Islam. We shall let you go, so long as you go abroad, but we shall not welcome you back until we have forgotten the part you played. Now make your decision. Will you take the cross of the crusader, or fester here as you deserve?"

"I'll go away," FitzWalter said. "By the time I come back, you'll very likely be dead."

"Very likely," Marshal echoed, "though the Saracens of the Holy Land are renowned for the accuracy of their shafts. Who can tell, upstart? You might never come back."

The foreign prince had left. The dowager queen had gone home. The rebel was on crusade. England breathed a pent-up sigh of relief and watched the child king grow to manhood.

But Marshal was not there to see it happen. He was taken ill in May 1219, and nursed in a manor he owned at Caversham, near Reading. It was not a sudden affliction so much as the languishing of his powers, and death knocked very gently at his door.

He had sired five sons and five daughters, and they all came to see him. But more than William, Richard, Gilbert, Walter and Anselm; more than Matilda, Isabel, Sybille, Eve and Jeanne, the old man wished for his wife.

She came early, and stayed all the while, and he found the strength to discuss things they had done together throughout the years of their marriage, and to tell her stories she had heard many times before, yet pretended were new.

Distressing those who had assembled, he worried about his youngest daughter, wishing she had married a less insolent suzerain. It was too late to change things, though he made provision for her to receive two hundred marks to lift her spirits, then fifty marks a year for life. She was to keep this award to herself, he insisted, lest her husband squander it.

He was visited by the world; by foreigners who had no reason to know that he was ill, by young men who pleaded with him to deliver the buffet of knighthood, then helped balance the sword that he touched to their shoulder. Stephen Langton came as often as possible, and Gerard de Barri had to be encouraged to sleep.

The young King Henry arrived, pressing the child's hand on an old man's chest. He insisted that Marshal lay back; there was no call for homage. Then, impeccably, the boy delivered a speech of praise, in which he described the warlord as "the guide of irresolute monarchs, the leader of strange armies, the founder and father of an incomparable line."

"We never had a man like you," Henry told him. "We never did. I wish, Earl Marshal, I truly wish you had been king. Yes, I wish *you* had been dominant hereabouts."

He grizzled at the bedside, and was led gently away, leaving the chamber empty for Isabel de Clare.

"It's an odd feeling," Marshal told his wife. "I'm in no pain, though the strength exudes from my body."

"I heard what the king said to you," Isabel murmured. "He spoke nothing but the truth." She turned away sharply, blinded by tears, and Marshal growled, "Kiss me, *belle amie*," and then more urgently, shouting *in extremis*, "It's the last time! Embrace me now!"

She leaned forward, sensing some movement in his lips. Or so she would ever believe.